"YOU'RE FAR FROM AREN'T YOU, LITTLE LADY?"

The speaker was a big, swarthy man with sharp eyes, who grabbed her arm as he addressed her. Kayla stared at him in stunned amazement. Where had he come from?

"Excuse me," she said, and tried to pull herself free. But the man held on.

"The word's out on you," he said. He pushed aside the flap of his green tunic. A laser pistol nestled in a sleek holster within easy reach. "Just stay quiet, do what the Blackbird says, and you won't get hurt." He rested his hand on the pistol's grip.

She tried to blanket his vision with shadow-sense, but either he was shielded or she was too distraught to concentrate. She began to panic. She lurched forward, but before she could get any leverage to use against him, he pulled her back to her feet.

"No monkey business," he said. "I know you empaths are tricky. But I've got a pulse-disruptor, so your damned nearsense can't work on me. And remember, I've also got my laser aimed right at your head. Now, c'mon."

"Where are we going?"

"To my ship. The Kellers've put out a reward on you, and I'm going to collect it." He yanked her arm sharply. "Walk or I'll stun and drag you. . . ."

WOMAN WITHOUT A SHADOW

Karen Haber

DAW BOOKS, INC.
DONALD A. WOLLHEIM, FOUNDER
375 Hudson Street. New York, NY 10014

ELIZABETH R. WOLLHEIM
SHEILA E. GILBERT
PUBLISHERS

For Marty and Roz, with love and gratitude, and for Lilith, blithe spirit, in memoriam.

"Our life passes in transformation."

—RAINER MARIA RILKE

Chapter One

Darkness meant morning in the caves. Deep beneath the furious, deadly surface of the world called Styx, stalactites cast purple rippling shadows across the hand-hewn passages as Kayla John Reed swung her coldlight lamp back and forth like a starry pendulum. The air had the cold tangy stone smell which Kayla had always associated with the beginning of a day in the mines. She took an appreciative sniff and her green eyes glowed with anticipation. Today was going to be a busy day. A good one.

"Yeouch! God's Eyes!"

White-hot pain shot up the length of her calf, forcing tears from her eyes. She had slammed her toe against a root outcropping of the glossy black stalagmite stump that the miners called "Old Bart's Nose." Cursing, she hopped, one-legged, long red hair bouncing, until she reached a niche where she could comfortably sit and massage her poor foot.

—*Kayla? What's wrong?*

Her mother's nearsense query, in narrowed mind-to-mind mode, came from a spot three kilometers down and to the right, from the deeper tunnels where her parents were prospecting.

—*Nothing. Just stubbed my toe.* Kayla was careful to modulate her nearspeech. Her empathic powers, already much stronger than those of her parents, were oddly amplified in the caves and she had been reproached more than once for giving her mother and father headaches during their telepathic conversations.

—*Watch where you're going. The caves aren't a playground.*

—*I know that, Mother!* Privately, Kayla wondered when her parents were going to stop overprotecting her. After all, hadn't they bought her a new cutter for her sixteenth birthday last year? She was an independent prospector now, searching for mindstone ore just like her parents and their parents before them. Why couldn't they respect that? Being an only child could be such a mammoth responsibility. Her thin shoulders had to bear the combined weight of both parents' worry. It would have been nice to share the burden with a sister or brother.

Her toe had stopped aching. She got up, dodged nimbly around Old Bart's Nose, and set down her gear.

The laser cutter looked shiny, almost brand new. She pulled it out of her sack and stroked the glossy casing as though it were a sleek animal pelt. Holding her breath, Kayla peered through the ultrasound scanner until she had located the marker she had left behind yesterday. Ah, there it was, a faint red circle that throbbed slightly on the yellow screen.

She pressed the trigger button and a thin, coruscating ray of green light surged from the mouth of the laser to melt away the smooth rock face. With practiced skill Kayla made clean, neat slices, wasting no movement, controlling the beam perfectly until she had carved an opening the size of a man's head.

She shut off the cutter and waited impatiently for the glowing incision to cool. When the sides of the rock cut had cooled to purple and brown, she inserted a probe. The readings made her whistle. The vein was even better than she had suspected, a find of the highest quality mindstone.

Her parents would be delighted. Kayla could imagine the look of barely-concealed pride on her father's face when she told him about her new stake. She paused, cocked her head, and used her empathic farsense to listen for the mental footsteps of her mother and father. There: they hadn't moved. Her mother was fretting over a balky laser while her father was puttering around, sifting through a pile of mindstone salt. Just another day in the midnight caves of Styx, where three generations of Reeds had been digging for mindstones.

The eighth planet in the Cavinas System, Styx was a fierce and icy demon of a world. Its surface was uninhabitable, swept by violent electrical storms and dotted by active ice volcanoes. But beneath its roiling skin, Styx was honeycombed by crystalline caves. Determined pioneers, Kayla's grandparents among them, had carved shelters out of the living rock, and fortunes out of the veins of rich minerals which laced the interior of Styx.

Although the earliest prospectors had merely hoped to eke a living out of their toil, they had become as rich as Midas through the discovery of an intriguing gem-hard crystalline stone. Ruby-blue with acid green striations, it was suitable, when cut, for costume jewelry. Called Cyrilite after its discoverer, Cyril Magnus, the rock was sold as pretty baubles, considered a curiosity until its first mind-altering effects were detected.

Something about the faceted stones affected the perceptions of some—but not all—of those who wore them. A savvy trader dubbed them "mindstones" and quickly made a fortune. Soon the entire Cavinas System was clamoring for the mind-altering jewels, and Styx was the only known source.

Kayla had grown up in the caves, wandering freely. Her parents were never worried that she would get lost. No one on Styx was ever lost for long, thanks to the miners' extraordinary empathic powers of near- and farsense: the ability to communicate telepathically over long distances, through layers of rock. These unique abilities seemed to have developed from their long exposure to the raw mindstone ore. Studies had yielded nothing more than confusing, tantalizing clues to the source of the miners' powers. All that was known was that the powers could not be duplicated in clinical tests elsewhere.

—*Kayla!*

It was her father, loud for nearspeech. His thoughts were clipped and there was a cold, unfamiliar feel to them that set Kayla's teeth on edge.

—*Quake, Kayla!*

She heard it before she felt it, a strange, low growl, as though a huge, famished animal had awakened. Kayla swept her equipment into her pack and pulled it across her back. Now she felt the deadly vibration. A hungry animal, yes. The planet Styx was awake and hungry, looking for miners to devour.

—*Get out. Hurry . . .*

But she was already moving, running as fast as she could on the slippery cave floor. It shifted and surged, bucking beneath her feet as stalagmites shivered and bounced, cracking all around her. Deadly pieces of blackened stalactite arrowed down from above, aiming for her back, her legs, any exposed and vulnerable part.

The cave mouth, where was the cave mouth? She couldn't see. Mindstone salt filled the air, getting in Kayla's nose, her mouth, making her cough, blinding her. Another few meters and. . . .

Something growled, roared, and knocked her sprawling in the suffocating dust. She fought to get up, to reach the safety of the braced and beamed outer passages. But even as she groped toward the light, the world went dark, dark and silent around her.

* * *

Kayla opened her eyes to blackness. Her body ached as though it had been pummeled. She felt, but could not see, an immobilizing weight which sat upon her left shoulder. Where was she? In the caves? No, the ground was too soft. A tentative touch revealed soft bedcovers. At home? Had she just kissed her father good night?

No, not at home. Not in her bed.

Memory came rushing back, pricking her mind, filling her eyes. The smell of the room was sharp, medicinal, no dream. She was in the hospital. But how?

"You're awake?" queried a soft voice. The familiarity of it put a huge lump in Kayla's throat.

A wall lamp came to life, casting a cool yellow glow across the small room, and Kayla saw Dr. Ashley standing in the doorway, strong, no-nonsense Carol Ashley, who had brought Kayla into the world. Her lips were a hard, white line in her ruddy face.

"How do you feel?"

Kayla tried to sit up, winced, and lay back again. The weight upon her shoulder was a pressure cast. "Terrible. Where're my mother and father? When can I see them?"

Dr. Ashley started to speak, stopped, shook her head gently.

"No!" Despite the pain, Kayla wrenched herself into a sitting position. Her head throbbed and the room swirled around her.

"I'm sorry," Dr. Ashley said. Her voice was suspiciously thick. She seemed unable to say more.

"Let me at least see them."

"I can't. We couldn't find them."

Kayla refused to believe what she was hearing. "If you couldn't find their bodies, then you don't know that they're dead, do you? You don't have any proof."

Dr. Ashley's face was a mask of pain. "We're reasonably certain."

"We could search . . ."

"No, Kayla. Two tunnels collapsed. The entire fourth sector's been sealed off."

"With my parents inside it? You can't do that! That's

most of our stake." Kayla took a breath. Her throat felt raw and painful, as though she had been screaming in her sleep. "Under whose authority was it sealed?"

"Beatrice Keller's."

"What? How could she?"

"Some sort of emergency powers act, agreed to long ago by the Guild."

"How convenient. But I still don't see how she gets off making decisions about the Reed stake. And if my parents are still alive in there, she's condemned them to death."

Dr. Ashley shook her head.

"They might be," Kayla said. "They might be unconscious."

"Don't you think we've been scanning for them? The strongest farsensers haven't detected a flicker from either Redmond or Teresa. Face it, Kayla. By now we'd have heard something, even the mental babble of delirium. But there hasn't been anything, not a whisper. No one could have survived this long under all that rock. If the initial cave-in didn't kill them, then the lack of oxygen would have. They're dead. Gone. They're not coming back."

"How did you find me?"

"Blind luck. You were close to the cave mouth and your mind was cycling loudly enough for Yates Keller to hear you."

Yates. The name brought uncomfortable associations, unwelcome longing, and confusion. There was no time for that, now. She closed her eyes. She didn't want to think about Yates, she didn't want to think about anything, but she didn't have that luxury. She took a slow, deep breath and stared up at Dr. Ashley. "What's my next move?"

An approving smile lit the doctor's face. "You'd better push for being declared a legal adult. It's your best bet for cutting through any red tape. And that way you'll avoid having somebody appointed as your guardian. You'll inherit all of your parents' claims immediately, and, I imagine, your father's seat on the Guild of Styx as well."

"My father's Guild seat!" Kayla winced. She wasn't ready for that, not at all.

Dr. Ashley took Kayla by the shoulder. "Do you want to see the Keller faction take over your father's seat? You've got to face up to your responsibilities, Kayla."

"But the Guild . . ."

"Yes, I know." Dr. Ashley's tone softened slightly. "It's difficult, a terrible shock. You're very young. But people have lost parents when they were younger than you are now. And you mustn't abandon the Guild to the control of the Kellers. Every seat that's absorbed by their faction limits the miners' power. That's the last thing Redmond would have wanted."

Kayla remembered sitting beside her father in the Guild Hall. How could she sit there alone, without him? She heard herself saying, "I guess you're right."

"All of us who were loyal to your father will be loyal to you. You know that."

"Yes." Yes, of course they would be. Who else was there for them? Who was left? "I wonder how the Kellers will react."

"Beatrice will probably expect you to align with her, now, or to sign over your voting rights until you come of age."

Not bloody likely. "I'm sure she'd like to get my voting rights."

"She wouldn't mind having your powers at her disposal, either," Dr. Ashley said.

Despite herself, Kayla smiled. It was common knowledge that she was one of the most gifted empaths of the younger generation, a tripath at the very least. The only one who even approached her skill level was Yates Keller. But he was only a duopath with near- and farsense capabilities, and the latter so weak as to be nearly latent, vestigial, useless. Not that that had prevented Beatrice Keller from crowing about her son after the testing. She had boasted for a week, until Kayla's results had come back.

Tripath. At the very least.

Her parents had warned her against pride—and the recklessness that accompanied it. But she was proud that she had such power. And that she was strong, stronger, even, than Beatrice Keller's precious son.

But Dr. Ashley was speaking, saying, "I think Beatrice will try to cooperate with you, Kayla."

"Why?"

"For starters, she's offered to cover all of your hospital expenses."

"I can pay my own bills," Kayla said sharply.

Dr. Ashley's mouth quirked. "I thought you might feel that way."

"Beatrice Keller must really want my cooperation."

"Don't cast her aside lightly," Dr. Ashley said. "An alliance with her might be useful. For all of us. But there's plenty of time to sort that out later." She pressed a derm patch against Kayla's wrist.

"What's that for?"

"So you'll sleep."

"I don't want to sleep. I want to go home." But her eyelids were already so heavy she couldn't keep them open. She thought she heard Dr. Ashley whisper, "Tomorrow," but that might have been just the beginning of a dream.

* * *

The entrance to her home looked exactly the same. What if she pushed it open and found Mom in the kitchen tending her hydroponic plants, or Dad fussing with a clogged ore cleaner? Would she yell, "Surprise!"?

No. They weren't there. They would never be there again. Kayla took a deep breath and unlocked the door. The familiar scent made her throat grow tight. Home.

It was still home even if there was only her left to fill it.

The warm familiar rooms cut from translucent green crystal were a welcome refuge, the very stone from which they were cut seemed to emit a comforting glow.

Shimmering lavender bambera-fur rugs, the finest grade from the best weavers of Liage, the plains planet, cushioned Kayla's footsteps. She had always loved their softness and had spent hours sitting on them, staring into their mandalalike patterns, dreaming of the bambera herds that roamed Liage, tended by their mysterious nomadic keepers under open skies where wind actually blew and rain fell from clouds.

But now they were just rugs. She walked over them blindly, and settled slowly into her father's big padded chair. The green and blue embroidered cushions smelled like him, and, for a moment, if she closed her eyes she could believe that she was a child again, sitting in her father's lap. Kayla opened her eyes and tears began to trickle down her face. She let herself go, huddling into the chair as though it were a human being, sobbing until she ran out of tears and a dry, cold grief filled her.

I've got to be strong, she told herself. *They're gone and there's nothing I can do about it.*

All around her were bits and pieces of her family's life: holopics, mine probes, the wall-hung tanks of hydroponics which her mother had so patiently tended under their pink growlamps. The imported wooden table and chairs, shipped all the way from the Salabrian System, which her father had ordered to surprise her mother on her thirty-fifth birthday—and paid for with the credits which would otherwise have purchased a new cutting rig. She didn't have the heart to put anything away. But the longer she looked, the less capable she felt of living with the painful reminders of her mother and father.

Stick to business, she thought. The quake had closed down a major portion of the Reed stake. She had to see how much was left, and what portion of that provided her with liquid assets. She picked up her father's strongbox: it was made of scented golden wood, elaborately carved into whorls, knots, and twining arabesques. She tried to open it, but the lock was set to her father's thumbprint and wouldn't budge. Dismayed, Kayla stared at the recalcitrant hardware and wondered what to do. She didn't want to smash the lid, but how else was she going to get at the family papers? Her eye fell upon her mining equipment and suddenly she remembered her laser. Use the cutter on the lock? If she were careful, she might be able to do it without even singeing the box.

She grabbed up the cutter and checked the levels. It was fully charged. She took careful aim and depressed the stud.

ZZZZZAT! A green-yellow bolt shot out of the laser's mouth, right at the strongbox lock. Kayla took her finger off the button and the cutting ray disappeared. The lock glowed white-hot, then red, then orange. Kayla tapped the side of the lid experimentally.

Snick.

It came halfway, nearly falling into Kayla's lap before she caught it.

Not a bad shot, she thought. *I wonder if Dad ever realized just how weak his strongbox was?* Of course he did. He could have gotten a nice little safe just like the one in her bedroom, but he loved old-fashioned things. Form had been just as important as function to Redmond Reed.

She paged through the files and vid cubes. It didn't take her long to realize that Reed Enterprises had just barely been keeping its head above water. All of their expensive equipment had been paid for with loans from the Keller family. Even their house was mortgaged to the Kellers.

Mortified, Kayla bowed her head. *Oh, Dad. Why didn't you tell me?* But of course she knew why, knew that her father had not wanted to worry her, had always believed that the next strike would yield enough money to cover everything.

Kayla felt hollow, drilled out by the discovery. Mortgaged to the Kellers. If she was lucky and worked nonstop, she might be able to pay everything off by the time she was ready to retire.

The box was nearly empty save for a cloth sack made of a surprisingly dense, soft blue material. She picked it up and nearly dropped it, surprised by its weight and heft. Something clicked musically from within.

Kayla tipped out the contents.

"Omigod."

Blue-red and green, gently winking in the light of the glow lamps. Mindstones. She had a fortune in finely cut mindstones sitting in her lap. There was enough here to settle all of the debts Kayla had just discovered.

Why hadn't her father used them? Why had he left them sitting at the bottom of a dark box?

She picked up a handful and felt the powerful effect of the stones begin to work upon her. The very air seemed charged, dancing with coruscating particles of yellow and red and gold and no-particular-color-at-all. Everything in the house had an aura, a nimbus around it of soft glowing light.

Across the room, something moved. She whirled and saw her parents climbing down out of their holopics and off the shelves to come sit beside her.

"I saved them for you, honey," her father said. "I couldn't just use those stones to pay off Beatrice Keller. They're the best stones ever cut from our mines. Your inheritance, Kayla. All for you."

Beside him, her mother beamed and nodded. They both looked so young and healthy. So alive.

Kayla laughed and wept at the same time. "Daddy. Mom, I love you so much. Why did you have to go?"

They didn't answer her, merely stared lovingly at her and smiled.

Somehow she remembered the mindstones in her hand. She allowed them to spill back into the bag.

When she looked up, the room was as it had been. The holopics were in their places on the shelves. The air was clear. The house was silent. Kayla grasped her father's precious gift, resealing the mouth of the sack.

"I understand," she said aloud. "Don't worry. I'll be okay." She tucked the sack beneath her pillow. For tonight, at least, it would be safe. She would figure out what to do with it tomorrow, or the day after that.

Chapter Two

Vardalia, a soaring metropolis of white domes and towers, was the capital city of St. Ilban, sole moon and offspring of the gas giant planet Xenobe.

Vardalia filled the only landmass on St. Ilban. Its towers spiraled up toward Xenobe's great purple belly, which hung in the sky like a swollen sack about to burst. At dawn and sunset an aurora of green, pink, and gold clouds wove strange and beautiful patterns against Xenobe's somber bulk and cast pale bronze shadows upon the city. At night, the many orbital suburbs winked down from above like tiny stars, friendly firefly companions.

Prime Minister Pelleas Karlson, head of St. Ilban's government and leader of the Trade Alliance, sat alone, locked away from the platoons of secretaries and undersecretaries, the petitions of the importunate, the querulous, and the needy, the crises and scandals of various dignitaries, in short, all the noise that filled the waking hours of a busy and powerful man engaged in public life. He had decreed that he not be disturbed, explaining that he was involved in business of the highest importance and delicacy, and now he sat in delicious isolation in his office, the largest suite of rooms on the highest floor of the loftiest tower in Vardalia.

A short man with a look of softness about him, Karlson might have been taken for someone's jolly, balding uncle. Only his dark, nearly-black eyes gave a hint of the dynamic mind behind the rounded flesh, the

determination and will to power that had brought him
control of the Trade Congress and politics within the
Cavinas System for nearly fifteen years.

Karlson bobbed gently in his padded null-g chair, all
of his attention fixed on a video cube whose
multiscreened surface showed the meticulous proce-
dures involved in cutting Styxian mindstones. A hunk
of cloudy reddish stone was being masterfully shaped,
faceted, and polished while spinning in the cool green
low-ion bath that prevented cracks from splintering the
rock during the delicate cutting process.

Mindstones, Karlson thought, *maddening mindstones.*
It became a litany, a chant he could almost hear, a
rhythm to which he could tap his toe. Such lovely, unpredictable gems, glowing blood red and blue in the lamp-
light, edging toward glorious purple when set, facets
winking, in precious metal.

The stones were the key to the greatest power in the
galaxy, Karlson felt that in his bones. Whoever controlled them controlled the worlds of the Cavinas System and worlds beyond that. And what if such power
were to fall into unscrupulous hands, say, the wrong
faction? Terrible, to think that all of his careful work to
create and maintain the Trade Alliance could be unbal-
anced by misguided management of the mindstone
trade. It was crucial that this industry be administered
carefully. Given their controversial effects upon people, mindstones should really be restricted goods. And
who was better suited than Karlson and his government to regulate all dealings in mindstones?

Of course, he reflected soberly, it would be a great
pity if his government were forced to seize all
mindstone stakes and holdings for the good of the
Trade Alliance. Sad, yes, but government control of
Styx might become necessary, if, for instance, there
was even a hint of illegal hoarding in an effort to force
already exorbitant prices higher. Yes, he would have to
look into that.

Mindstones. What was their secret? People who could afford the jewels often wore them constantly—even to bed—in the hope that they would develop empathic powers like the miners of Styx. But that never happened.

What exactly did happen varied: Some wearers swore that the stones increased their latent extrasensory perception. Lunatics, obviously. But some folk claimed that their aesthetic senses were sharpened, their appreciation of beauty refined. For a lucky few, sex was reportedly better, deliriously better. Some claimed that the stones gave them terrible headaches. Others went into trances. For the unluckiest of the wearers, a strange shattering of personality and sanity seemed to take place. And for still others, there was no benefit, no effect at all.

Karlson had heard the tales of euphoria, the bonding between wearers, the ecstatic communion which the gems seemed to facilitate. He had also heard the darker reports of flawed gems which induced madness, paranoia, even death. But which was truly flawed, he wondered, the stone or the wearer?

And what really caused it all? Light frequencies, oddly refracted, or subsonic sounds rebounding off the gems? Whatever it was, obviously, something about the stones triggered strange reactions in some—but not all—of their wearers.

Even stranger, even more frustrating: the damnable things didn't last. At least, some of them didn't. From the moment the gems were separated from their parent rock, their potency apparently ticked away until eventually—no one could calculate when it would happen—most of them would blacken and crumble like dust. Most, but not all.

And what about the miners, those molelike folk who worked and lived near the stones, day in and day out? Their long-term exposure resulted in tangible and seemingly permanent benefits: extraordinary, startling telepathic abilities about which rumors abounded. Why didn't some of them go mad? Or did they, and was that all hushed up somehow? Even the Styxians who handled the stones directly, cutting them and preparing them for market, seemed to remain untouched and safe from psychic nightmares.

The buying public ignored the possible dangers. The stones drew the attention—and money—of anyone who could afford them.

To Karlson, mindstones presented endless questions and tantalizing possibilities. He knew that it was only a matter of time before the stones' secrets were unwound, analyzed, and employed. Once their power was tapped, they would become the most valuable material in the Trade Alliance. Whoever controlled them would wield unfathomable power. Pelleas Karlson fully intended to be that person.

He stared in fascination at the emerging gem with its graceful sweep of whorling facets and green striations. Hypnotic, attention-capturing.

The sparkling, hypnotic facets.

Karlson stopped rocking and sat bolt upright, nearly pitching himself over and out of his floating chair while one thought echoed in his mind: Could the pattern of the facets have something to do with the unpredictable effects of the stones?

Quickly, Karlson ran the vid sequence back and played it once more, and then again, Why not? Why in the nine worlds not? It was a plausible theory, as plausible as any he had heard. Yes. Yes, he must look into it right away.

A yellow light flashed from the recessed pad on his desktop: the prime minister's private line. He pressed a button on the side of his chair to throw a shield around all communications in the room, and switched on his personal screen.

"Yes?" Karlson snapped. "What is it?"

"Good morning, Excellency."

The voice was deep, its tone both insolent and insinuating.

"Merrick," Karlson said. "I expected your call yesterday. Where were you?"

"I couldn't get to a shielded screen, alone, before this. And it's important, all right. I've got what you asked for."

"Information?"

"Yes. As you suspected, the miners are experimenting with the tailings. They call it mindsalt."

"Mindsalt?"

"That's what I said. They crush it to powder and eat it."

Karlson's eyes widened in surprise. "You don't say. How ... unexpected. Any conclusive results?"

"Too soon to tell consistently, but it seems to have a certain, shall we say, potency."

"Very, very interesting, Merrick. Please keep me informed on this mindsalt. Now, what about the stones themselves?"

"I've got a hold full of 'em. Way beyond the legal shipment weight."

"Do you, now. And where did you get them?"

"I thought we agreed, Prime Minister, that we wouldn't ask too many questions."

Karlson smiled sourly. Merrick was almost as able a fencer as he. "Which means you probably didn't just stumble over them by chance in some dark alley. Well, I don't need to know their pedigree. Just get them here."

"The usual drop point?"

"No," he said. "I'll send you new coordinates. Screen to screen."

"And payment?" the trader said.

"As always, unless you've changed accounts ..."

Merrick chuckled. "No, but the price has gone up, Karlson."

"What?"

"It's harder and harder to arrange these shipments," the smuggler said, his voice gone hard and flat. "When I take on more risk, you pay more."

Karlson hesitated, debating what to do. If he rejected Merrick and his shipment, he would waste time and probably credits before he found another shipment of contraband mindstones. "Very well," Karlson said. "How much do you want?"

"Two hundred thousand credits."

"You must be joking."

"No, sir."

"You're a pirate, Merrick. This is outright robbery."

"Whatever you say, sir."

"Don't be so smug about it. I could have you arrested, you know."

"So? Cage me and I might sing."

The prime minister's voice softened dangerously. "Singers need tongues, yes?" Karlson disliked resorting to overt threats, but this bandit needed to be slapped down. "You're not irreplaceable, Merrick, and you know it. I have at least five people lined up and eager to do your work. Remember that. And I'll pay you one hundred and eighty thousand credits, not one credit more."

There was silence.

Finally Merrick drawled, "It's a deal."

"Good." Without further discussion, Karlson relayed the location of the drop point and switched off his screen.

He bobbed slowly in his chair, floating before the floor-to-ceiling window. Outside, Vardalia was putting on its show of lights and shadows, but Karlson might as well have been staring at a stone wall.

So the Styxians were experimenting with ground mindstones, were they? What effect would this peculiar condiment have on people? If the stones themselves were believed to enhance the intellectual, sexual, and psychic prowess of the wearer, why, then, not the eater as well?

But to eat mindstones? For a moment Karlson was repelled. He was fastidious in his dining habits and ingesting crushed rock had little appeal for him. Nevertheless, he was intrigued as well. What would it be like? Would there be hallucinations? Fabulous dreams? Might he discover untapped mental abilities?

But what if something went wrong and he was reduced to imbecilic babbling? No, no, no. He couldn't risk himself, that would be foolish. But he would like to see its effects on someone else. Yes, he would enjoy that very much.

His office com line chimed two liquid notes and the voice of his secretary, Norris, came over the speaker. "The trade delegation to Styx is ready for their briefing, Prime Minister."

"Send them in."

The door slid open and Coral Raintree, chief negotiator, solidly built and blonde, and Robard Fichu, her lieutenant and rumored lover, sleek and handsome, walked in. They were wearing their official gray uniforms with the gold shields at either shoulder.

Both were quite tall, at least a head taller than the prime minister, forcing him to raise his chair a full five inches until he was hovering with his knees at their waistlines.

"Please sit," he said. "I want to show you something."

Without further introduction he activated the vid cube and both negotiators watched closely. Everyone, no matter how sophisticated, was fascinated by mindstones.

When the clip ended, Karlson asked, "How large a shipment of stones can Styx muster at any given time?"

Raintree and Fichu exchanged startled glances.

"Well," Raintree said. "I'm no expert, but I think they send several kilos."

"Let's say three."

She shrugged. "More or less. I wouldn't want to be held to that estimate."

"You won't be. Just for the sake of discussion, let's imagine that such a load is worth three hundred thousand credits. What if we doubled the amount of mindstone ore brought to market? Tripled it?

The agents stared at him. "The market would be flooded," Fichu said. "Practically destroyed."

"But that couldn't happen," Raintree interjected. "There simply isn't enough stone available at any one time."

"What if there were?"

"I don't understand."

"Suppose the mining of Styx was done by state of the art techniques rather than the slug-slow methods currently employed by those telepathic tunnel rats?"

"We should tell the Styxians how to do their work?" Raintree's tone suggested, politely, that her employer had taken leave of his senses. "Aside from the fact that Styxians are notoriously clannish, they shun all outside interference in the mines."

"And what if they thought it was being spurred by an insider?"

"Such as?"

"Beatrice Keller. She seems like an ambitious, progressive-minded woman. I'm certain she would welcome some support of her mining operations."

"Not if it meant relinquishing control."

"She can be made to see reason."

"I don't know . . ."

Such negative thinking infuriated Karlson. "It's in the highest interests of the government that we maintain some sort of control over the mindstone trade. If the Styxians won't allow us to purchase mine rights directly, then we must do so through a third party. I think that Beatrice Keller is our best bet. But if she won't cooperate, we can and will take control."

Robard Fichu squirmed in his seat. "Seizing those mines might not be easy as you think. Don't forget those empaths—those miners and their mind powers. A spooky bunch, if you ask me, living in their tunnels like rats, reading each other's thoughts. Who knows what they could do to normal people?

Raintree leaned toward the Prime Minister. "Are you actually suggesting that we take over? Interfere directly with the miners' operations?"

Karlson looked pained. "No, not yet. We would aid, direct, persuade. Perhaps the rumor could be planted, gently, that efforts at synthesizing the gems are nearing fruition. That might spook them."

"You want us to lie during negotiations?"

"It won't be the first time, will it?"

"What if they don't believe us?" Raintree said. "We have no proof."

"You're a resourceful negotiator, one of my best agents," Karlson said. "I'm sure you'll find a way." His voice was caressing, almost obscene in its silken intonations. "And be on the lookout for any signs of hoarding."

Raintree's smile was sardonic. "Look as in find?"

Karlson pinned her down with his gaze. "I think you understand me clearly."

Fichu and Raintree nodded. They knew that if they didn't produce the desired results, the prime minister would find others who would. And they would quickly find themselves back among the rank and file of Karlson's security force.

Fichu said, "With all due respect, Prime Minister," he said. "I don't see how we can convince the Styxians to turn out more stones. They know it will lower the price they get at market. In all my years of negotiations I've never met a tougher bunch."

"Of course it's difficult to deal with the miners. I'm

not saying it isn't. But you're seasoned people, the best I have. I couldn't imagine anyone else better qualified for this job. And I'm counting on you to get it done right." He paused, watching the flattery do its work. He didn't bother to add that what was important here was gaining control of the mines, not the increase in stone production. "So," Karlson said. "The Styxians simply must improve their output, with our help. Surely they don't want to be labeled uncooperative isolationists. If that happened, certain parties might call for tariffs against them, raise prices on the goods they need, and so on."

Raintree sighed. "We could always imply bottlenecking. Restricting the flow of necessary goods throughout the systems."

"I think the key here is Beatrice Keller," Karlson said. "She's always been a reasonable woman, and she controls a large interest in the mines."

"But it's not her decision alone," said Fichu. "There are other miners with major holdings."

"None so large as hers. She must be made to understand that Styx simply doesn't produce enough stones and people are in need because of it," Karlson replied. "Other market forces could close in and force her to sell her interests. Stage a hostile takeover. Surely that's simple enough to convey?"

Fichu blinked as though wondering whether he had been insulted.

"Honestly," Raintree said. "You'd think anybody in the Trade Alliance would be delighted that we were literally begging them to increase their output and offering them the means by which to do so."

"Don't make it sound like we're holding out a blank check," Karlson said. "It will mean more expense for us than I like to think about, even if we act through a third party. Bea Keller is smart enough to figure out where her best interests lie. What I'm interested in is the increased stone production which we, not Keller or the other Styxians, will ultimately control. I don't want them swinging their weight around at the next Trade Congress."

Raintree nodded, but her smile was cynical. "Difficult to have one without the other, isn't it? But we'll see what we can do."

"For the good of the market," Fichu said.

"For their own good," said Raintree. "After all, if demand for the stones is increasing steadily while output remains level, there's potential for a market imbalance and retaliation by other traders. Better that Beatrice Keller ride the wave of the future—into our hands."

"That's the ticket." Karlson gave her an approving look. "Concentrate on Beatrice Keller. If you can convince her to agree to our participation, then she'll convert the other miners in their guild."

He swept them cordially out of his office and turned back to his video cube. Mindstones, lovely mindstones. It was a friendly refrain in his head. Sooner or later, he would control them.

Chapter Three

Kayla made a desultory search of her parents' possessions, flipping through old vid cubes and equipment, but she didn't really have the heart to take a total inventory. Not yet. Not until she could move through the house without crying.

She saw him before she heard him, saw Yates with her mind before she heard him fumbling at the front door.

His smile was sheepish but still potent at only half-power. "Hi, Kayla."

She felt her heart leap. "What are you doing here?"

"I wanted to say that I'm sorry. About your folks. I wanted to know if there was anything I could do."

Yes, she wanted to say. *Yes, there's something you could do for me. Bring them back, Yates. Get your mother to take all her millions and buy my parents' lives back. Buy yesterday, and the day before, and make it all come out differently. Could you do that for me, Yates? Could you do that, please?*

Instead, she said, "Thanks. Do you want something to drink?"

His smile went to full wattage. "Great." He looked down at the rugs and his eyes widened. "Hey, that's a nice rug."

"Yes, my parents had good taste. Even if they didn't have money."

"I didn't say that."

Kayla felt her cheeks heating up. "No, I know. I'm

just all confused. I'm angry and I'm looking for some-body to blame." She pulled a fat red bulb of flavored nectar out of the wall-hung cooler. "Here.

Yates slid his fingers into the handhold and opened the bulb's seal. "Thanks." He took a long, appreciative pull.

What was he doing here? Kayla's mind reached out toward his. But just before she touched him, she re-coiled. Long training made her cautious. She knew bet-ter than to probe, uninvited. But what did Yates want? He sat in her house, big, handsome, unreadable. A Keller, here. Why?

Even among empaths, Kayla was an anomaly. Not only could she employ nearsense and farsense, both sending thoughts and listening at great distances, she had the much rarer capacity to use shadowsense as a means of confusing the minds of others.

Her mother, Teresa, had been a monopath. Her fa-ther, Redmond, a weak duopath. Despite their repeated warnings that Kayla rein in her powers, both of them had been proud of their daughter's abilities. Hadn't she read that emotion clearly, seen it glowing like a beacon in their minds?

Kayla's parents had been proud, yes, but they had discouraged her from flaunting her skills or conde-scending to her friends and classmates.

Don't mind-peep.

Don't show off.

Don't give your friends headaches.

Protect them.

Protect yourself.

It was an endless litany. What good was it, Kayla had often wondered, what good to be the strongest empath in the class if all it got you was a list of things you shouldn't or couldn't do? The message was clear. With great ability came great responsibility. And she might be exceptionally skilled, but she still had to do her allotment of work each day, help her parents clear

away the rocksalt tailings, test their ore for the best
and purest stones, and carry their cuttings home. Those
were the rules.

But everything was different now.

"Kayla? Kayla, can you hear me?"

She came to herself with a shudder. Yates was staring at her, frowning. He probably thought she was
some sort of greeb, staring off into space, ignoring
him. She felt a pang of embarrassment and irritation.
What did he want anyway?

"Sorry," she said. "Guess I just sort of wandered
away."

"I understand."

"Do you?"

"Yeah. I was that way, myself, after my father died."

Their eyes met in a quick and easy bond. Kayla had
forgotten that Yates' father had died, suffocated in a
dust pit. And that her father, Redmond, had helped res-
cue Yates' mother before she suffered the same fate.

"That was a long time ago. You were maybe nine
years old."

"Yeah," he said. "But you never forget something
like that." He reached out and took her hand. "I know
what you're going through, Kayla. I'm sorry."

She got a sudden, intuitive flash that Yates not only
identified with her but felt the loss personally. She
squeezed his fingers. "Thanks."

"Do you want somebody to go with you tomorrow?"

"To the funeral?" She made herself say the word.

"Yeah. I could come get you, to walk you over."

"I'd like that, Yates. I really would." She squeezed
his hand again.

"Good. Me, too."

The two of them stared, suddenly out of words.
Yates leaned closer.

Kayla shut her eyes.

He kissed her, gently, on the forehead. "See you,
then." He moved toward the door. "About noon?"

Kayla started breathing again. "Right."

She stared until she could no longer make out his shape in the empty air. Then she turned back to the silent, empty house.

* * *

They sat in rows, Kayla with Yates beside her, his mother Beatrice and the other miners behind them, in the cavernous chapel carved from living rock.

Chaplain Emery, bald-headed and round-shouldered, worn to bone and skin by a lifetime of caring, murmured the ritual phrases.

"Life is given and life is taken away . . ."

Kayla hardly paid attention to the words he said. There were no graves nor graveyard. Space was too precious. Usually, bodies were cremated, ashes scattered in space, and the names were added to the plaque of the dead. This time, there hadn't even been bodies to burn.

She stared dully at the names and dates: Redmond Reed, 2938–2978. Teresa Reed, 2942–2978. What did they mean? What, really, did they signify? Her parents weren't here. They would never be here. Missing in action, lost somewhere just out of sight.

"Ashes to ashes," said the chaplain.

Ashes? Kayla thought. There were no ashes to tuck away under a mattress or shoot out into the clean vacuum of space. But there was plenty of dust in the tunnels of Styx. Dust and tears.

She felt obligated to weep, but her eyes were dry, her heart numb. Yates squeezed her hand and she smiled briefly. The memorial service was unsentimental: Death was a given in the mines and the people who lived and worked on Styx were a stoic bunch, accustomed to hardship and peril. She felt her attention wandering and told herself to pay attention.

* * *

—Pay attention, Kayla!

She was a child again, her hair in tight braids, sitting

on a hard bench and swinging her legs restlessly as her
parents instructed her in the ways to control her burgeoning mind powers.

"Kayla," her mother had said. "Pay attention. This is
how you build a mindshield." A pentagonal structure,
pink, glowing with marvelous light, appeared in
Kayla's mind. "And this is how you break one." The
thing imploded silently, was gone. "Now you try."

It was harder than it looked. Beads of sweat rolled
down her forehead and into her eyes, stinging, as she
tried, time and time again, to construct the five-sided
shield. And once she had done so that was just the beginning.

Do this. Don't do that. Yes. No. Rules, rules, rules,
when what she really wanted was to go down into the
mines with her father and press her cheek against the
smooth, cool rock.

Cool, cool rock.

Her mind looped around, over, and up to her first
visit to the Guild Hall. It was a vast and shining space,
magical-seeming to a child of ten. The long table, the
red tapestries hung upon the walls, the soft carpet of
bambera-fur underfoot. Grand, grand and glorious.

"You'll sit here beside me one day," her father had
whispered.

The thought was pleasing. Kayla pulled herself up
into the woven black sling and pole seat and felt suddenly different, important and mature. Sitting at that
long table she was a solemn adult, no longer a child.
She watched Beatrice Keller preside over the meeting,
blonde, regal, aloof. Her handsome son, Yates, caught
Kayla's eye and winked. Kayla blushed, but she
couldn't stop looking at him. He seemed transformed,
almost grave, no longer the playful, flirtatious boy who
was three levels ahead of her in school. He was the
heir apparent. His calm assurance made Kayla feel
strange and quivery. She had always liked Yates, perhaps even more than liked him.

Her father had nudged her mentally: —*Kayla, pay attention.*

She wanted to, but Yates was filling up the room, smiling, staring right into her soul. She wanted to climb into his blue eyes and drown.

—*Kayla!*

She came to herself in a hurry. This was the Guild of Styx, a place for important, adult matters, not foolish schoolgirl yearnings.

Beatrice Keller was speaking, saying in low measured tones, "We've got to increase our production of mindstones. This is a good moment to push for tariff breaks at the next Trade Congress. We'll finally be able to expand our market penetration beyond the Cavinas System. Redmond, you'll be our representative."

Her father had nodded. "Yes, I said I would do it. But you know how I feel about pushing our markets too far, Beatrice."

Her smile was icy as she stared at him. "I thought we were in agreement on this."

"We are, we are," Johannes Goodall said quickly. His eyes flashed an unspoken message to Kayla's father.

Kayla began to understand that things were not very simple at the Guild.

Later that night, long past when she should have been asleep, she had heard her parents arguing about the Kellers. Her parents never argued aloud, and they would have been mortified to know that Kayla could tap into their intimate mind-to-mind nearspeech frequency.

—*She goes too far, Terry.*

—*You've known Beatrice for a long time. Why are you so surprised whenever she shows her greed? She's crazed for money and power. The only thing keeping her off our backs is her gratitude to you for saving her.*

—*She's not really that bad, I know it. There's a spark of decency in her, dammit.*

—She never lets it rule her.

—No? She could have foreclosed on us any time. She didn't.

—Don't start defending her now.

—Don't be jealous.

—Jealous? That's the last thing I am.

Kayla couldn't bear it; she had to interrupt them. She crept out of bed and walked, yawning elaborately, into the main family room.

"What are you doing up?" her father demanded.

"I couldn't sleep," she said. "I thought I heard somebody talking."

Her parents exchanged a quick look and then her father was shooing her back to her bedroom. "You were dreaming," he had said. "You didn't hear anything. Now get back in bed before you stunt your growth, squirt."

* * *

With a start, Kayla returned to the present just in time to see Chaplain Emery bow his head and end the funeral ceremony with a prayer.

"Great and unknowable powers that formed the Universe
Take the energy, the life and light that were two good people
And shelter it reverently.
May their essence glow always in greater space,
As their memories shine forever in our minds."

Redmond and Teresa Reed had taken their places in the book of the dead. Kayla rose and the crowd rose with her.

The group at the chapel's mouth was a blur of old friends and colleagues. Beatrice Keller looked most peculiar, pale and tight-lipped, stunned. Kayla peered from under half-closed eyelids at the imposing figure with long blonde hair and icy blue eyes. She appeared to be thirty-five and was, perhaps, twenty years older than that, but her slender body and creamy, unlined skin gave no hint of her real age. She could have been Yates' sister.

Kayla watched Beatrice push her way through the crowd until she was close enough to place a possessive hand upon her son's shoulder. Why, Kayla wondered, had she come? Beatrice Keller had never been a friend to her parents. In fact, she and Redmond had frequently disagreed at Guild meetings. With Redmond Reed gone, the Kellers were free to dominate the mines. The loudest voice against them on the Guild had been stilled now and forever.

Beatrice smiled down at Kayla. "Darling," she said. "We're all so sorry, so terribly sorry. You must come and visit us soon. Our home will always be open to you." Her voice was tinny and strained.

Kayla stared at the ground and said nothing. The woman's fierce gaze was disconcerting and the reading Kayla got on Beatrice Keller's emotions was confusing and unpleasant, a jumble of greed, anger, and fear. Kayla didn't care to probe farther.

"I've called a Miners' Guild meeting for tomorrow afternoon," Beatrice said. "Business never stops. Of course, the matter of the open seat must be settled."

"My father's seat, you mean?" Kayla met her eyes, not bothering to conceal her dislike. "What is there to settle?"

Beatrice seemed caught by surprise. "Why, we have to fill the seat, dear. Surely you understand that."

"There's nothing to fill. I'll be there to claim it."

"Claim it?" The older woman frowned. "You? Don't be ridiculous. You're barely of age."

"The lawyer said that the courts will declare me an adult, and I've already told him I want to maintain the family business. Why shouldn't I have my father's seat on the Guild of Styx as well?"

Kayla felt the woman attempting an empathic probe

in direct violation of all rules of polite empathic society. Kayla held her own shields firm, just as her father had taught her. Beatrice Keller was not a particularly strong empath, and Kayla knew she could keep her at bay. Still, it was a blatant discourtesy, a way of communicating that, legalities aside, she saw Kayla as a child undeserving of the etiquette reserved for adult empaths.

"It's a complicated situation," Beatrice said. "We'll explain that to you tomorrow." All pretense of kindness had vanished from her face. "This is certainly no place for it."

Kayla stared back at her defiantly. "I'll see you tomorrow, then."

Yates offered to walk her home, earning an outright glare from his mother, but Kayla refused. She wasn't in the mood for any company right now, especially if that company went by the name of Keller. Besides, she wanted time alone. She needed it to go through her father's records and study every dealing he had ever had with the Guild. So Beatrice Keller considered her a child undeserving of even the slightest courtesy? Well, she might just find a few surprises waiting for her at the meeting tomorrow.

* * *

The next morning, Beatrice Keller had a meeting with the Trade Congress representatives from Vardalia, Coral Raintree and Robard Fichu.

She sat behind her massive stone desk and eyed her visitors with ill-concealed disdain. The two agents for Pelleas Karlson, Fichu and Raintree, sat across from her in her office, smiling like idiots. They were doing their best to seem ingratiating while actually attempting to intimidate her. The nerve of them, to try and force the Keller family business into a partnership with Karlson. It might have been amusing if it weren't so damned annoying. She was accustomed to these periodic forays by the prime minister's operatives, but she had never cared for them. They took up too much of her time.

She reflected sourly over the horrendous week just past. First the cave-in, which had come close to endangering her own family's holdings. Then the deaths of the Reeds and the funeral that she had forced herself to attend. Beatrice hated funerals and avoided them whenever possible. She could never forget that Redmond Reed had helped her cheat death years ago when he had pulled her out of the dust pit that had claimed her husband. Ever since, she had felt that every funeral that was held should have been hers. Death had touched her for a moment, and she bore that mark forever, regardless of the rejuvenation treatments she submitted to at regular intervals.

Redmond Reed, dead. It was difficult to take that in. She had disliked the man, found him contentious, righteous, and narrow-minded. Always an obstacle to whatever she had proposed in the Miners' Guild. But she owed him her life, and therefore she had attended his funeral, as unpleasant as that had been. Respect must be shown, the appropriate rituals must be observed. The exchange with his brat of a daughter hadn't improved her mood, though. One would think the girl would know better. Hadn't Redmond told her about all the money he owed to the Kellers? Only foolish sentiment had kept her from foreclosing on the family and sending them packing. And sentiment had spurred her on to offer to pay the girl's hospital bills. But there had to be an end to it. Now that Redmond was dead, it was time to call in the loan and assume the Reed holdings. That silly child Kayla would never be able to manage those mines alone.

She thought of the girl's thin, heart-shaped face, the large green eyes so like her father's, and that shock of unruly red hair. Perhaps she would grow into her looks. But it hardly mattered. She was a sharp-faced child, graceless and clumsy. Yates had been charitable, perhaps too kind, in accompanying her to the funeral when he knew how his mother felt about those occasions!

And now, on top of everything else, these unwelcome visitors had descended upon her, uninvited, from the lofty towers of Vardalia. Soft, pampered offworlders, accustomed to balmy breezes and two suns in the sky, bringing their velvet-wrapped threats. They would never last a week in the mines. Five minutes alone in the dark and they would begin whimpering. As would their owner, Pelleas Karlson.

"Mrs. Keller," the scrawny male, Fichu, was saying. "We are in a position to support your enterprises with quite considerable resources—"

With an irritable gesture, she cut him off. "Mr. Fichu, I'm fully aware of the wealth available to the prime minister. But as you know, we are a small, family-owned operation." *And we like it that way,* she thought.

"Precisely our point," said the other agent, the big blonde named Raintree. "We are authorized to help you expand that business to insure its dominance in the marketplace."

Beatrice smiled coldly. "Why do we need your help to maintain what we already have?"

Raintree didn't miss a beat. "But that's exactly it. Yes, you dominate the market today. Possibly even tomorrow. But what happens next week, when the stones are synthesized, or a rival miner agrees to outside sponsorship? It's dangerous not to have powerful friends."

"And just as dangerous to have them," Beatrice shot back. "Sometimes they can protect you right out of your own best interests." She paused and, with exaggerated attention, looked at her watch. "I'm terribly sorry. I have a meeting scheduled with the Guild of Styx."

"We'd be happy to wait," Raintree said, smiling a trifle too brightly.

"I'm afraid that would be pointless," said Beatrice. "Please tell the prime minister that I appreciate his interest, but the answer is still no."

"But—"

"Now, if you'll kindly excuse me." She stared them out of her office.

What pests, she thought. Let them report to Karlson that she was a stubborn woman. Perhaps the Prime Minister would do someone else the honor of targeting them for his silly power plays and allow her to get her work done.

The door to an inner closet opened and Yates walked in.

"You heard all that?"

"Yes."

"Good. And what did you think?"

Her son's expression was guarded. "That we should, perhaps, accept Karlson's friendship."

"What?" She stared at him in disbelief.

"Mother, if we ever need him, we might find the cost of his patronage greater than we can bear. If we join with him now, we'll be invulnerable."

"We're strong enough."

He shook his head. "I disagree. We're never strong enough. Arrogance is dangerous, Mother. By refusing Karlson's offer—and insulting him—you weaken us."

Beatrice turned on her firstborn with amazement and anger. "I suggested that you listen to my business dealings so that you could learn, not criticize."

He met her fire with his own. "Don't order me around like some flunky if you expect me to learn. You only deal with the present, Mother. I'm concerned about the future."

"Is that so? And why, if you're so concerned about the future, do you waste your time buzzing around that little Reed girl?"

Yates seemed amused rather than angry. "Mother, you really are blind, aren't you?" He started to say more, stopped, and shrugged. "Come on. We'll be late for the Guild meeting."

She swallowed her angry retort. She didn't want to fight with Yates, especially right before an important Guild meeting. He was young. With time and tempering he would come to see that she was right. She could afford to be understanding.

Chapter Four

The lump in Kayla's throat grew with every step she took toward the Guild Hall entrance. *My father should be doing this,* she thought. *Not me.*

She pushed the pad beside the studded doors and waited. Would someone greet her?

The doors slid open, obviously keyed to allow general entry. Heart pounding, Kayla stepped inside.

The gleaming table with its burnished golden surface, the soft, curved chairs, the glowing translucent walls of the carved chamber—she had seen it all as a small child, visiting with her father. To walk up and take a seat at the table as sole representative of the Reed family stake was unthinkable. Yet she was doing it, feet moving in dreamlike cadence, right up to the chair marked "Reed."

For a moment the room swam in her vision. She swallowed hard. Already, several Guild members were ranged around the table: Johannes Goodall, Miriam Crown, and Rusty Turlay. All of them had worked side by side with her father and mother. They stood now in a determined show of welcome.

"Kayla," Miriam said. Her wide brown face crinkled with affection. "It will be good to have you at our table."

Bald, brawny Johannes Goodall reached out to tousle her hair as he had so many times before. Halfway through the motion, he froze, as if remembering that she was now legally an adult and an associate. He put the offending hand behind his back and shrugged. His face was bright red.

Rusty gave her a grin through his beard and winked a bright blue eye. "Just one big family," he said.

"And, boy, do we have some family fights," Johannes added. He rolled his eyes. "Watch out for Beatrice. She's got sharp teeth."

"Hey, don't discourage the kid before the meeting has even begun," said Miriam. "Kayla, don't pay any attention to them. The first Guild meeting is always a little confusing. Don't worry, you'll get the hang of it soon enough."

Kayla smiled gratefully. They were making it easier for her to be there, embracing her as a colleague and friend. She took a deep breath and sat down. It wasn't as difficult as she had expected, not by half.

Just as she was beginning to relax, Beatrice Keller swept in with Yates and the rest of the Guild members.

Beatrice gave Kayla a cool smile. "I see you're determined to join us. Well, a vote will have to be taken on that. But as Guild president, I welcome you as an observer on behalf of us all," she said. "If you have any questions about protocol, feel free to ask me or anybody else here."

"Thank you, Beatrice," Kayla said pointedly. She had never before called Beatrice Keller by her first name, but she wanted to make it clear that her status had changed. Nevertheless, it felt odd.

Only a few chairs were empty: miners who were busy with their stakes or, more rarely, off-world. Kayla knew that not many of the miners enjoyed traveling far away from their tunnels: as empaths, they found it uncomfortable—if not unendurable—to be near large numbers of unshielded minds.

"Let's talk about the proposed mindstone salt deal, shall we?" Beatrice said. "As I told you, we have buyers already lining up for the salt."

"I'm for it," said Wilson Kurland. "It would make

use of the tailings from our mines, and of stones which aren't good enough to be cut. Just grind 'em down and sell the powder, I say, if anybody's fool enough to want it."

"Have we discovered yet just what, if any, euphoria-inducing properties the salt has?" Miriam asked.

"I don't think that matters," said Yates Keller. "As long as there's demand."

Rusty gave him a disgusted look. "And if there was high demand for poison, would you knowingly sell it to the highest bidder, laddie?"

Yates flushed. "Of course not. I'm not suggesting we sell untested salt. But I don't see why we should be concerned about its effects so long as there's a proven market for it."

"Have you tried it?" Miriam said.

"No. Why should I?"

Miriam's face had turned bright pink. "How can you expect anyone else to use it if you don't know its effects? No one, aside from a few nuts, has ever eaten mindstones before. Can the human system tolerate it?"

"Hell, Miri, the Vardalians will love it," Johannes said soothingly. "They'll probably sprinkle it over their breakfast steaks. They'll bathe in it. They're absolutely crazy for mindstones."

"I told you, the market is there for the salt," Beatrice said. "Yates is right. We know it's harmless stuff. We've all been inhaling it for years. Why not sell it rather than dump it into the dust pits?"

Kayla sensed a deep undercurrent of mistrust and resentment welling up from the group in response to Beatrice's comment. Never before had she realized how thoroughly some of the miners disliked Beatrice and her family. The Kellers had pioneered Styx. Beatrice's great-grandfather had been one of the first prospectors on-world. Small wonder that the Kellers held some of the best stonebeds. And smaller wonder that they were so resented.

She remembered her father explaining some of the group dynamics to her. "It's natural for all the little dogs to hate the big dog," he had said. "But somebody's still got to run the pack."

Apparently, nobody in the Guild was willing to challenge Beatrice outright. But that didn't mean they were happy about her leadership.

"Let's vote on it," Yates said.

"Seconded," said Wilson Kurland.

The vote was nine for, three against.

"Good, that's settled," Beatrice said. She looked even sleeker, eyes gleaming with satisfaction. "Now, there's the matter of a shipment of gems that caused temporary psychological disorders in the purchasers. Rusty, I believe you mined those gems. I thought you agreed to leave that vein alone."

"There's nothing wrong with my stake," Rusty said. "It's the cutters. They must have damaged the stones. Once I sell the lot, it's not my responsibility how badly they're cut."

"We do like to try and use reputable cutters rather than cheap, illegal shops. After all, we'll get blamed, regardless of whose fault it is."

"Hell, Beatrice, I know you'd like us all to use the same cutters you do. You've probably got some sort of sweet little deal worked out with them."

There was stunned silence.

Beatrice reared back angrily. All the color had drained out of her face. "I beg your pardon. Are you implying that the Keller family enterprises are engaged in illegal schemes to line our pockets at the customer's—and your—expense? And are you willing to back that up in court?"

"Whoa now, calm down," Johannes said. "Come on, you two. This is a Guild meeting."

Rusty tensed, as though preparing to spring right at the Guild president. Then, all of a sudden, the fight went out of him. "Hell," he said. "I'm sorry, Beatrice. I just spoke without thinking, that's all. You know me."

She stared at him, but he would not meet her glance.

"I do know you, Rusty," she said. "That's why I won't take what you said seriously. At least not this time. By the way, your payment's late."

"Dammit, I told you. I'll get it to you on the fifteenth."

Kayla stared miserably at the tabletop, humiliated for poor Rusty's sake. She could tell that he had meant exactly what he had said to Beatrice. In fact, she sensed that he had the proof to back up his accusations. Why, then, didn't he use it? Why was he so frightened of Beatrice Keller? What was even more puzzling, Kayla could read similar fears in the minds of almost everyone present. Why were they all so terrified? Did she hold the mortgage on every mine on Styx?

She glanced down the table. Even Yates was wary and well-defended around his mother. She looked at his handsome face and felt his dark eyes lock onto hers with an almost palpable shock. She had always found him attractive and there was no mistaking the voltage in his gaze now. To her chagrin, Kayla felt her face get hot. She didn't want to think about Yates. She wanted to concentrate on Rusty.

Before she knew what she was doing, she heard her own voice saying, "I don't think that's fair."

Beatrice Keller turned toward her and Kayla had the impression of a great beast of prey opening its jaws.

"Pardon me?" Beatrice said softly.

Kayla forced strength into her voice. "I just don't think that's fair."

"What isn't fair?"

"Using your influence to shut Rusty up like that."

Miriam was shaking her head frantically, and Johannes sent a sharp warning through nearsense: —*Kayla, stop it.* But she was too wound up to pull back now.

"Let her speak," Beatrice said.

"Well," said Kayla, "if Rusty has a complaint, he should be allowed to air it."

Beatrice sighed. "Now listen carefully, dear. Rusty's complaints are all well known to me. Do you realize that what he just said to me was slanderous? I could take him to court over it."

"But it's true!"

Beatrice closed her eyes as though mastering herself with effort. "You are not a child any longer," she said. "Stop acting like one, or I'll be forced to have you removed from this meeting."

"I won't shut up, Beatrice! Just because you hold the loans for half the people here doesn't mean you can lord it over us like we're peons—"

"Damn you, girl," Beatrice snapped. "Be quiet!"

Kayla couldn't believe it. No one had ever talked to her in that tone of voice before. And not one member of the Guild dared to oppose Beatrice, nor did anybody dare make an attempt to defend Kayla against her. Well, she didn't care. She met her cold gaze and said, "You're a bully, Beatrice. I don't know why the Guild puts up with it."

"I've had about enough of this," Beatrice said. "I was going to suggest that we formalize your assumption of the open Guild chair, to give you the benefit of my doubt. But I don't think you're ready. I make a motion that we table this issue for reevaluation."

"Seconded," said Wilson Kurland.

Beatrice wasn't finished. "What's more, I want full payment on the loans I gave your father or I'll foreclose."

Kayla looked around the table. Miriam trembled on the verge of tears, red-faced Johannes stared at the floor, and Rusty scowled and made a disgusted sound but no one said a word.

"Fine," Kayla said. "Keep your precious Guild seat, Beatrice. I don't want it if I'm expected to just rubber-stamp your decisions. And don't worry, I can pay you. I'll pay you right away."

An excited buzz rose around the table as what she had said sank in.

Beatrice stared at her, astonished. "Pay?" she said. "Exactly how do you propose to do that?"

"My father left me something that should satisfy the debt. I'll go get it." She stood up, pushed back her chair, and without another look at the group hurried from the chamber.

The harsh artificial light of the tunnels washed over her, casting long shadows as she raced home. Tears of fury nearly blinded her. She would show Beatrice Keller—and all of those cowards on the Guild. She would rattle her bag of mindstones right in their faces and watch their jaws drop. *You want payment, Beatrice? Watch. I'll pour out the finest mindstones you've ever seen, right onto that burnished table. You'll beg to buy them from me. And you'll beg me to come back to your stupid Guild, too!*

She pressed the palm block at the front door and slid through the aperture into the house.

The mindstones waited in the small safe she kept in her bedroom behind a holopic of sunrise on Liage. She whispered the combination into the lock speaker and the door sprang open.

Ah, what a satisfying heft the bag of stones had in her hand. She rattled it triumphantly.

"What have you got there?" said a low male voice.

Kayla jumped.

Yates stood in the doorway, leaning carelessly against the green carved wall.

She hadn't heard or sensed another presence. He must have come in fully shielded. But how had he gotten there so fast? Had he followed her right out of the Guild meeting?

"What are you doing here? Aren't you afraid that your mother will find out?"

He shrugged, leaned down, and took hold of her shoulders. Gently, he raised her up until she was standing, face-to-face with him, mere inches away. He didn't remove his hands and she realized that she didn't mind.

"You mustn't take Mother so seriously," he said softly. "Oh, she doesn't like insubordination, and she's a bear for protocol, but she just lost her temper. She doesn't really mean all she says."

"Which parts didn't she mean?"

Yates chuckled. "She likes you, you know. She's always had a soft spot for your family."

"Not the way I heard it."

He shook his head mildly. "That was just political. You know that. He saved her life. She'll never forget it."

"My dad didn't like to talk about things like that."

"He didn't talk about how pretty you were, either. But I've noticed."

Kayla didn't know what to say, and she was afraid that she would start blushing again.

"Seriously," Yates said. His dark eyes met hers with hypnotic power. "I like you, Kayla. I always have."

Before she knew what was happening, he was kissing her.

When they came up for air, he whispered, "I love you, Kayla. I want you. Come back to the meeting. I'll protect you. I promise."

Her senses swirling, Kayla tried to make sense of what was happening. She had always thought Yates Keller was the handsomest man on Styx, but he had never seemed to pay much attention to her. Now he was holding her, kissing her, and telling her he that he loved her. He had followed her from the meeting to comfort her. She felt excitement flaring in her chest like a tiny sun.

Yates pressed her close and she didn't fight him. When he kissed her again, the touch was electric.

Kayla wanted to stay there for hours, kissing him, feeling his hands stroking her hair. But her restless empathic senses were less easily tethered, and they bounced and rebounded off his shields.

Why was Yates so thoroughly shielded? Idly, with only half of her concentration focused, she made a stronger attempt to get through.

When that failed, her interest was really piqued. What was he hiding? Kayla was determined to find out. Even as he pressed his lips against hers, she sent a powerful probe lancing into him.

He was aroused. She saw that clearly, and couldn't help feeling an answering pang. But she probed deeper, deeper, broke through into memory and saw him as a young boy watching his parents, saw his sorrow at his father's death and his awe of his mother. Saw, too, his casual attraction to Kayla, and also his amused condescension to her childishness. That stung. But as Kayla recoiled from that, she touched something dark and terrible, something that she couldn't see clearly, and as she tried to focus on it, Yates' mental shields intensified and she couldn't proceed without alerting him to her probe. But there was something harsh and ugly in him, something ruthless and devouring hidden from view behind that handsome face and easy smile.

Kayla pulled back slightly and saw that he didn't love her. He liked her, sort of, but he was drawn to her more out of curiosity and impulsive desire which he was romanticizing. More compelling to him was a strange sense of guilt which permeated his mental processes but whose source was lost in the formless darkness behind his defenses. There was also a lurking desire to please his mother, Beatrice, by bringing Kayla back into the fold. Beatrice, the queen of the mines, who was afraid that Kayla might somehow find a way to pay off the loans—perhaps by borrowing from sympathetic friends of her parents—and thereby elude Beatrice's control. It made an ugly sort of sense.

If Yates successfully wooed and married Kayla, that would really bring the Reed stake into the control of the Kellers.

Kayla reeled from the knowledge. He had been toying with her, the entire time, just playing with her emotions.

His arms felt like steel braces around her. "Let go of me!"

He grunted and tightened his grip.

Again she saw that dark place deep within him, and the half-glimpsed horrors that lurked there.

How dare he treat her this way! Who was he to think he could take over the Reed stake? Rage flooded her mind—a wild surge of overwhelming anger and repulsion. No one could play with her like this, no one!

Kayla tore herself from his grasp. "You son of a bitch!"

Before she knew what she was doing—and against all of her careful conditioning—Kayla attacked, flinging a storm of anger at Yates, a mindbolt of such intensity that he gasped like a drowning man and fell to his knees.

She struck at him again.

Yates waved his arms feebly, trying to ward off the frontal attack, his face a mask of shock and terror.

Once more Kayla lashed out at him.

With a groan, Yates crumpled to the floor and lay there, facedown, eyes closed, unmoving.

"Yates?" Kayla poked him with her foot. He didn't respond, but she saw to her relief that he was still breathing. Not dead, just unconscious.

She felt nauseated and dizzy, drained by the power of her effort, by her fury and confusion. Her father had warned her never to use her powers against other people. But in one moment of blind rage she had thrown aside all his of his teachings.

It would ruin her.

The kind of assault she had just committed was punishable by confiscation of all the family holdings and years in prison.

I've played right into Beatrice Keller's hands, she thought miserably. *Now she'll be able to take everything.*

What should I do?

In despair she cast around the friendly rooms where she had grown up. Oh, why weren't her parents here, why wouldn't somebody tell her the right thing to do?

She gazed distractedly at the walls and ceiling, at the objects that she had known for her entire life. Lost to her now—all of them, everything. The disaster was complete. She was alone, surrounded by enemies, and she had just given Beatrice Keller an excuse for annexing the Reed stake and imprisoning her. Run! She had to leave, get away, hide.

Get away, she thought. *Get away before Yates comes to. I can't let them catch me and lock me up. I won't!*

A lump grew in Kayla's throat. She stamped her foot. *There's no time for this now,* she thought angrily. She grabbed up the bag of mindstones—her parents' legacy—took one last look at the place where she had spent her childhood, and ran for her life.

Chapter Five

Styx Port bustled as robot cranes and loaders crawled along the shiny beetle-brown carapace of a shuttle, swinging pallets and crates into its loading bay. The cruiser was poised for its return to the mothership hovering in orbit far above the surface of the planet.

A shuttle track had been carved from the extinct volcano whose ancient caldera enclosed the main Styx landing strip. Two sets of massive space doors kept the area safe from total vacuum. The shuttle would pass through those on its way back to the outer worlds of the Trade Alliance.

Still reeling from her encounter with Yates, Kayla steadied herself against a metal pylon, leaning her cheek against it until the coolness penetrated the fog in her brain. She reached into her pocket and heard a few credits rattle. Too few, not nearly enough to buy passage off-world. And if she used any credits, that would leave a trail, one the Kellers could follow. She had no choice, really. She would have to sneak aboard, somehow.

She studied the entrance to the ship: two massive barrels of shielded mindstones provided cover near the shuttle's open bay. Kayla ducked out of sight and waited for her chance.

A slim, white-blonde woman wearing a silvery pressure suit walked briskly out of the shuttle and hurried down the loading dock, out of sight.

Using her farsense, Kayla probed the interior of the

small spacecraft. No mental activity in there. It was empty. She took a deep breath and scrambled through the door.

The ship was crammed with barrels set in holding pens. There was barely enough room for the cockpit. Forcing her way around the cargo and behind a row of empty pressure suits, she found a webbed couch at the back of the ship onto which she could hook herself during acceleration. With the suits hanging over her she might not be seen.

Must not be seen, at all costs. She knew that.

I could use shadowsense to prevent anyone from seeing me, she thought, and felt an immediate pang of conscience. Her father wouldn't have liked it. But he was gone and she was here, faced with problems he'd never had to think about.

Dad, I don't want to! I don't want to disregard all you taught me! What should I do? What would you do?

Clattering footsteps distracted her. The pilot returning? Kayla slid down even farther beneath the suits, wrinkling her nose at their peculiar sweet/sour metallic smell.

Clank!

The door of the shuttle was thrown to and locked. Kayla heard someone—the platinum blonde?—in the cockpit. The walls of the shuttle hummed, vibrating as the engines came suddenly to life. The crackling voice of the flight controller announced: "Shuttle *Endor,* you are cleared for departure."

"Thanks," said a firm female voice. "*Endor* beginning departure sequence now."

"Roger, *Endor.* Bringing mindstones to the stars, are you? Where are you headed?"

"After rendezvous with the *Seiko Maru,* we're going to Brayton's Rock. For starters."

The controller chuckled. "I know you'll have an interesting time there. Safe trip, *Endor.* Styx Port out."

The shuttle gave a sudden brief shudder. Kayla felt

her weight shift back gradually against the couch and
realized that the little spaceship was sliding forward
along its magnetic tracks, up the long tunnel to the surface of Styx.

Despite her turmoil, she was intrigued. She might
see the suns of the Cavinas System, perhaps even the
stars! How she had longed to see the stars, had badg-
ered her parents, demanded vid cubes, and light shows.
Now, finally, through the most unimaginable circum-
stances, she might actually get her childhood wish. She
sank down beneath her camouflage of space suits, impatient for her first glimpse of the world outside.

* * *

Nighttime in Vardalia with its swirling clouds and
glow globes winking in the sky like the younger brothers of the orbital colonies high above. Pelleas Karlson
walked the paths of his private zoological garden, one
of the greatest luxuries to be had on land-starved St.
Ilban.

He saw the leonine prides of moccicats from Acturus
nesting quietly, the green and slender Carew cattle settled for the night, the purple-feathered bat parrot of
Endor asleep on its perch. Finally he came to the Liage
pens. John Kavorkian, his zookeeper greeted him at the
gate. "Evening, Excellency. Our new shipment is
here." With a nod he gestured into the shadow of the
pens where something seemed to be stirring.

"And have you made our new arrivals comfortable?"

"As comfortable as I know how. Not that they would
ever let on for a moment how they feel."

"An enigmatic bunch."

"In all my years as a keeper, I've never seen a stranger lot. They just stare at me with those huge purple
eyes and make tiny sounds, like birds."

Karlson patted him on the shoulder. "I'm sure you'll
give them everything they need. Any problems, you
know who to come to."

"Yes sir."

"Carry on." Karlson continued his evening stroll.

"Good night, Prime Minister."

He felt the tension in his neck knotting up—a twinge every time he turned his head—and cut short his walk. Back to his quarters, to the lift which brought him home, and Ti-ling.

Beautiful Ti-ling, of the golden skin and satiny hair.

* * *

Karlson leaned back against the pillows and enjoyed the sensation of supple hands rubbing his flesh.

"A little higher, Ti-Ling, and to the left."

Trained as a body worker, his golden-skinned mistress, Ti-ling, pressed down upon his neck and shoulders. Her silky dark hair hung over her face and tickled the back of his neck. Karlson groaned happily. When she had finished he lay still, eyes closed, for several minutes. But his was not a relaxed nature and there was only so long he could stay immobile.

He swung his legs over the side of the bed, and stood up.

"I've brought you a present."

Her almond-shaped eyes glowed with pleasure. "Pelly, you didn't. Where is it?"

He handed her the shiny box and watched her tear at the wrappings, eager as a child.

Her face fell as she stared at the contents. "A box of purple sand? Is this a joke?"

Karlson's lips twisted in amused impatience. Of course she didn't understand. "No, my dear, it's certainly not. I've brought you the latest, most exciting thing. Everybody wants to do it. Mindsalt."

"Mindsalt?" Her pretty face was clouded, confused. "I've never heard of it."

"It's ground mindstones. You put it in tea or liquor and drink it."

"Drink sand?" Ti-ling wrinkled her nose in disgust.

"The effects are supposed to be ... quite special."

The corners of Ti-ling's mouth curved upward. "Pelly, we don't need any aphrodisiacs."

"Still, I'd like you to try it."

She sighed indulgently. "Okay."

He poured her a glass of bubbling wine and dropped a palmful of the mindsalt into the libation. "Down the hatch."

Ti-Ling swallowed the mixture in two gulps. "Hmmm. Not bad. Just a little gritty."

"How do you feel?"

"I don't know." She held up her glass. "I'd like more wine."

"Let's not dilute the stuff." He sat back, watching her in fascination. How would the effects first manifest themselves? He felt as giddy as a child opening a birthday present.

Ti-ling's eyes began to glaze over. Her complexion grew pallid, her breathing swift and shallow. She gasped.

Karlson leaned forward eagerly. "What is it? What do you see?"

When she answered him, it was in a language he didn't understand. She didn't see him, didn't respond to his voice or the pressure of his hands. She was lost in some private, inner world.

Damn, he thought. Where was his universal translator? Did he even keep one in the bedroom?

Frantically he scrabbled through his headboard's compartments. Ah, there it was, long unused in its sleek metal casing. He pulled the translation device forth and held it near Ti-ling's mouth.

"I can hear you singing, Grandmother. I can hear your voice in the stars, calling to me."

Karlson stared at his slender mistress in chagrin. She was babbling, speaking nonsense.

Ti-ling turned and seemed to focus blurrily upon him. "No, not nonsense," she said. "You should try to understand. You should try much harder."

Karlson stared at her, aghast. He had said nothing, yet she seemed to know what he was thinking. Was she reading his mind? No, no, it was sheer coincidence. The mindsalt couldn't possibly work that way. Karlson felt a chill pass through him. Ti-ling's eyes were strange, unblinking. She began to say something else. Then, with a sigh, she closed her eyes, curled in upon herself on the high, white bed, and began to snore gently.

—*You should try to understand. . . .*

If only I could, Karlson thought. *If only I could.*

* * *

The voice cut into her dreams. "Get up! You there! Come on, get out from under those suits. I can see you. Don't think you can hide!"

Groggily, Kayla fought her way up to wakefulness. Where was she? What was happening?

"Hurry it up!" The voice was shrill, angry, and female. The shuttle pilot.

It all came flooding back to her: the assault on Yates, her mad dash to freedom, and stowing away in desperation. But her hiding place had been detected. *Shadowsense,* Kayla thought. *Use it!*

She took a deep breath to clear her head. This had always been the most difficult of her empathic powers to summon. She reached deep within herself and waited for the energy to form its familiar coil within her mind. It took longer than usual—*Come on! Come on!*—but finally Kayla felt the tingling in her neck that meant she was ready. Exhaling, she expelled a numbing shadow field that blanketed her would-be captor like a dense fog. With some luck, all that the woman would remember was something half-glimpsed, less than a ghost lingering briefly at the edges of her memory. The effort left her nauseated—an unfamiliar aftereffect—but she fought down the bile in her throat.

The pilot gasped and staggered back against the inner wall of the ship.

Clutching her mindstone hoard tightly against her chest, Kayla gathered herself and sprang out from under the suits, past the woman's outstretched hands. It was the same woman she had glimpsed on the docks at Styx Port. The printed label on her red suit said "Samuelson." She stood, seemingly hypnotized, gazing into the middle distance, beyond the shuttle's shell.

The door of the ship gaped open and Kayla dived through it, remembering at the last moment to scan for other mental activity nearby. She caught peculiar glimmers high overhead and beneath her, but nothing in the immediate vicinity. As soon as she got out the door she saw the reason for her odd impressions.

She was standing in a huge, deserted shuttle bay. At least two other shuttles, sleek, gray, and identical to the *Endor* sat on their launch tracks. But they were dark and silent. The *Endor* must have docked within its mothership while Kayla slept. Her first glimpse of space would have to wait.

The bay was huge: Kayla had never been in a room with such a high ceiling before. Some of the caves of Styx had been enormous, yes, but never like this: square with regularly spaced rows of light fixtures and metal casing lining the walls.

The mutter and purr of hundreds of minds filled her head before she slammed down her shields. The noise! Where were all these people? Their thoughts seemed to come from above and below her, all around.

Don't stand around gawking, she told herself. *You've got to find a better hiding place until you figure out what to do next.*

At the double portal she paused and used her farsense to listen; the outer passage seemed to be clear. She took a step closer to the door and it flew open with a hiss. She was in a hallway of the *Seiko Maru*. At first glance, it didn't seem much different from one of Styx's tunnels, just better lit and carpeted with some ugly gray stuff which muffled footsteps. An odd, thrumming seemed to pulse through the corridor. Was that the throb of the engines? There was a sweet, canned quality to the recycled air that was different from the tangy darkness of the atmosphere back home.

I'm on a spaceship somewhere between worlds, Kayla thought. Try as she might, she couldn't quite grasp the fact. *Funny, I thought it would feel more alien than this.*

She crept along, casting her farsense before her like a net. Two people were coming down an adjacent corridor. Panicking, Kayla hurried to the nearest door, pressed the keypad, and thrust herself through.

Rows of jumpsuits hung from floor to ceiling like a strange metallic forest. She was in some sort of storage facility. A whirling click startled her, and she jumped again as a row of suits began to move, swinging gently, left and right, until a purple-and-silver-striped suit emerged, was grasped by robot arms, and flung down a chute. Kayla stared in wonder. What was this place? A laundry?

I need to blend in, she thought. *Maybe one of these suits will fit me.*

She began to inspect the rows of limp pantlegs. This one? No, it looked too big. This one? Too bright. Finally, she found a gray suit with lime stripes at the wrists and ankles. That seemed safe enough. She shrugged into it and was pleased to find that it even had a compartment where she could stow her mindstone sack. She pulled her hair back into a neat braid and took a deep breath.

Back out in the corridor, she felt a little less conspicuous than before. Now, if she could only find a porthole or viewing platform and get a look at actual space.

"Jump in one minute," a hidden loudspeaker announced. "Jump in one minute. Please secure quarters."

Kayla wondered just how one went about securing

quarters on a ship this large. She was beginning to imagine doors slamming and locking when, without warning, the walls contracted around her and time seemed to stop.

She was frozen in mid-step, a long row of similarly frozen Kaylas extending back behind her down the corridor and out of sight. Her stomach spasmed, cramping and knotting. She couldn't breathe. Couldn't think. She felt as though she were being pulled apart but, try as she might, she could not move. It was agony.

Far away, an alarm sounded, muffled by layers of air.

As she began to wonder how long it would take her to finish dying, the corridor lights blinked, the engine purr resumed its reassuring rhythm, and time crashed back down upon her.

The alarm howled a moment more, than stopped.

Kayla's legs wouldn't support her and she stumbled to her knees as her stomach surged in protest. Gagging, she vomited until she had the dry heaves.

Weak, shaking, she wiped her mouth on the back of her hand and got to her feet. *If that's what jump is like,* she thought, *I don't want any part of it.*

A blue light blinked at the bottom of a wall panel. The panel swung inward and a swarm of mechanical bugs rolled out, chittering angrily. Before Kayla could do more than gasp, the bugs had swirled all around her, cleaned up the mess, and returned to their nest in the wall.

"All medical personnel," the loudspeaker blared. "Report to sick bay immediately. Repeat, all medical personnel to sick bay on the double."

Kayla sensed a mass of people in the corridor just beyond her. A crowd had formed at the mouth of an elevator as crew members crammed themselves into the cab. The doors slid shut. A moment latter, they opened. The cab was empty. A man in a suit just like Kayla's raced toward the lift. When he saw Kayla, he held out his hand.

"C'mon, don't dawdle. You heard them."

Kayla stared at him. "Excuse me?"

He gestured impatiently. "You're going to sick bay, aren't you? That damned power surge during jump screwed half the crew. We've got people puking all over the ship."

Kayla realized with dismay that she must be wearing a medic's uniform. She played along and hurried into the elevator. The doors shut with a lingering hiss.

They opened on bedlam.

People were running back and forth across a wide, gray room. All along the walls, people lay upon cushioned platforms, some moaning, others stiff and unmoving, while still others convulsed, screaming for help.

Kayla staggered as the mental assault hit her: it was like stepping into a terrible vortex as minds cried out in long, sobbed passages of wordless lament. Strange echoes ebbed and roared: breaking glass, screeching winged creatures swooping and diving against a howling wind, terrible discordant music.

Kayla fell back under the mental assault. It was too much, there were too many hungry minds here threatening to suck out her consciousness. It felt as though someone was pounding on the top of her spine, trying to get at the marrow in her bones. Gasping, she shielded herself as she had been taught. But the brief exposure left her badly shaken. Kayla put a trembling hand to her forehead. She was drenched in sweat.

Got to watch it, she thought. *There're too many damaged people in the room. I'm not prepared.*

"You, medic," snapped a gray-haired man with a craggy face. He seemed to be a doctor. "Get over here and help me with this one."

Me? Kayla thought. *Okay, here goes. Don't look him directly in the face.* "Yessir."

The doctor scarcely glanced at her, merely held out a length of flexible tubing filled with blue fluid. "Hold this. Anaphylactic shock here, a damned close call, too. And they're still bringing in colonists going through every stage of jump sickness. I've got to get patches on them all. Didn't anyone warn these damned greenhorns to take their pills?"

He didn't really seem to expect an answer and Kayla didn't offer one, although she could have told him that her brief contact with their minds had revealed that all of these people had taken their antishock pills. No medication could have protected them from the jump malfunction. Even seasoned spacers had been brought to their knees by it.

Kayla grabbed the tubing—it was repellently warm and fleshlike—and held it above the writhing figure on the couch, a middle-aged man with a thick, reddened face. As she watched, the doctor pressed the end of it against the patient's forearm, penetrating the flesh, and squeezed the bulb to initiate the flow of liquid. Apparently satisfied, he leaned back and nodded. "Convulsions should stop in a minute or two." Then he turned, squinting as though he was taking his first look at her. "Forgot your nameplate? Don't let the captain see that unless you're looking to pull extra duty. What's your name?"

Kayla froze. *Name. Think of a name, quickly.* "Kate. Jeffries."

"Jeffries?" The doctor looked momentarily puzzled. "You must be one of the new kids we picked up at the Temple Base. This your first shift in sick bay?"

She said nothing, just nodded and gazed down at the now-unconscious man on the couch.

"I'm McAndrews," the doctor said. "People call me Mac. I run this place. Keep your nose clean and we'll get along."

Another five colonists were brought in, vomiting and screaming. Kayla helped the doctor to sedate them, using her shadowsense to temporarily numb the colonists' pain receptors until the derm patches could be applied.

"Okay, Jeffries," said Dr. McAndrews. "It looks like things are simmering down around here. You might as well help me with the androids."

"Androids?"

The doctor gave her a sharp look. "That's right. We're carrying a full shipment, bound for Malania."

"But that's in the Admanan System."

Dr. McAndrews gave her a strange look. "So?"

"But that's out of bounds because of the radiation."

"You really are a greenhorn, aren't you? Where'd you come from, kid, the dark side of Styx? Malania has been open for years. These androids are being used to terraform it for major colonization."

Kayla blushed. The doctor was right, she really was a greenhorn.

"So," he said, "a bunch of these androids are bad. Have to be kept deactivated. I'm running out of room, so they're in the cold ward."

"In the cold ward?" Kayla began to feel as though he were speaking a foreign language.

"Yeah, the freezer. If their body temperatures rise too high they go haywire. They need refitting. The captain nearly had the entire bunch of them jettisoned."

"A bad shipment of androids." Kayla tried to keep the wonder out of her voice. She had heard about androids, but she had never, ever before seen one.

Dr. McAndrews snorted as though he was tired of talking to amateurs. He led her into a smaller room. The far wall was completely taken up by a smooth white door with a lock panel and what looked like temperature readouts.

He punched out a quick series of numbers on the panel, and the door slid open. Tongues of green mist seeped through the aperture, and with them came the cold.

Inside, the room was softly lit and oddly peaceful. Kayla's breath came out in great frothy pale green plumes.

A dozen bald, sexless, inert bodies were stretched out on slabs as though they were hunks of meat. Kayla scanned them carefully but detected only minimal mental activity.

The room was hushed. Kayla sighed with relief. It was quiet here, so wonderfully quiet. The relentless mental babble of the starship's passengers and crew was scarcely audible, a murmur. Kayla closed her eyes for a moment and savored the silence. She was tempted to lower her shields and relax.

"Am I keeping you awake?"

Kayla's eyes flew open.

Dr. McAndrews was staring at her mockingly. "You like cold places?"

"Yes. I guess so. It's . . . nice in here."

"You've got a strange idea of nice." He unrolled a length of derm patches. "Here you go. Break them off and put one of these behind their right ears. Keeps their metabolic systems ticking while they're in coldsleep."

Kayla touched the android closest to her: it felt rubbery and unreal beneath her fingers. *They're not really people,* she thought. And not really not, either. Biological systems. She was grateful that they were deactivated.

Without a word, the doctor left her alone with her motionless charges.

Kayla peeled the first patch away from its backing and pressed it into place. The android never moved. Was that a tiny smile on its face? The thing looked dead and embalmed. Kayla shuddered and peeled off another patch. She wished that Dr. McAndrews hadn't left her alone. She no longer found the cold room to be such a restful place. It reminded her of a morgue. She finished her task and hurried out, nearly bumping into the doctor.

"All done?" His face softened, almost made it to a smile. "Good. You can take a break, kid. The lounge is up the hall and to the left. The regular staff can handle things."

"Thanks." She waited until his back was turned and, not bothering to conceal her relief, hurried out of the sick bay.

Chapter Six

Outside, the corridor was empty and surprisingly quiet. Kayla lowered her shields gratefully. It was a relief to have solid steel doors between her and the noisy minds in sick bay. It was hard work to maintain her mental defenses against so many people for such long periods of time. Maybe with practice she would get better at it.

She found the lounge McAndrews had mentioned and slipped inside, hoping for a few quiet moments in which she could collect her thoughts.

It was a big, empty room lined by wall seats upholstered in a sparkling red material. The air was filled with the scent of coffee and the muddled whisper of an unattended vid cube. But what caught Kayla's attention was the huge bowed window that opened out upon the black bowl of space. She took a step toward it and caught her breath.

A shooting star trailed a shower of gold as it curved across the face of the void.

Beautiful, she thought. *I never knew that it would be so beautiful.*

She had seen the planets of the Cavinas System before, watched them on her vid cubes. Her parents had given her a library full of cubes, whatever she wanted. Scenes of St. Ilban. Flora and fauna of the three worlds. Prehistoric life-forms of Liage.

But that wasn't the same as seeing the real thing, she realized. Not even remotely.

Space, she had thought, would be dead and black, an

empty vacuum through which distant planets made infinitesimal progress along slow loops of even more distant stars. Instead, it was alive and sparkling like dark crystal lit from within by a million white pinpricks of light.

Where are we? she wondered. *Moving through the Cavinas System, on our way out toward—what had that pilot said?—Brayton's Rock.*

And there, off to the side and far away—were those really the rest of the planets spinning around those tiny twin suns? She gazed in wonder at the first real suns she had ever seen. They looked like tiny glow lamps set deep in the heart of the darkest mines. Not dead. Not at all.

And those precious, tiny planets rolling like rock marbles around two spots of burning light. Which one was Styx? Which one?

"Nice view, isn't it?"

She turned to see a crewman in a blue uniform standing next to her, smiling. He was handsome in a sort of generic way, with blond hair, blue eyes, and a square jaw cleft by a dimple, and very, very confident.

"First time in space?" he said grandly.

"Is it that obvious?"

"Only to a career spacer."

His nameplate said Donan Fraser. Kayla had no clue as to his rank or specialty. With a quick probe she saw, to her dismay, that he was the assistant lieutenant in charge of security.

"That coffee smells wonderful," she said quickly.

"It's probably been recycled twice," Lieutenant Fraser said. "Let's get some fresh stuff."

She watched him press a panel. Two yellow cups were extruded and filled with steaming liquid.

"Here," he said. "Not too bad for ship swill." He took a sip, and another as he looked her up and down. "What's your name, Red?"

"Katie."

"New here?"

"Yes. Just got on at Temple Base." She blessed Dr. McAndrews for giving her enough clues to get by on.

Fraser nodded easily. "Thought you looked unfamiliar. We took on a ton of crew after that blowout at the Ice Cluster." He peered at her. "You must have just gotten out of the med academy. Probably don't even know your way around the ship, yet."

"Not yet," Kayla said truthfully. "I've been kind of busy. I just finished helping them mop up in sick bay after the jump."

"That was one hell of a mess. Whoever arranged passage for those colonists should be shot: It's criminal not to warn groundhogs how to prepare for jump."

Kayla fought back the urge to correct Fraser and point out that the ship's power fluctuation, not the colonists' naiveté, had been the source of the problem. "I guess you're right," Kayla said. "Will we have any more trouble during the next jump?"

"Not likely. Besides, we won't be jumping for a while. We'll be at Brayton's Rock soon. The passengers will have to wait until we've picked up more fuel and food. Then we can head on to the Admanan System. That's a one-jump."

Kayla looked at him with admiration. "Have you really been there before?"

He preened. "Sure."

"But I thought it was dangerous. Contaminated."

"Where've you been? That was years ago, right after their Dust Wars. The only planet too hot to touch now is Dickinson, the fifth, where all the big action was. That leaves Malania, Gorvus, and Bixtang for the colonist. Not that I envy them, poor groundhogs."

"Maybe they like being groundhogs," she said. Lieutenant Fraser's self-regard was beginning to annoy her.

"Good thing," he said. "Since that's all they'll ever be. Now I'm different. I knew I wanted space and that one day I'd get out here. And someday I'll have my own ship, I can guarantee you that. You see, some people are meant for travel, for new things and challenges . . ."

A red light came on at his waist and began to flicker while a high chirping sound filled the air.

"Your belt is beeping," Kayla said.

"Damn. Somebody wants me on the bridge. Listen, we'll be at the Rock in two hours. I know a maxxed club there, a little place called the Red Eye. Want to go?"

"Sure." Kayla had absolutely no intention of ever seeing this overstuffed peacock again if she could help it. But it was easier to say yes and just assume that he would scarcely notice it when she stood him up.

"Great. See you then." With a wave he was gone.

At least he had told her something useful. Landfall on Brayton's Rock would be in two hours. She could hide until then, and when they opened the doors she would mingle with the crowd and get off the ship. Easy. And there was even time for one more look out the window.

* * *

Brayton's Rock was a lumpy planetoid in an irregular orbit on the edge of the Cavinas System. Although technically it belonged to Cavinas, it was neutral territory, wide-open, and Kayla saw at a glance that the main street was filled with every amusement a wandering space jockey could want. Null-g parlors, rental marriages, organ banks, temporary or permanent personality grafts, cyberodeos, hard and soft augments, stims. Real coffee. Anything.

The atmosphere was contained by a series of interlocking domes that circled the port. The air was thick with smoke and humid cooking odors, as though too many circulation pumps had malfunctioned.

Her first spaceport! Her first visit to another planet—or rather, planetoid. Kayla stared and wondered why she didn't feel more awe. It just looked like some busy, gaudy marketplace. Someone jostled her, nearly knocking her off her feet. She spun around, furious.

An android hurried past with its peculiar, rickety-tickety gait. Kayla felt a momentary chill. She didn't like those half-alive, brain-neutral things, she decided. When active, they gave off an unnerving mental vibration that was almost worse than the clamor of unshielded human minds.

Instinctively, she pulled away, deeper into the flow of *Seiko Maru* crew members as they eddied here and there among the shops and taverns. She wanted to get far enough from the crowd to be able to buy some new clothing and ditch her distinctive ship uniform, but she really couldn't do that right under the eyes of her supposed crewmates.

Nice and easy, she thought. *Just keep drifting until you're out of sight.*

She turned down a side street and was relieved to find it relatively deserted. Midway down the block a sign blinked, blue on red, "Clothing Bought and Sold." It was a tiny shop, crammed from floor to ceiling with bales of clothing, and smelled of old rags. She convinced the bearded proprietor to take her medic suit in exchange for a dull green unitard and tunic. She was halfway out the door when a hand grabbed her arm.

"You're far from home, aren't you, little lady?"

The speaker was a big, swarthy man with sharp eyes and dark hair parted so that it sat like two shiny bird wings upon his wide skull. His voice was deep and unexpectedly silky. Kayla stared at him in stunned amazement. Where had he come from?

"Excuse me," she said, and tried to pull herself free. But the man held on. "Let go of me!" Desperately, she looked behind, her but the bearded shopkeeper was nowhere to be seen.

"I saw what you did in there, trying to go incognito. Smart move, but it'll never work. The word's out on you." He pushed aside the flap of his green tunic. A laser pistol sat nestled in a sleek holster within easy reach. "Just stay quiet, do what the Blackbird says, and you won't get hurt." He rested his hand on the pistol's grip. Kayla saw in his mind that he would use it on her without any compunction.

She tried to blanket his vision with shadowsense, but either he was shielded or else she was too distraught to be able to concentrate. She began to panic. Maybe she could pretend to stumble, kick him, and get away. Yes, that was it. She lurched forward, almost squatting, but before she could get any leverage, he pulled her back to her feet.

"No monkey business," he said. "I know you empaths are tricky. But I've got a pulse-disruptor, so your damned nearsense can't work on me. And remember, I've also got my laser aimed right at your head."

Kayla tried to swallow. Her throat was dry with fear. If only someone would walk down the alley!

"C'mon," the Blackbird said.

"Where are we going?"

"To my ship. The Kellers've put out a reward on you, and I'm going to collect it." He yanked her arm sharply. "Walk or I'll stun and drag you."

She was afraid he would make good on his threat when around the corner came an elderly woman, heavyset, gray-faced, almost bald, wrapped in shawls and laden down with packages, her eyes clouded by cataracts.

Without stopping to think, Kayla used nearsense to penetrate the woman's memory and find an image she could use.

—*It's your brother, Jed! You haven't seen him in years! You thought he'd died on a freighter near St. Ilban. But it's him, right here, living and breathing before you!*

Kayla hammered away until the old lady stopped,

dropped her bags, and gasped in breathless amazement, pointing at the bounty hunter.

"Jed!" she cried. "Jed, is it really you?"

The Blackbird glared at her. "What the hell do you want, old woman?"

"You're alive. It's a miracle." She clutched at his arm and managed to hang on despite his efforts to shake her loose.

"Leave off, I say!"

"Don't you know me? Your own flesh and blood! You don't recognize your own sister Martyl, after all these years. I can't believe it." She pulled him into a bear hut, nearly lifting him off his feet.

"Dammit, I'm not your brother. Crazy old biddy!" Blackbird bellowed and swore. But his hand was no longer on his laser pistol and his attention was no longer on Kayla.

She tugged herself free, turned, and bolted down the alley. She could hear the Blackbird's outraged roar, but it faded with every step she took. In a twinkling she was across the main street, zigging and zagging through the side streets. She ran blindly, heedlessly, until she was out of breath.

"There you are," said a familiar voice.

She whirled, expecting to see her captor, ready to kick him in the chops and devil take the consequences.

"Hey, take it easy, you're right on time." It was Lieutenant Donan Fraser, grinning and patting her on the shoulder as though she were some sort of pet. "But you're nonreg, out of uniform. Don't let the old man see it. In fact, I should really turn you in. I could get in trouble myself." He winked. "But I'll let you off, seeing as you're my date." He began to laugh as though he had said something especially witty. "Poor form, that, to report your own date."

Kayla said nothing. She was trapped by this loathsome Fraser. If she made a scene or pulled away, it would only call attention to her, the last thing she wanted. Of all the bad luck!

"Come on, let's go inside and get a table."

Kayla bowed to the inevitable.

"Hey, let's sit down," Fraser said. "The show will start any minute. I'm telling you, these are the best g-dancers in the quadrant. You'll love 'em."

At least she was indoors. Kayla hoped that the Blackbird was still trapped in his "sister's" embrace. She settled into a hardbacked chair near the stage and merely nodded at Fraser's offer of a beer.

The light-field curtain blurred and flipped through a wild spectrum. Then it slowed, slowed and became translucent, finally dimming to transparency. There was only a thin illumination now, enough to show the silhouettes of three men and a woman, all naked, all coated with some reflective material so that they flashed red and blue and purple right along with the stage lights. They were wearing devices upon their heads that occasionally flared with a bolt of silvery light of incredible intensity.

As Kayla watched the dancers kicked off from the stage one by one to hang suspended in midair. They turned lacy cartwheels, wove slow-motion arabesques around one another, and twirled, together and separately, in slow-moving orbits.

They were wearing null-g rigs, Kayla realized. She had heard of these machines but had never expected to see naked dancers onstage wearing them.

The pace picked up and the dancers began to link in erotic configurations. Kayla squirmed in her seat. It was a live sex show. Of course Fraser would suggest something like this for a first date. He probably thought he was being clever.

A shadow loomed in front of them.

"Hey," Fraser called. "Down in front. I can't see."

"Excuse me, spacer, but I want a word here." The voice was deep, silky, and familiar.

The Blackbird! Kayla froze.

Fraser glared at the intruder. "We're busy."

The bounty hunter leaned closer, dark eyes glinting hungrily. "This girl is not what you think."

"You're not getting my message, friend." Fraser stood up. "Now get lost before I call the management."

"You have no idea what you've—"

"Right. That does it." Fraser grabbed the man by his collar. "I'll handle it myself. Be right back, Katie."

"Katie? Her name isn't Katie," the Blackbird sputtered.

Fraser ignored him, dragging him toward the door.

"She's wanted, I tell you. For empathic assault. There's a reward out for her."

"What are you talking about?" Fraser said.

"Listen, we can turn her in, we can claim the reward together." The bounty hunter pawed at Fraser's shoulder. "She's a renegade empath from Styx."

Fraser rolled his eyes. "Are you nuts? She's a medic on the *Seiko Maru.*"

"Really? Did you ever seen her onboard before you made your layover at Styx?"

"Well, now that you mention it—"

Kayla's heart began to pound. She had to get away. But she knew she couldn't use her empathic powers against the Blackbird. Not directly.

The first image that came to her panicked mind was fire, and without hesitation she brought that illusion to life. A wall of fire flared suddenly at the foot of the stage, roared like a maddened beast, and raced toward the audience. Sparks scattered, red flames capered, and blinding smoke was everywhere as the sound of shrieking winds filled the room.

Pandemonium. People ran, screaming, clawing, desperate to get out of the way of the ravening holocaust.

The room swirled around Kayla as the effort to project the mass illusion drained her severely. She staggered and nearly fell, but propped herself up against a table, pouring herself into the terrifying spectacle.

Fraser pointed at the fire and swore. The Blackbird scowled, but before he could do more, both he and Fraser were swept up in the chaos. It seemed as though everyone in the club was trying to get out the door at the same time.

Dizzy and nauseated, Kayla staggered out the door as well, but it was the back door. She forced herself to run until her lungs felt ready to ignite and burst, until the club was lost in the gloom behind her. Only then did she stop to lean, gasping, against the back wall of a storehouse.

Dusk had come and the street was lined by ropes of yellow lamps. Stars winked above in the hazy sky. Kayla stopped for a moment and stared. *Night sky,* she thought. *My first.*

A man, obviously drunk, stumbled past her. Kayla tensed, ready to flee, but all he did was mumble, "Evening, Red," and move on to the next bar.

I've got to do something about this hair. It's like a beacon announcing "here I am." That bounty hunter will be looking for it. And Fraser will probably be right behind him.

Her stomach grumbled, reminding her loudly that she hadn't eaten in almost a day. She shoved the thought away. No time for that now. The Blackbird might come pounding around the next corner any second.

Warily, she roamed the back streets. *I've got to hide,* she thought. *At least stay out of sight until the* Seiko Maru *is gone and Fraser can't arrest me. And stay out of that Blackbird's way.*

She had wandered far from the center of town. There were shuttered warehouses here, closed shops: evidence of former prosperous times on Brayton's Rock. Behind one warehouse she found a pile of packing boxes twice her height. She arranged them carefully and bedded down, out of sight.

Surprisingly, she slept soundly, save for one interruption: the sound of footsteps in the middle of the night. They came close, echoing like thunder, and, as Kayla cowered, paused just beside her hiding place.

—*I'm not here,* she projected. *No one is. Nothing. Ghosts and shadows.*

After a moment, the footsteps resumed, the leaden echoes faded, and were gone.

Chapter Seven

Light, weak and fitful, played against Kayla's eyelids. She sprang up, awake, wondering what that strange glow was. Then she knew. Sunlight. Even at this distance the light of the twin suns could still reach her through the main dome of Brayton's Rock. For a moment she forgot the strangeness of the place, her discomfort, and her predicament, lost in the wonder of actual sunlight.

A growling roar drowned out any other sound or thought. The ground shook. Dust and dirt trickled from the eaves of the buildings to the ground. Windows rattled in their casings, bottles joggled against porch rails.

Quake? Here?

Kayla prepared to hit the ground, but the rumbling eased, softened, faded, was not.

She looked up. A huge firefly was dwindling as it moved up, up, up beyond the domes through the brightening sky. A white-hot flash and it was gone. The thing had vanished, simply vanished.

It took her another moment to understand.

The *Seiko Maru*. It had gone into jump, taking its cargo of inert androids and puking, grav-sick colonists on their way to the Admanan System.

I hope they remembered to take their pills, Kayla thought. Despite her relief that at least one potential pursuer—Fraser—was gone, she felt oddly bereft and abandoned, and tears welled up suddenly in her eyes.

Don't be ridiculous, she told herself. *You didn't be-*

*long there any more than you belong here. Any more
than you belong anywhere, really. You're a ghost. A
woman without a shadow. Now stop sniveling and figure out what your next move is.*

Kayla got up, stretched, and relieved herself by the
far corner of the warehouse wall where, she observed,
others had been before her.

A shower and meal would have been heartening. But
she was afraid of attracting too much attention at a tavern. Slowly she moved down a broad, dusty street,
wondering what to do next.

She came around a corner and came face-to-face
with herself. It was a vid kiosk listing fugitives wanted
by the police. She saw that the Kellers had put up a reward of a hundred thousand credits.

Kayla backed away and cut down another alley.

A pink light flashed over a null-g display announcing "24-Hour Beauty. Hair, Eyes, Implants, and More."

She took a step toward the shop. The last of her
credits rattled in her pocket. If she did this, she
wouldn't be able to pay for food or anything else.
Kayla started to turn away. But the words of her
would-be captor, the Blackbird, echoed loudly in her
mind: "dangerous . . . empath."

Do it, she thought. *Now.*

Kayla pushed the door open and walked in. The
clerk at the front desk had the most extraordinary hair
she had ever seen, a three-tiered multicolored confec-
tion of curls, blinking lights, and strings of tiny jewels.
He was intent upon a vid cube and didn't even look up
as she came in.

"Excuse me," Kayla said.

"What do you need?" the clerk asked, yawning.

Kayla smiled. "A cut. I want it short. And dye it."

He was still staring raptly at the vid cube. "What
color? Orange with red streaks? Gold shot through
with black and silver? Green and purple stripes?"

"Brown."

Startled, he momentarily abandoned his vid cube to take a look at her. He frowned in obvious disapproval and shook his head. "With your coloring, black would be much better."

"Brown," Kayla said. "Good old unremarkable brown."

"Suit yourself. But nobody will look at you."

It was well past noon when the clerk finished with her.

Kayla gazed in wonder at the stranger in the mirror. The woman with a neat cap of brown, lusterless hair looked back at her. Kayla swung her head experimentally. What an odd, feathery feeling. Her head felt so light. Her features seemed suddenly much less sharp, her green eyes tamed to unremarkable hazel. She looked like a mouse. Perfect. No one would ever give her a second look. Perhaps not even a first.

"Nice job," she said.

The clerk shrugged, and bells tinkled madly. He managed a listless smile, but his eyes were back on the vid cube. "Glad you're happy. Most of my customers would kill me if I gave them what you asked for. That'll be ninety credits."

She paid him, thanked him again, and pocketed her change. Twenty credits left. Her stomach rumbled. *Food,* she thought. *Even ghosts need to eat.*

The streets were almost deserted. Brayton's Rock seemed geared to afternoon and evening activity. Everybody must be inside sleeping off last night, or the night before, Kayla thought. She wandered until she found a small tavern that was open and went in. It was dark and smoky inside, so dark that it reminded her of the mines. She didn't enjoy the memory.

The scent of cooked meat made her mouth water. She hesitated only a moment before ordering food from the bleary-eyed owner.

"I want something to eat," she said.

"We've got roasted vatmeat. That's it."

"I'll take it." She settled at a table near the fireplace and stared at the dancing flames. Her stomach groaned. When was the last time she had eaten?

The meat was dry, colorless, and nearly devoid of flavor, but she devoured it gratefully, mopping the greasy plate with a crust of stiff bread, and washing it all down with warm, sour beer.

In minutes she was back on the streets with a full stomach. It was a good feeling. For a moment she relaxed.

A dark-haired, heavyset man walked down the street toward her.

Kayla tensed. Was it the Blackbird? Would he see through her disguise?

The man, a complete stranger, walked past without giving her a glance.

She exhaled noisily. That Blackbird was undoubtedly still looking for her, and Brayton's Rock was a small place. She had to keep moving.

The sound of voices rising and falling in harmony floated to Kayla. The young empath found it strangely compelling.

She crossed the street, turned left, walked down a dusty alley, made another left, and came to the source of the voices. It was a gray and weathered building, unremarkable save for a small sign on the door. CHURCH OF THE INNER LIGHT.

The miners of Styx were resolutely secular, but Kayla had heard about different religions, about churches and other houses of religious worship. Weren't all priests and priestesses sworn to secrecy? Maybe she could find help and guidance here.

She tapped on the door. No one answered.

The lock panel was rusted solid. Kayla pushed against the door and it gave under her touch.

Inside, the house was hushed except for the sound of many voices twined in lush harmony.

"Om nimra om. Om nimra om."

Like a sleepwalker, Kayla moved, transfixed, through the entry hall and into the main gallery. It was a spare room, empty of furniture. The floor was covered by knotted yellow mats. Roughly twenty celebrants were in there, clad in loose robes, eyes tightly shut. They all were floating at least five feet above the floor.

A woman with blonde hair in many braids looked over her shoulder at Kayla and smiled broadly. "Welcome, pilgrim." Slowly she lowered herself until her toes touched the floor and she was standing mere inches away, a short, stocky figure in pale green sacking.

Kayla drew back. "What makes you think I'm a pilgrim?"

"All who pass through that door are pilgrims of one sort or another," said the blonde. Her round face glowed with some profound inner serenity. "Make yourself easy. I'm Sarah. Please, come join us. The afternoon session has just begun."

"How do you do that? Floating?" Kayla said.

"Simple. It's a null-g field. We wear belts which can neutralize gravity. See?" She pushed aside a loose fold of cloth to reveal a silvery mesh girdle studded by winking green lights.

"Does it only work in here?"

"Yes. Why would we want to float anywhere else? The gravity on Brayton's Rock has to be enhanced as it is."

Despite herself, Kayla chuckled. "I see." She paused, liking the bright-eyed blonde with her welcoming smile, but wary nonetheless. "Are all who come here allowed inside?"

Sarah gave her a knowing glance. "Well, all are welcome. But we don't allow weapons. Or any use of force. We are nonviolent and will not tolerate any deviation from that among those who dwell beneath this roof."

Better and better, Kayla thought. Despite her fears, she felt herself relaxing. At least the Blackbird couldn't barge in and capture her here. "Is this some kind of religion?"

Sarah's face crinkled into outright amusement. "Why don't you see for yourself?"

"Are you a priestess?"

"We don't have any of those."

"What about the guy up in front?" She pointed at the slender short-haired man who faced the group and whose tenor voice was audible above all the rest.

"That's Nator," Sarah said. "He's just the chant leader. Come on. Here's a belt. It doesn't cost anything. Just try it. The words are on the wall over there."

Kayla peered at the orange holo letters. "Om nimra om." What does it mean?"

Sarah laughed aloud. "Nothing. They don't have to mean anything. We just like to chant for the high we get."

Strapping the belt around her waist, Kayla felt herself beginning to float upward, bobbing gently in the null-g field. It was a curious, not altogether comfortable sensation. "How do I control it?"

"More pressure for less gravity," Sarah said.

"What about the spinning?

"You get used to that."

Once she grew accustomed to the oddness of it, Kayla spent several happy hours floating in null-g. The chanting left her ears ringing, but she felt peaceful and light-headed, almost giddy. Afterward, she helped sweep the room and wipe down the walls. Dinner was a simple affair fixed in the communal kitchen. Kayla munched on her bread and cheese and began to feel as though she had found a safe hiding place at last.

The rest of the evening passed quickly in cleaning and chanting. Kayla was given a spare sleeping mat in the large dormitory and she drifted off while others were still whispering in the dark.

She awoke, in the middle of the night, to feel a hand slipping under her robe.

"What?" she gasped.

"Shhh!"

It was Nator, the chant leader. Was this part of the ritual as well? If so, Kayla wasn't having any of it. She had grown muscular in the mines, lifting heavy loads of rock, and she used those muscles now against the slight, wiry frame of her unwelcome visitor. In a moment she had him in a stranglehold. She squeezed his throat until he made choking sounds. Then she released him to cough and sputter on the mat beside her.

"Are you crazy?" he said. "All initiates are welcomed by me. That's the way it's done."

"In that case, I quit."

Without a word, Nator got to his feet and padded away toward his own mat. Eventually, lulled by the other sleepers' steady breathing, Kayla relaxed and she, too, slept. She awoke before sunrise, took some bread from the kitchen, and walked out, alone, into the predawn neon-riddled gloom.

* * *

Tired, hungry, and more than a little homesick, she wandered the main street past holo parlors, cyberpalaces, and bars where drugs were sold alongside drink at any hour, day or night. Every now and then she saw a vid kiosk and once she saw her face staring boldly back at her. Who was that strange girl, that redhead?

She thought she saw the Blackbird coming out of a doorway and she ducked into a cross-dress salon, pretending to browse the merchandise while ignoring the unfriendly squint of the double-chinned proprietress. When Kayla peered out the window, the bounty hunter was nowhere to be seen. A quick empathic scan showed no sign of his mindtrail.

She moved slowly down the street, aimless and light-headed, and paused, her attention drawn to another vid kiosk.

QUIK MARRIAGE 'N DIVORCE.
TOTAL HOLO ENVIRONMENTS FOR RENT BY DAY OR HOUR.
AUCTION OF CONFISCATED GOODS.
TEMPORARY ROOMMATES WANTED.
GUNS BOUGHT, NO QUESTIONS ASKED.
THREESOME LOOKING FOR FOURTH, FIFTH, AND SIXTH.
NEED A NEW FACE? TRY DON'S PLASTIC SURGERY PARLOR: QUICK AND PAINLESS. NEW I.D. FREE WITH EVERY PROCEDURE.
JEWELRY PURCHASED.
LASER STIMS
MEMORY IMPLANTS
BAIL BONDSMEN/LEGAL REFERRALS
PROXY MARRIAGES
STIMULANTS, TRODES, MASSAGE
ISOLATION TANKS
ESCORT SERVICE
S&M MATES AND MATCH-UPS WHILE U WAIT
SHIP FOR RENT
HELP WANTED.

The last category caught her—she certainly needed to make some money somehow—and she pressed the tab for a thorough scroll-through. The first ads weren't promising: **Cyberpalace mount. Waiter. Masseuse. Prostitute/Accounting clerk.**

Kayla paused and requested more information about an ad for a weapons officer on a trade caravan. She canceled the scrolls when she saw that previous experience and a grade three weapons license were required.

Navigational aide-trainee. What was that?

Her face fell as she saw that the position offered no wages, only board and training. She started to scroll past the listing, then stopped.

Why not? she thought. She could earn her keep and learn a profitable skill. It was certainly more savory than any of the other possibilities. And it might even get her off the Rock and away from bounty hunters.

Before she lost her nerve, she punched in the number on the ad and was told to apply in person. A small map showed her where to go.

The storefront address was unpromising: a poured-foam building in need of a paint job with opaque black windows. Kayla pressed the buzzer.

A big, burly man with a graying beard and long hair drawn back into a ponytail opened the door. "Yeah?" His voice was a hoarse, unmusical baritone.

"I'm here about the job," Kayla said.

He gave her a suspicious look. "What's your name?"

"Kate N. Shadow."

"What's the N. stand for?" he said.

"No."

"Huh? You bein' funny?" He looked as though he were about to slam the door.

"Not at all."

"Ever navigated a ship before?"

"Yes," she said quickly. "But it was a long time ago."

He squinted at her. "It couldn't have been too long ago unless you did it when you were still in diapers."

"I was old enough."

He nodded to himself as if to say: Yeah, sure you were. "Ever been on a ship?"

"Yes!" She hoped that he wouldn't ask how many times.

"And how old are you, anyway?"

"Nineteen."

"You look fifteen. Ever been in jail?"

"No."

"What are you doing on Brayton's Rock?"

She hesitated for a second, then told the truth. "Running away."

"From what?"

"A lot of things."

"You sure you're of age? I don't want to tangle with angry parents looking for their cub."

"My parents are dead."

"Sorry." He shrugged. "Why do you want this job?"

"I need it," Kayla said. She couldn't keep her voice from quavering a bit.

He stared at her for a moment and his expression softened slowly. "That's the best answer I've heard yet. Okay. You're hired."

Kayla couldn't believe her luck. "That's it?"

"Yeah."

"Don't you want to ask me anything else?"

"Nope." He grinned at her obvious confusion and his blue eyes twinkled. "You look okay to me, kiddo. Probably trainable. And if you manage to screw up too badly, we'll just kick you out the nearest air lock."

"Um, I might need a little refresher on your navboard," she said. "Systems differ."

"So I've been told." His lips quirked for a moment as he nodded.

"When do I start?"

"Right away." He stepped inside, grabbed up a jacket. "How much time do you need to get your things?"

"I travel light."

He smiled again. "Whatever you say." He locked the door behind him, pulled a choba stick from a pocket, bit off the end, and jammed it in his mouth. "I'll get you an off-world pass at the port. C'mon. If we're lucky, we'll be able to catch the next shuttle."

"Okay . . . um, what's your name?"

"Barabbas. Call me Rab, it's easier. We'll get along fine so long as you don't call me Barry. Now hustle, lady. I don't like it here any more than you do."

She ran to keep up with his long strides. "What happened to your navigator?"

"Died. Third one this year."

Kayla began to wonder what she had walked into. "Is the job really that dangerous?" she asked.

"Not if you're careful. Besides, your predecessors didn't all die on the job. The last one got caught at the wrong end of a vibroblade during landfall. And if first impressions mean anything, Miss Kate N. Shadow, you don't seem much like the type to engage in bar fights." Barabbas stopped to purchase two tickets for them. "Here. Stick close. The shuttles fill up quickly and we *do* want to get out of here."

She followed in his wake as he bulled his way through the crowd and claimed two seats near the front of the small craft. She wasn't sure why she was trusting this big genial stranger, but she felt completely safe with him. "Where are we going?"

"To Shepherd Station. Edge of the Salabrian System," he told her.

"And then?"

"Somebody will meet us."

"Who?"

"I won't know until I see," he said. He seemed cheerfully unconcerned. "Hey." He nodded toward the window. "Check it out, babe. You don't want to miss blastoff. Best sight of all, watching this hellhole get smaller behind us."

The shuttle doors slammed shut and locked and the cabin filled with pressurized air. The shuttle trembled and, with a muffled roar, rose straight up through the cloudy atmosphere.

Kayla watched, openmouthed, as the planetoid dwindled to a boulder, then a ball, and finally, a pea, before winking out behind them. She leaned back in her seat and took a deep breath. She had gotten away from the Blackbird. And into who knew what?

Chapter Eight

The noise was fierce, nearly deafening. But it was nothing compared to the smell. Kayla stood in the half-lit hallway outside the air lock and wrinkled her nose.

"That's from our recycling vats," Rab had said. "You'll get used to it."

"If you say so." She didn't believe him. She would never grow accustomed to this rank odor of sweaty bodies, overripe fruit, and decomposing garbage. No one could, and live. "How can you stand it? Don't you faint occasionally?"

"Home is home," Rab said. "You can get used to anything. Your bunk is down here."

The ship, the *Falstaff,* was a jumbled affair. It looked like the bastard child of a group marriage among several salvaged cruisers. Doorways began halfway up walls, and the ceiling and floors seemed to cant at strange angles. Gargoyles and cherubs carved from cast aluminum glowered and winked from cubbyholes and corners. Hydroponic moon ivy, variegated red and purple, trailed in garlands along the walls, looped around doorways, and hung down from light fixtures.

Boom-chukka-boom-chukka-boom.

"Does that noise ever stop?" Kayla asked.

"You'd better pray that it doesn't," Rab said cheerfully. "Those are the engines."

The racket coming from the engine room provided a

steady percussive accompaniment to every conversation, every motion, every thought.

Kayla looked over her claustrophobic surroundings and shook her head. This was even worse than the mines. She followed Rab gloomily down one dim hallway after another, half expecting him to bunk her in the latrine.

"This is it."

The small cabin was clean and neat, the floor covered by green macrofiber matting that was surprisingly bouncy underfoot. It contained two beds, a small desk, and a battered yellow easy chair. An embroidered orange tapestry covered one wall. Its swirling pattern seemed to shift and move when Kayla stared at it, and she looked away quickly.

"You're rooming with Greer," Rab said. "She's a little extreme, politically, but okay, our cargo specialist and port liaison. She's on duty right now. Stay out of her politics and don't bug her and you'll be all right. Oh, mess is at seventeen hundred, and the john is down the hall."

"Wait. What about my training?"

"Don't worry. They'll come get you." He gave her a wink and turned down a side corridor, out of sight.

The right-hand bunk was covered with a faded green blanket and appeared unused. Kayla sat down gingerly and found that it was softer than it appeared. Deliciously soft.

She was aware of the tick and murmur of other minds, but there weren't many of them, they were safely distant, and the thrum of the engines drowned out most of their nattering.

Inch by inch, Kayla relaxed as she counted off the day's events: She had managed to escape the bounty hunter, had found a job, and had even gotten off of Brayton's Rock. The transit from the shuttle to Shepherd Station had passed in a blur of excitement. Once on-station, Rab had hailed a tall, taciturn, long-faced man—Kelso—who had led them to a tiny cruiser and conveyed them to the *Falstaff,* her new home.

That seemed like plenty to accomplish in one day. She would deal with the mysteries of the *Falstaff* and its crew later. The bunk was well-padded and she slid down gratefully into it. How long she lay there, insensate, she had no idea, but she was awakened by a bright light and the sound of rustling, like a thousand trees in a high wind. It took her a moment to realize that it was nothing more than somebody nearby changing her shirt.

A tall, olive-skinned woman of middle years stood next to the bed. She was buttoning a tired-looking brown jumpsuit over a stained white underblouse. Her close-cropped hair was brown flecked with gray and her eyes were a flinty green. She had flat cheekbones, a high forehead, and thin lips which looked as though they rarely smiled. Her only ornament was a small golden ring in her right earlobe from which a sparkling red gem depended. It looked to Kayla rather like a mindstone. She turned as Kayla sat up and gave her a half-smile.

"You're alive?" The voice was sharp, the accent clipped. "Good. I'm Greer. It's time to eat so hustle. You know the way to the loo?"

Kayla nodded and stumbled down the hall into the bathroom, still groggy. A few minutes later she emerged, feeling a bit sharper.

Greer was leaning against the wall, waiting for her. "Tonight's Salome's turn to cook. I hope for once that she deigned to follow a recipe."

"Who's Salome?"

"Captain. She owns this tub. Inherited it from her crazy uncle when he died. In jail."

Before Kayla could digest that information, a blurred white-and-orange mass came dashing down the hall, stopped, and turned into a four-legged animal with a pointed face and ears, and a long sinuous body ending in a tail. Bright green eyes with reflective irises regarded her cautiously from a triangular face.

Kayla stared back in amazement. "It's a cat," she said.

Greer glanced at her oddly. "Yeah, old Pooka. She belongs to Morgan. Probably looking for her right now, aren't you, piggy? Looking for some chow." Greer scratched the animal under the chin and Pooka made loud, vibrating noises of obvious approval.

"I've never seen a live cat before," Kayla said. As she watched the graceful feline, she couldn't resist making a gentle probe. She penetrated the small glowing mind easily to find it filled with cheerful carnivorous urges.

The cat gave her a startled look and Kayla quickly pulled out.

"Fssst!" Pooka said. With her tail expanded to three times its regular size, she streaked away down the hall.

Greer frowned. "That's strange," she said. "Pooka usually likes everybody. You must have spooked her somehow."

"I hope not." Kayla peered wistfully after the vanished animal. Perhaps she would come back later.

As they made their way toward the mess hall, she noticed that many of the walls had strange designs painted on them: some were abstract, others nothing more than graffiti. The slogans were mostly illegible, but Kayla could puzzle one out that seemed to say "Free Trade Now Not Later." Just past the graffiti was a fairly accomplished portrait of a dark woman with yellow catlike eyes and long golden hair set into a trompe l'oeil gilt frame with the words "The Mother of Us All" scrolled in elaborate old-fashioned script on the bottom of the frame.

Greer smirked. "Admiring our art gallery? Everybody takes a turn when cabin fever sets in. I hope you've got more skill than I have."

The mess was a large circular room with several couches and a long table in the middle. Food was served through a wall unit which must have concealed both food processing and kitchen facilities. A tantalizing scent of sweet and potent spices made Kayla's mouth water.

A small-boned, slender, dark-eyed woman sat at the table, intent upon her plate. She gazed brightly at Greer and Kayla and, without any obvious curiosity, went back to her meal. She had no hair, but her face and skull were covered by spiraling patterns in several pigments which looked like tattoos. Her posture was graceful and erect, like a dancer at rest.

"Where is everybody?" Greer said.

The woman shrugged.

"Not very friendly, is she?" Kayla whispered.

"Don't mind her. That's Morgan. She's a mystic. Doesn't speak very often. It goes against her yoga practices. She handles our hydroponics and recycling, which is good, because she doesn't have to speak much to plants and garbage. But she's also our medic. You might want to brush up on your sign language."

Kayla nodded at the woman, and Morgan smiled but said nothing, chewing quickly.

"This the new trainee?" said a deep booming voice. The owner was a plump, cheerful man of middling height with a full head of curling dark red hair. "I'm Arsobades. Court musician. In my spare time I'm the ship engineer. Also handle security around here, so please don't cause any trouble." He waggled a shaggy eyebrow at her. "What's your name and do you play an instrument?"

"Katie, and no, I'm afraid not."

"Too bad. But you can probably sing."

"I don't—"

"Everybody can sing. They just think they can't."
With that he picked up a platter, filled it from a tureen
in the wall unit, and sat down at the table.

Kayla followed his lead and loaded a dish with a
juicy, fragrant stew. She settled down at the table and
dug in.

The meat had been cooked until it almost melted on
the tongue and the vegetables were soft and tender.
Kayla couldn't remember the last time she had eaten.
She chewed in silent bliss.

"Salome must be making up for last week,"
Arsobades said between mouthfuls. He grinned at
Kayla. "You're lucky you missed it, Katie. The worst
meal we've ever had on *Falstaff.* Nobody would eat it,
not even Pooka. Morgan refused to contaminate her
recycler with it. Rab finally had to send it out the air
lock, space litter laws be damned." He cackled briefly.
"It was that or mutiny."

"I seem to remember that you managed to choke
down a few bites," Greer said acidly. "In fact, you
were practically weeping as Rab delivered us from that
foulness."

"Well," Arsobades said. "I came up during the famine on the orbitals. Can't stand to see food wasted."

"Famine?" Kayla said, startled by the thought.
"Where?"

"Elysia. Orbital suburb of Vardalia. One of the first.
And don't let the name fool you, Katie. It was a floating hog trough."

Rab swept into the room, trailed by Pooka and a
cloud of cigar smoke. "Ah, yes, the topless towers of
Vardalia," he intoned. "Above which poor Arsobades
spent his boyhood, looking up to look down, hoping
that one day he, too, would merit a bit of groundspace
in that fabled city. But it was not to be." Shaking his
head sadly, he filled a plate and settled down next to
Kayla. "Good thing, too. Otherwise, he'd have been ar-

rested long ago for being a public nuisance with his bagpipes."

"Remind me to set up your laser with a feedback coil, smartass. We'll see how well you like getting shocked every time you reach for your pistol."

Greer wrinkled her nose in disgust. "Must you smoke that thing while we're eating?"

"Guys, stop that." A beautiful woman with skin the color of chocolate and long shimmering golden hair appeared from behind the serving unit. Her face was the same as the one in the wall portrait, but she wore a golden nose ring which linked, via hoops, with a ring in her left ear. Her eyes were a startling shade of amber. She looked at Kayla and smiled brilliantly. "Hello, Katie, I'm Salome, the captain. Glad you're aboard. I've been doubling as navigator. It'll be a relief to hand it over to you."

Kayla thought, but did not say, that Salome looked capable of running the entire ship all by herself. Maybe even two ships.

Salome joined the group at the table and gave Rab a sharp look,

He sighed and stubbed out his cheroot.

"Hallelujah," said Greer.

"Hey," Arsobades said, his mouth full. "This is good grub. Salome, you've redeemed yourself."

"Thanks, I think."

"Where's Kelso?" Arsobades said.

"Monitoring ops," said Salome. "Somebody's got to mind the store while the rest of us eat."

"Is he a pilot, too?" Katie asked.

Rab started laughing. "Him? Kels couldn't nav his way out of a latrine, blindfolded. The only place he knows his way around is his credit records."

"Then how can he monitor navigation?"

"It doesn't take much to check a digital readout. Any problem and he'll get on the horn to us. Besides, there's the knowbot to keep him company. If we're about to hit an asteroid or police cruiser, the "bot" will trigger our deflectors."

"We hope," Arsobades added. "It usually works."

"Well, now that Katie's here we'll have less margin for error, won't we?" Salome said. She blotted her mouth delicately, turned to Kayla, and said, "If you're finished, I'd like to show you around ops, where you'll be working."

"Sure." Despite her exhaustion, Kayla got to her feet and followed Salome through the maze of hallways.

Soon they were in a broad room lined by instrument panels. Kelso was sitting at a screen making notes as lights blinked in configurations of red and blue that almost—but not quite—made sense.

"This'll be your station," Salome said.

Kayla stared at the navboard in dismay. It seemed to be covered with buttons and bisected screens, all of them flashing. "This board is really different from the one I'm used to," she said, improvising rapidly.

"It can't be that different," Salome said, staring. "They're all fairly standard, aren't they?"

"Well, yes."

"Then you'll catch on, won't you?" Salome nodded. "Here, you'll sit next to me. At first I'll just want you to get used to the equipment. I'll show you the basics. Just mime what I do. When I think you're ready, I'll let you handle certain easy maneuvers. But not until I think you're ready."

Fine with me, Kayla thought. Her face must have revealed her relief because Salome laughed and patted her on the back.

"Don't worry, you won't have to memorize all of this tonight. Get some sleep, you look like you need it. But I'll expect you in here tomorrow morning at eight sharp."

Kayla nodded. Her eyes were burning and she was beginning to feel like she hadn't slept in a month.

Somehow she found her way back to her bunk. Greer was nowhere to be seen. Kayla didn't even try to remove her clothing. She just tumbled into bed and for the next ten hours she was blissfully unconscious.

Chapter Nine

The days passed quickly for Kayla, filled with new equipment, routines, and relationships, and the peculiarities of puzzling out all of them.

The first morning in ops had been the hardest: putting on the headset which connected her to the navboard through a tangle of plasteel umbilici, cut her off from the real world, and thrust her into the nonplace of cyberspace.

The room vanished, and Kayla plunged into an unfamiliar landscape filled with strange approximations of things: plunging canyons, spiked towers, sheer slick walls, sudden dead ends, vertiginous angles, and confusing perspectives. And there, glittering like a waterfall, the jump interface. Vivid colors, fugitive, crawling as though half-alive, made her eyes hurt. There was no smell or sound, nor were there any shadows.

It was nothing like the tiny rig her father had given her to play with: that had been in black and white, and she had quickly tired of it. But this: how could one ever come to know this vast, dizzying space?

It's not real, she thought. *Not any of it.*

But it felt real.

She was deep in a shining canyon between turreted outposts, gazing across to another canyon whose walls sparkled with marbled silver ice.

A huge orange triangle came tumbling down a sheer wall, blotting out the light. It would crush her with its vast bulk. At the last possible moment it caught a spur in the wall overhead, bounced up and over Kayla, and catapulted out of sight.

She took one cautious step, bounced against a sleek wall, and then against another. Her next move was not nearly as cautious, and soon she was speeding along golden byways, darting from canyon to canyon, caroming off of unexpected walls into alleyways, and bouncing, exhilarated, into spiraling subjump interfaces.

Down this electric pathway, around this onyx corner, and into a new, more complicated canyon whose walls bristled with triangular protrusions. Kayla paused to scan the area and, to her chagrin, could not locate any familiar landmarks. Where in cyberspace was she?

Rolling along the bottom of the canyon, she cast probes forward, hoping to find something that would help guide her. This looked like the way to go, she had been here before, hadn't she? But when she came to the base of a broad tower she stopped, confused. She could feel a faint vibration, growing stronger, a growl turning into a roar. There, a dark shadow, racing toward her, coming closer. Kayla was terrified.

Suddenly, a bright red sphere, big as a boulder, bounced back-and-forth, back-and-forth between canyon walls and came to rest beside her. Somehow Kayla knew it was the cyber equivalent of Salome's consciousness.

Gently, Salome nudged her until she was moving along a specific path, retreating from the growling, gathering darkness. Soon they had rolled into a brighter canyon whose walls were smooth blue mirrors, wonderfully clear.

The Salome-ball went halfway up the wall of the canyon and began to bounce from tier to tier, leaving a glowing trail wherever she touched, executing maneuvers in a vibrating, choreographed sequence.

What was she doing?

Kayla made a quick feather-light probe of Salome's

consciousness, a tickle really, not powerful enough to trigger recognition of an empathic contact, and saw that she was initiating a scan of near space.

So that was how it was done. Kayla filed the information away for later use. She also saw that she had nearly trespassed upon restricted Trade Police routes and the threat she had encountered was from their defense systems.

She came up out of the navboard gratefully, surfacing into the air of the real world like a swimmer too long below the surface of a strange sea. The electrodes came off with a loud pop, and she sniffed the rank air with pleasure. Fingers. Toes. Real movement, light and shadow, familiar things. No careening triangles coming over the horizon to flatten her.

"So what do you think?" Salome said.

"Easy," Kayla lied. "No problem."

* * *

Luckily, the navigational controls were easier to understand than Kayla had expected once she learned to gently pick the minds of those around her for information.

By carefully probing and watching, she was able to make the appropriate moves and convince Salome that she knew far more about the navboard than was really the case. And, as time went by, she took to the odd mathematical science of charting the *Falstaff's* course with surprising ease. To her amazement, she seemed to have a natural affinity for the work. Salome stopped hovering at her elbow and relaxed, allowing her free rein with the navboard.

Sinking into the interstices of the board became a curious pleasure and plotting a course was a puzzle to be pieced, with occasional clues from Salome's helpful mind, and nudges from the ops knowbot. Despite the "bot," Kayla wondered how nonempaths managed the work. It must be twice as hard without any sort of farsense.

She could cast her farsense ahead of her along the vast reaches of space, scanning for hidden obstacles, strange anomalies, police cruisers. It made it all so much easier.

Away from the navboard, Kayla goggled openly at the wonders of space. Her more seasoned fellow crew members teased her mercilessly about the amount of time she spent on the observation deck.

Puzzling out the human factor aboard *Falstaff* took her a bit more time than did mastering the intricacies of piloting. However, she soon grew accustomed to having crewmates nearby, came to know their distinctive mind signatures, and how to shield against them in groups.

It soon became obvious that Salome and Rab were lovers, quite thoroughly absorbed in one another. Although they accepted the presence of their crewmates, they were obviously a unit. Salome was quick-tempered, even a bit imperious, tough and ambitious, and always thinking about the welfare of the ship. Rab was a bit easier-going, more flexible, but deeply cynical.

Kelso was a dark, sardonic man whose sole interest seemed to be money. Silent, tattooed Morgan liked to perform acrobatics nude in null-g, and didn't seem to care who watched her. Her cat, Pooka, continued to avoid Kayla, much to her chagrin.

Greer maintained a cool, aloof demeanor unless prodded about her politics, about which she felt passionately, and then she was anything but cool. Her attitude toward Kayla was amusement tinged with a faint degree of condescension. Of the entire crew, cheerful Arsobades seemed easiest to get along with, and the best company. He teased Kayla at every opportunity, telling her, "I know there's a singer in there just waiting to be let out."

All in all, not a bad crew nor ship. More troubling was the exact nature of cargo which the *Falstaff* carried. Officially listed as a merchant vessel, it was, as Kayla slowly realized, a smuggling ship conveying contraband around the Three Systems, Cavinas, Salabrias, and Admanan, and beyond. The *Falstaff* was equipped with cloaking shields and radios set to the Trade Police frequencies. The ship danced along the perimeter of the legal trade lanes, plying the black market with various goods through Cavinas and its neighboring systems, even visiting the distant Mergui Cluster and the Satsuma Nebula.

One month they carried a load of retooled screenbrains once intended for the dike mechanisms of St. Ilban but now scheduled to run milking machines on a squatter's ranch on Liage. And on dry and dusty Liage they filled their hold with purple bambera-fur rugs, tapestries, and blankets destined for the street markets on Salabria VI.

Kayla grew less worried about their cargo as she realized that her shipmates had no more interest in mixing with the authorities than she had. In fact, the *Falstaff* was a near-perfect hiding place. Where better for an outlaw to hide than among others of her kind?

* * *

Within the first month of her sojourn on *Falstaff*, Kayla was lured into participating in the evening songfests that Arsobades arranged after dinner.

"C'mon, Katie!" Arsobades strummed a lively arpeggio on his battered lute. "Anybody can sing. I know you can, you've got the look of a born alto."

Perhaps it was the food and her full belly, perhaps it was the glass of wine, or maybe even the good-natured hoots of Rab and Salome, but Kayla felt her inhibitions melting away. Somehow she was standing up, agreeing to warble an old song, a favorite of her father's, "The Green Hills of Earth." She made her way through the chorus without wavering, and even hit most of the notes. Arsobades was delighted, and as the others applauded, he gave her a big hug.

"She's a natural," he said, beaming. "I knew it! Katie-my-dear, we'll have you performing madrigals before we make landfall."

Kayla warmed to Arsobades' words. It had been a long time since she had felt so comfortable with anybody. Emboldened by the applause, she tried another tune her father had loved, "My Love is Like a Red, Red Rose." Halfway through it, she noticed that something was troubling Arsobades: his ruddy complexion had gone pale, almost ashen. Distracted, she hurried through the rest of the song, stumbling badly over the chorus, and ended on a reedy, wavering note that somehow also managed to be flat.

Arsobades said nothing, merely stood up and left the room.

Kayla stared after him. "What's wrong?" she said. "Was it my singing?"

Rab shook his head sadly. "Nah. That was his wife's favorite song, that's all."

"Arsobades' wife?" At first, Kayla couldn't take the notion seriously. "Oh, sure." She smiled and looked around the room, but nobody seemed interested in sharing the joke.

"His wife, Anna. They sang together in Vardalia," Salome said. "In the clubs, in the streets. Then she started fooling with breen, and after a while she died, or finished dying. So Arsobades took to space."

"I didn't know," Kayla said. She felt terribly stricken. Why, of all songs, had she chosen that one to sing?

"Know?" said Rab. "There was no way you could have known. Don't worry about it."

Arsobades was cool to Kayla for what seemed like weeks. Then, one day, he winked at her, picked up his lute, and was back to his old rollicking self. They put the episode behind them. Kayla settled happily into the routines of the ship and began to forget life underground.

* * *

Between landfalls, Kayla was forced to maintain her disguise and dye her hair herself. She watched carefully for the first telltale red-gold roots to appear and, in the middle of the night, when the ship was quiet and no one prowled the hallways, she crept into the bathroom and locked the door behind her. It was a messy business, daubing the dye mixture upon strand after strand of hair, and the sour smell made her eyes water. Afterward she spent a good hour removing any trace of the dye from the tile walls.

The next day she would yawn over the navboard, bringing comments from Salome and Kelso, but she didn't mind. At least she was safe and secure as brown-haired Kate.

* * *

The stars were red and green and blue through the observation bay. Kayla sat, staring raptly. When Rab came up behind her she hardly noticed.

"That red one's Aries IV," he said. "And the green is Minerva. That little white speck's its planet, Minnow."

"Have you ever been there?"

"Yeah. It's weird: green air and blue ground. Yellow lakes. It rains chartreuse most of the time. Nice, kind of."

Kayla smiled at the thought. There was so very much more to the universe than she had ever imagined. She might see and do more, in hiding, than ever she had seen living under her real name in full view of the law. She made Rab tell her the names of the stars again and repeated them to herself, silently, like a litany and a promise: someday she would see those places for herself. Aries IV, Minerva, and Minnow. She would see and feel green rain, and walk over blue ground. Someday.

* * *

At night she dreamed of purple tunnels, translucent, mysterious, and filled with shadows which groped toward her but never quite managed to reach her before she awoke. She would sit up in bed with the echoes of footsteps still in her head, and only after she had listened for the ship's engines would she hear the reassuring boom-chukka-boom which chased away the shadows of the night.

But one night the dream lasted longer than usual: she was caught in the cave-in, tons of stone falling, crushing her. Kayla cried out, and came awake to feel Greer's hand on her shoulder.

"You were screaming in your sleep."

Kayla put her hand to her face and found tears. "Bad dream."

"Yeah? Must be a recurring one. You've been thrashing around in your sleep every night since you got here."

"I'm really sorry. Do you want me to move out?"

"Did I say that?" Greer sat down on the side of her bunk. "So do you want to tell me about it?"

Kayla felt a sudden yearning to unburden herself. The hours, the closeness of quarters . . . why not? But no, she couldn't. No one must know, ever. "No."

"You're awfully young to have such a big secret."

"I wish I could, Greer. I just can't."

Her roommate sighed. "Okay. Life's a bitch, and it only gets tougher as you get older." She got to her feet and crawled into her own bed. "Remember, I'm over here if you need me."

"Thanks." Kayla lay on her back in the dark, eyes wide open and listened as Greer's breathing grew deep and regular. *If only I could confide in her,* she thought. *If only. . . .*

* * *

Of all the *Falstaff*'s cobbled-together innards, the place Kayla liked best after the observation bay was the hydroponics section: the cool smell of growing things, the musical trickle of water, the odd pink light, and reflective surfaces. It all reminded her of her mother. With Morgan's permission, she puttered among the plants, snipping dry leaves, inhaling the fresh oxygen.

Occasionally, Pooka would wander in, cast a yellow, suspicious glance in her direction and, tail swishing, settle under a table in a far corner.

"I'm harmless, Pooka. Really," Kayla said. She held up her hands. "See? No cat-killing weapons here."

Pooka ignored her and began washing a hind leg.

"Well, at least you're not leaving. That's progress, I guess." Kayla had a sudden urge to squirt the cat with the spray tube she held, just to see the look on the smug beast's face.

Peace, she told herself. *Perhaps someday you'll pass Pooka's test and be admitted into her good graces. Or at least be allowed to stroke her tail.*

Humming, Kayla turned her back on the cat and squirted nutrient on a shimmering white space pea instead.

*   *   *

It was on their third landfall, on Westerby, second world of the Salabrian System, that Kayla saw her first alien.

It was a Sinx, native to the place, bright orange-pink, with three mouths, or what looked like mouths, rimming its neck. Kayla told herself not to stare, but she was fascinated, transfixed.

The thing moved in a series of undulations, not completely snakelike thanks to its small legs. It seemed more like a low-slung quadruped, its legs pumping to move it along.

Rab saw her staring and nudged her playfully. "You're not on Brayton's Rock any more, kiddo."

"No," she said. "I'm a long way from there." *And from home.*

"Better get used to it," Rab said. "You'll be seeing a lot more, and stranger."

But Rab's words faded as Kayla's attention fixed

upon a corner vid kiosk, upon the face of the screen. Pointed chin, red hair, vivid green eyes. It took her a moment to realize that she was looking at herself.

"Wanted," screamed the red hololetters. "Wanted, wanted, wanted. Reward."

Kayla stared at herself and felt as if she were looking at a ghost. *I'm not Kayla,* she thought. *My name is Katie. Kate N. Shadow. That person on the kiosk isn't me, she's somebody else.*

Rab bumped up against her. "Hey, what're you doing, sleepwalking?" He looked over her head at the kiosk, but the image had scrolled over to the next fugitive on the list. "See somebody you know?"

"Somebody I used to know." Kayla took a step, then another, turning away. "C'mon," she said. "Let's get something to eat."

* * *

As time went by, Kayla grew more and more content. Everyone had welcomed her and made room for her. She was beginning to feel like a member of the family.

One night Kayla, Salome, Barabbas, Greer, Morgan, and Arsobades were relaxing together in the rear viewing bay after dinner. Arsobades began to sing a rollicking ballad about the "mind catchers and thought-spies of Styx, stamp 'em out, stamp 'em out, stamp 'em out"—and everybody joined in heartily on the chorus. Everyone but Kayla.

She glared at her crewmates in disbelief. "Would you mind telling me what's wrong with empaths?" she demanded.

"They're damned spies for Pelleas Karlson, that's what," Rab said, scowling. "Salome almost had her brains fried by one in a bar the last time we were on St. Ilban. I nearly killed the guy." He pulled Salome against him protectively, ready to mangle any rampaging empath who dared to come near.

Salome leaned against her lover's broad shoulder

and smiled. "He was probably a scout," she said calmly. "Trolling through the crowd, probably just fishing for tasty bits of information that he could sell."

"Or smugglers he could turn in," Greer said.

"Most people wouldn't even have noticed," said Salome. "But I'm especially esper-sensitive. Didn't know what had hit me."

"Empaths working for the prime minister?" Kayla said. She was stunned. Who could it have been? "I don't believe it."

Rab nodded at her over Salome's head. "Sure. They're used as interrogators. Karlson pays their way off-world and they jump to it. Who wouldn't want to leave Styx? Especially if it was for glorious Vardalia."

"I think those miners go loony in their tunnels," Morgan said.

At the sound of her voice, everyone turned and stared at her in amazement.

Morgan shrugged and turned back to her vid cube.

"I don't know," Kayla said carefully. "Maybe it's not so bad there."

"Of course it is," said Arsobades. "Imagine living underground. No sky. No sun. Like rats in a maze."

"Just imagine," Kayla said. *Just imagine,* she thought.

Later that night, as she and Greer were preparing for bed, Kayla decided to ask her roommate what she really thought of empaths.

Greer gave her an unreadable look. "I haven't known that many," she said. "I met one or two of them, long ago. Strange folk. They're probably all right, as far as that goes, but they give me the creeps. Who would really want to eavesdrop on another persons' mind?"

"Where did you meet them?"

"On St. Ilban. When I was a delegate to the Trade Congress."

"You?" Kayla said. "You hate government traders. You told me so yourself."

"Yes, me." Greer smiled one of her infrequent smiles. "Hard to believe but there it is. I was a social worker on St. Ilban. Young, idealistic. We were going to change everything, right every inequity. Hah! As soon as we started talking about the smaller trading partners being exploited by the larger ones, Karlson began to force us out. It was all so corrupt. And it hasn't gotten any better, let me tell you. So we formed the Free Traders. We're committed to a free market without tariffs or restraints. And maybe someday we'll get it. Until then, we pass the time smuggling and giving the Trade Police the middle finger." Without another word, she got into bed and turned off her light.

Kayla lay awake long into the night and Arsobades song echoed in her mind. "Stamp 'em out, stamp 'em out, stamp 'em out."

Yes, it was tempting to relax her guard, to feel friendly and at home on the *Falstaff*. But as much as she was coming to like these people, she reminded herself that she had to be careful. They must never, ever know her true nature.

* * *

"Come here," Kayla said in her softest, most appealing voice. She crouched in the hallway, almost at eye level with Morgan's cat. "Nice Pooka. Come on, kitty. See what I've got for you." She sent a nearsense pulse of friendliness in the cat's direction. "Don't be afraid. I'm harmless."

The orange and white tabby stared at her suspiciously and twitched its whiskers.

"Yum," said Kayla. "Yummy food for Pooka." She held out a handful of mashed rehydrated fish which she had taken from lunch. "Mmmm." She hoped that the cat would find its overpowering odor tantalizing and come nearer.

Pooka sniffed the air.

"Come on."

Pooka came a step closer.

"That's right."

Pooka sniffed again, hissed, and walked away, tail held high in disdain.

Damn, Kayla thought. *That didn't work. It's been months. When will that cat warm up? I'm not exactly a stranger any more.* Sighing, she wiped the food from her hands and went to take up her post.

Salome had picked up a load of weapons scavenged from a derelict cruiser and wanted to get it across the Salabrian System to Dolmec, the fifth planet, pronto. She was planning to rendezvous with a buyer there. But that required taking some risks, flying close to government radar and checking stations. Salome had given Kayla the first leg of the journey. But when Kayla got to ops, she was surprised to see the captain sitting at the navboard, already plugged in.

"No offense," Salome said. "I want to steer us past the police checkpoint."

"But I've been doing this for almost a year," Kayla said. "You've never had a problem about it before."

"I know, Katie. But don't take it personally. It wouldn't matter how long you were doing it. I'm just funny about this. Call it superstition. When the heat's around, I don't feel comfortable unless I'm at the wheel."

Kayla subsided into mild disappointment. She had hoped that Salome would trust her more thoroughly by now.

"Don't look so sad," Salome said, laughing. "I'll let you sit in, all right? Here." She tossed her a set of board jacks. "Plug in."

With Salome beside her, Kayla plunged into the familiar electronic cyberscape of the navigation board, its turrets, canyons, spiked walls, frustrating cul-de-sacs, and breathtaking shortcuts. The jump interface loomed to the left, a huge glittering door requiring special keys and passwords, but she wasn't interested in that now.

A bright red sphere bounced past her: Salome. The Salome-ball left a glowing trail wherever it touched, executing a perfect ignition sequence. It jumped here, jumped there, then paused in midair as if considering the options.

Kayla felt a twinge of impatience. Salome's next moves were obvious. Why wasn't she setting the heading that would take them up and over the rings of Chaat's moon?

Come on, Salome! What are you waiting for?

Green security lights began to flash, rippling across the face of a wall. Kayla tensed, realizing what it meant.

A Trade Police cruiser had appeared onscreen, coming around the far side of Chaat.

Why wasn't Salome taking an avoidance path? There was still time to elude them.

But the red sphere beside her was motionless, frozen in mid-bounce.

Orange flashes superseded the green lines of a moment before. The *Falstaff* was being scanned. In a moment the police would locate the weapons shipment, gauge the metal/plastic content, and inquire further.

Salome, where are you?

A shrill alarm went off, a high shriek that set Kayla's nerves vibrating. The knowbot, sounding the alarm.

The police were signaling them to come about and be boarded.

Kayla watched the inert red sphere, feeling helpless. They had to get away. Why wasn't Salome responding? They had weapons and sufficient cloaking shields. But they had to do it now, right away, before the police cruiser got any closer.

She gave Salome a subtle nudge with nearsense.

Nothing.

That was odd.

Next, she tried a probe but met some sort of strange interference, impossible to penetrate.

We can't just sit here, waiting. Got to do something right now!

Taking a deep breath, Kayla overrode Salome's linkage and pulled control of the *Falstaff*'s navigation away from her. Desperately she calculated the most efficient escape trajectory and ordered the ship to take it, fast.

The engines' whine built to a roar. The knowbot reminded her about the dangers of subjump speed when engaged near another vessel.

—*Faster!*

The comboard speaker crackled with the police cruiser's objections. Kelso cut it off.

As the *Falstaff* pulled away from the cruiser, Kayla ventured a farsense probe of the ship. And nearly fell out of her seat.

Impossible. She had to be mistaken. But no, those were the distinct emanations of another empath coming from the police cruiser, a stranger. Kayla didn't recognize his mind signature at all. He was intent upon Salome, brutally probing her—probably the reason for her complete immobilization. Furiously, Kayla sliced through his probe, deflecting and dispersing it. Before the unknown empath had time to refocus, the *Falstaff* gave a shudder, the engines roared again, and the ship's cloaking shields came up as it fled far beyond Chaat.

The police cruiser diminished and became a small dot on their screens. Before it could fix on their ion trail, they were safely hidden by Chaat's huge bulk. Apparently the police empath didn't have tremendous farsense capacity: Kayla scanned cautiously but found no trace of his emanations. They were safe for now.

She came spiraling up out of the navboard, dizzy

and sweating. The lumpy yellow face of Chaat floated in the viewing bay. Only gradually did she become aware of Salome slumped in the seat beside her.

"Salome!"

There was no response. The *Falstaff*'s captain was unconscious, breathing raggedly, slumped in her seat.

Kayla punched the intercom for Morgan. "Medic! We need a medic in the main cabin right away."

Morgan's reply was clipped. "Coming."

Kayla was torn between monitoring their escape and keeping an eye on Salome. She decided that no one would be served if they were caught by the police while she was patting the captain's hand. She submerged once more into the navigational interface.

They were secure behind their shields. Nevertheless, she warned Arsobades to arm the main laser cannon. Then she plotted a quick and dirty course to Dolmec with a few extra evasive maneuvers thrown in just to be sure they had slipped away from the police. By the time she resurfaced, Salome was gone. She was alone in ops.

Kelso relieved her at six.

"How's the captain?"

"Better," he said. "Still a bit wobbly. Barabbas is going to handle the unloading, with Greer as backup."

"With Salome out of commission, maybe I should relieve you at two," Kayla said.

"Suit yourself. But you'll be doing two shifts without sleep."

"I don't mind."

"See you at two, then." Kelso took the headset from her and settled into the captain's chair.

Kayla wanted to see Salome, but she felt exhausted and desperately in need of food. *First things first,* she thought. *Grub, then the captain.*

The mess was deserted. She helped herself to a heaping plate of noodles and meat from the wall unit.

As she ate, Rab came in the door and leaned against it. His face looked weary.

"There you are," he said. "That was some nice piloting, kid. Real nice."

"Thanks." Kayla accepted his praise easily, amused by the knowledge that, six months ago, she would have blushed with pleasure.

He settled down next to her on the banquette. "What happened?"

"I wish you would tell me," she said. "All I know is that one minute the captain was there, the next she was gone, and a police cruiser was on our tail. I decided to risk a demerit and get us out of there."

"Why were you on the navboard at all?"

"I guess Salome felt sorry for elbowing me aside. She told me to watch and learn."

"Then here's to guilt: It's the only thing that saved us." Rab stole a noodle from Kayla's bowl, toasted her with it, and slurped it with gusto. "One thing that bothers me, though."

"What's that?"

"Salome's reaction. Reminded me of that time the empath tried to read her mind." His eyes were like twin blue lasers burning into her.

Kayla met his gaze without flinching. "Could there have been an empath aboard the police cruiser?"

"What makes you think that?"

"I don't know. You told me that empaths were working for the prime minister."

"Guess I did," Rab said. "Well, I wouldn't put it past 'em, that's for sure. Anyway, Salome got good and spooked by this one. She's decided she wants a backup navigator so that she doesn't have to worry about it."

"Does that mean you have to recruit someone?"

"Yep. I'm going down to Dolmec tomorrow, check things out, take a look at the prospects."

Kayla wondered what it would be like to have someone sitting and watching everything she did. She had the feeling she wouldn't enjoy it, but she decided to keep quiet and see what happened. "Good luck," she said. "Don't bring back any jerks."

Rab laughed. "I'll do my best."

Chapter Ten

The next day, true to his word, Rab left early and came back late. And with him came a new crew member, a blond, tanned young man of about twenty-three. Barabbas led him into the mess where the assembled crew was eating dinner.

"This is Iger," he said. "He's from Liage, originally. Says he got tired of running the bambera, decided to see the galaxy instead, and hopped a freighter to Dolmec. Now he wants off. So we'll let him ride backup on the navboard auxiliary. He can learn by watching Katie." He paused, smiled sardonically. "I hope he meets with your approval, Madame Navigator."

Blue eyes in a square-jawed, deeply-tanned face. A strong, graceful body, broad of shoulder, clad in purple bambera-cloth tunic and leggings.

Kayla gazed at the Liagean and felt a sudden flash of attraction, unexpected and embarrassing. Flustered, she turned her attention to his companion.

What was it? Violet-flesh, two-limbed, with a triangular head, lipless mouth, and huge purple eyes.

"This is Iger's pet," Rab said.

The newcomer coughed politely. "It's not a pet," Iger said. "Not exactly. It's my companion, Third Child. A dalkoi. I don't know if it's a he or she. I won't know until it comes of age." His voice was a high baritone, smooth and appealing. He gave Kayla a quick smile, white teeth flashing.

"Is the dalkoi from Liage, too?" she said.

"They're the only real natives."

"I didn't think they went solo," Greer said. "What about its family cluster?"

"Gone," Iger said. "It came wandering into our campsite one day, years ago. We never found a trace of its cluster mates."

An orphan, Kayla thought. *Alone, like me.* But she amended the thought. Third Child had Iger.

The dalkoi padded toward her and stood, inches away, the point of its head twitching as it stared up at her. After a moment it made a high chirping noise.

"What does that mean?" Kayla said.

Iger smiled. "It likes you. That's rare. It's usually very shy around strangers."

"Should I pet it?"

"Go ahead, if it'll let you."

Kayla reached out hesitantly and touched the dalkoi's neck. Its flesh was warm and silky, not at all like what she had expected. She moved her palm slowly up and down its long sinuous neck. Third Child closed its eyes and chirped a bit louder. "Does that mean it's happy?" she asked.

"Definitely," Iger said. His teeth flashed again. "You must have the touch."

Odd though it was, Kayla felt drawn to the strange creature. It was certainly friendlier than Pooka. How would the cat react to the dalkoi, and vice versa? She was tempted to try an empathic probe of the dalkoi. But then she remembered Pooka's reaction and decided against it: she didn't want to frighten Third Child away, too.

Salome was staring at the dalkoi with frank displeasure. "Is that thing housebroken?"

"Of course." Iger sounded mildly insulted.

"What does it eat?" she said. "I can't afford to support any exotic diets here."

"Grains and vegetables. Don't worry, it's not fussy. But no meat."

"Good," Arsobades said. "I'd hate to see our meat rations get divided even further."

"Eat more vegetables," Morgan said suddenly. "You'll live longer." Her voice was a thin, reedy soprano.

The crew stared at one another in amazement. Morgan was talking again!

"Speaking of food," Rab said, "Are you hungry, kid? Help yourself to grub in that wall unit."

The Liagean nodded appreciatively and looked around the table for a place to sit.

Kayla got up. "Here, you can have my seat."

"Thanks."

Was it her imagination, or did his smile and glance linger on her a bit longer than necessary?

She smiled back. "If you're not doing anything after dinner, you're welcome to come up to ops and take a look at the navigation board."

"Can I bring Third Child along?" Iger said.

"Please." Glowing just a tiny bit, Kayla left the mess to take up her post and await her company.

* * *

Iger arrived so swiftly that she suspected him of bolting his food. He was bright-eyed and interested in everything, and Third Child was right behind him, poking at buttons, sniffing dials, weaving around her in a disconcerting manner.

"Does it always do that?" Kayla said.

"Only when it's happy."

"How can you tell?"

"Oh, I can tell."

Kayla watched him move with easy grace and could almost imagine him walking through the sunlit fields of Liage. Before she could stop herself, the question was out of her mouth: "Why did you leave home?"

Iger didn't seem to mind her curiosity. "Didn't want

to tend bamberas for the rest of my life." He noodled with a bit of electrode cable and smiled. "Where'd you come from?"

"Styx." It slipped out without her thinking. Kayla glanced around nervously but Kelso, intent on his screen, gave no indication that he had heard anything.

"Really? The underground world?" Iger's eyes shone. "Tell me about it. I'd give anything to see it."

"Maybe later. I don't really like to talk about it." Why, oh why, had she said that? What was it about Iger? She felt instinctively that she could trust this attractive newcomer. But that didn't mean letting down her guard completely. "I've got to link up to the navboard now," she said. "I'm sorry, I've really got to check something."

"I could hook up, too," Iger said. "Y'know, sort of listen in."

She stared into his eyes, nearly getting lost in the blue depths. With difficulty, she broke away. "It might be too complicated. And don't you want to get settled in your bunk?"

"Can we meet later?"

"Sure." *Please,* she thought, *there's not enough oxygen here, just go away and let me breathe and think clearly for a minute.* She turned to the board, waved casually, and attached the electrodes. Before the valleys of cyberspace had formed around her, Iger and Third Child had left ops.

Got to watch that, she thought. *He's cute, but that doesn't mean I have to park my brain at the door. And that goes double for when we're linked through the navboard.*

To distract herself she began running practice escape drills until all she could think of was how to avoid hitting a large red trapezoid that was really a merchant ship.

* * *

Cyberspace had quickly become familiar territory to Kayla and she came to know its nooks, corners, and shortcuts, growing ever more comfortable and confident at plotting course maneuvers.

It was on a jump to the Salabrian System that she learned an uncomfortable truth.

The automatic countdown to jump had begun and all the crew were strapped into their stations. Iger was sitting behind her, hooked into the board. Salome gave the go-ahead and Kayla plunged into the canyon just below the jump interface.

She floated past the blue diamond twirling to her left, pivoted around a yellow and green square, and saw the archway at the entrance to jumpspace glowing with its own peculiar energies. She took the first step through it and. . . .

Space stretched nauseatingly before her with no up, no down. She drifted, an infinite number of selves, each immobilized, the bottom falling out of her stomachs, the top of her heads coming off. She couldn't see forward, nor backward, in nor out. She was impaled upon the present moment, isolated, frozen, and alone.

Help, she thought. *Help, help, help. Iger, do something. Can't you hear me? Doesn't anybody hear me?*

She tried to reach out through nearsense, but her empathic powers were frozen, too.

How long she hung helpless in cyberspace—aeons?—she didn't know. Time had swallowed itself and disappeared, seconds stretching into lifetimes, until strange and sudden energy rippled like ball lightning through the jump interface and released her. She was falling, flailing, to smash on the hard floor of the canyon.

Kayla blinked. She was in ops, sitting in her chair in realtime and realspace. The chronometer showed that only moments had gone by since she had entered cyberspace. Jump had been completed. The red Salabrian sun was a small light, growing brighter, onscreen.

Salome nodded. "Nice jump, Katie."

Kayla forced herself to smile. *I'm in trouble,* she thought. *Big* trouble. *There's something about jumpspace, something that I'm allergic to. How can I pilot this ship when I can't take us through jump without freezing?*

When they were parked in a comfortable orbit around the red dwarf star, she pulled off her electrodes and saw that Iger was absorbed in the board—he hadn't even noticed her dilemma. Good.

"You can monitor the board for a while," she told him. "I'm off duty."

She made a quick trip to the ship's library to do a little research. Most of what she learned left her in despair.

JUMP SICKNESS. Complaint of uncertain origin, possibly psychological, most often afflicting the empathically gifted. Can be treated with some success by somatics, tranquilizers, coldsleep. See equilibrium, motion illness.

Kayla shut down the vid deck in disgust. How was she supposed to pilot the ship on tranquilizers? She decided to consult Morgan on natural remedies.

But what if the medic questioned her too closely? Jump sickness was peculiar to empaths.

Kayla would find some way to conceal the truth. Grimly, she headed for the hydroponics lab.

Just outside the lab, Kayla caught her reflection in a polished bit of bulkhead and didn't like what she saw. Her hair was growing out again. She had taken to dyeing it once every two months to cover the bright red roots, but her dye supply was nearly exhausted and she wasn't certain when the *Falstaff* would next make landfall.

The lab was empty, silent save for the drip-drip-drip of water and rustle of leaves on the ever-moving salvia. Morgan was nowhere to be seen.

"Hello! Anybody home?"

Silence.

Kayla left a note on the lab's screen. Perhaps she would pick a few minds at dinner and see what they knew about jump sickness. But that was hours away. Again she noticed her reflection, the red roots on brown hair just starting to show. There was still time. She could dye it now. That might take her mind off of her problems.

The bathroom near her room was empty. She could commandeer the place.

She dumped the last of her dyestuff into a container, stuck it under her arm, and ducked into the loo.

Whistling, she stripped off her clothes, combed the dark green goo through her hair, and settled down with a vid cube she had borrowed from Arsobades.

Greer walked in. "Hey."

Kayla jumped, startled. How had she forgotten to lock the door? Before Kayla could cover herself, Greer saw the triangular empath tattoo between her shoulder blades.

"What the hell is this?" Greer grabbed her arm and swung her around sharply. "Why do you have an empath's mark on you? Are you some damned spy for the prime minister?"

"No." Kayla pulled free from Greer's punishing grip and prepared to defend herself. *What should I use,* she wondered. *A mindbolt? Can I blank out Greer's memory with shadowsense? What if Greer is as sensitive as Salome? What if I killed her? No, don't be foolish. Just do it. No, I can't. This is Greer, my roommate for over a year. I owe her the truth.*

"No," Kayla repeated. "I'm an empath, all right. But I'm no spy."

"No? Then what the hell are you doing on this ship?"

"Hiding. Running away."

"From what?"

"Well—" Kayla told her about about the cave-in and

her parents' deaths. About Beatrice Keller, money owed, and her attack on Yates. And about the price on her head.

Greer listened silently, frowning. Finally she said, "Why should I believe any of this?"

"Because it's the truth." Kayla said, her voice rising. "Because you have no reason not to."

"You've been lying to me, to everyone here, ever since you got aboard."

"Not because I wanted to. Because I had to. Don't you see? You hate empaths so badly that I thought I'd better not reveal who I was. I figured you might toss me out of an air lock. Or turn me in."

"What makes you think I won't do that anyway?"

"Because you're not like that. And you can see I'm no threat to you. Come on, Greer. If I'm a spy, why didn't I just turn you all in when the Trade Police tried to stop us?"

Greer leaned against the wall, arms crossed, eyes hard, her mouth a grim straight line. "You must have me figured for some kind of sucker."

"Or why shouldn't I just erase your memory of this whole encounter? Why am I wasting my time telling you this if it's not the truth when I've got a whole arsenal of scary empathic tricks I could use to ensure your silence?"

"Because you're young and foolish."

"But—"

Greer held up her hand. "Just shut up and let me think about this for a minute." She paced angrily, back and forth. "How do I know this isn't just some elaborate setup? Maybe you were exchanging information with the empath on the police cruiser, or maybe there wasn't even an empath there at all. Maybe you were transmitting information right to them."

"You're completely paranoid," Kayla said. She would have laughed if she hadn't been so frightened. "What would I tell them? That this is a smuggling

ship? They already know that. And how do you think
I felt, finding an empath working for the Trade Police?
And there was an empath on that ship, believe me. Or
do you think I made Salome go into convulsions as
well?"

"Somebody or something did."

"Yes, but it wasn't me. Although now I can see why
you've come to hate empaths. If they cause some of
the effects I've seen in Salome, and if they use their
abilities to interrogate Karlson's enemies, I don't
blame you for how you feel. My father would have
been horrified. It was one of the things he always
feared: that the government would subvert the empaths
and use them as a secret weapon against everybody
else in the Trade Alliance."

Something in her voice or in her face must have conveyed to her roommate all the horror she felt. Greer
stopped pacing and stared at her with narrowed eyes.

"You really understand?"

"Didn't I just say that?" How could she break
through Greer's paranoia? "If you're going to report
me to Salome, why don't you just go ahead and get it
over with?"

"If you got sent back to Styx, you'd go to prison for
life?"

"Probably."

"Gods' Eyes, I don't know what to do," Greer said.
"I trust my instincts, and they tell me to like you. But
I don't like empaths, and I don't trust them."

"And I don't blame you, if all you know of them is
what you've learned through the government's spies.
But there are other empaths. Believe me, Greer. Men
like my father, Redmond Reed."

Her roommate held up her hand. "What did you say
his name was?"

"Redmond—"

"Reed!" Greer's eyes widened. "I met a Redmond
Reed once, years ago. Back on St. Ilban. He was part

of a trade delegation from Styx. A decent guy. Honest, spoke straight from the hip. It would have been great if he had been our liaison with Styx. Instead we had to deal with that Keller bitch. If the son is anything like the mother, small wonder that you knocked him out. So Redmond Reed was your father?"

"Yes."

"And after he and your mother died, you had to run from Keller and son? Pretty gutsy, weren't you? Yeah, I'm beginning to get the vid."

Tears of relief welled in Kayla's eyes and threatened to spill over. "Good."

Greer's mouth quirked slightly. "Stay right there. Don't move. I'll only be gone a minute."

She returned with a clinical-looking metal case and a small opaque bottle, which she set down upon the sink. "Lock the door. Then come here and lean over the sink."

"What are you going to do?"

"Cover that tattoo."

"No!" Kayla backed away.

"Don't be stupid," Greer said. "Somebody else might walk into the bathroom just like I did."

"I'll be more careful."

"Bull. You'll be smart and listen to me, Katie, or whatever-your-name-is."

"It's Kayla. Kayla John, after my grandfather."

"That's nice. But let's keep it Katie, just to be safe and avoid confusion."

Greer's fingers were deft and strong. The cleanser was cool against her back. But the hypo stung as it punctured the skin, and the dye swabbed on over the puncture hurt worse.

"Ouch!"

"Sorry. Want a painkiller?"

"Yes, please." Kayla grimaced until the touch of another hypo left a warm, numb place where the burning ache had been. She had half-expected this to feel the way her initiation and tattooing had. She remembered her mother's hands, her father's gentle grip, the ameliorating mindtouch that erased all pain. Now, for a moment, she could close her eyes and pretend that her mother was making each precise cut in the design, whispering words of encouragement, stroking the dye evenly until it formed the sign of the empath.

"Okay," said Greer. "You'll do."

Kayla stared at her back in the mirror. A black star had obliterated her telltale tattoo. "What's the star for?"

"The Free Traders."

"That anti-tariff group you told me about?"

"The very same."

"You must be pretty well organized if you've got secret tattoos. What else have you got, handshakes and passwords?"

Greer chuckled, a rare sound. "Not a bad idea. I'll pass it along." She rolled up her sleeve. A black sunburst covered her forearm. "Everybody on the ship has one. I had to outline Salome's in gold so it would show. She wanted it between her breasts. Rab complained at first, but he likes it fine, now." She gave Kayla an amused, approving pat. "So, Katie, you're one of us now, like it or not."

Kayla felt both hilarity and disbelief. She had finally found a home for herself, a hideout among people who were sworn enemies of all empaths. But it felt oddly appropriate and, somehow, she couldn't imagine a better hiding place in the entire galaxy.

Chapter Eleven

Early, too early, Kayla awoke, stretched under the covers, and then remembered the date. Her birthday. Today, right this minute, she was eighteen. She lingered a moment longer before opening her eyes, and remembered how her mother had always let her sleep late on her birthday, how her father had prepared a special breakfast, spiced flatcakes. She could almost smell them . . .

She opened her eyes and saw the outline of Greer curled in sleep in her own bunk. No pancakes. No parents. Good morning.

The *Falstaff* was docked at Buffalo Port on Salabria III in the Salabrian System. Kayla had monitor duty in ops. A quiet morning, then. She would check the navboard relays, scrub the deck, polish the brass. Happy birthday.

She hadn't been in ops more than ten minutes when the com line sputtered and squawked, pulled her out of her funk.

"Rab? Salome! We've got trouble." It was Kelso's voice, high and frightened. He and Arsobades had gone into port right after breakfast. "We're pinned down between a bunch of crazy pirates convinced we've got a load of mindsalt on board. They won't listen to reason, and the port police must be asleep. We've got one gun between us. Is anybody listening? Hello?"

Kayla stabbed the com button. "Kels, where are you?"

"About two meters from the big gantry near the end of the dock."

"I'm scanning for you," Kayla said. Where was he? What if she couldn't find him? No, wait. A red blip on the screen. "There. Got you. Hang on. Help's on the way." Even as she said it she was hitting the ship intercom, signaling madly: all hands to ops on the double.

In minutes the room was bustling as her crewmates, newly apprised of the crisis, grabbed weapons and strapped on body armor.

"Iger, Kayla, you come with me," Rab said. He handed Kayla a heavy disruptor. "Salome and Greer will cover us with ship's guns. Move it."

He led them down the ramp and out of the ship. "Stay low," he rasped. "Don't shoot unless you have to. Katie, Iger, you stay on either side of the deck and cover me."

Iger ducked right, Katie went left.

She could feel her heart pounding in her chest. Each breath she drew was like thunder in her ears.

The whine of disruptor fire filled the air, then shouts, then silence. More shooting. More silence.

A moment later, footsteps, faint at first, growing louder, coming closer.

Kayla's heart beat harder, but she kept her weapon steady.

Arsobades came toward her at a dead run. As he ran past, he saw her and gasped. "Right behind me."

Kayla saw the man, heavily armored, gaining on her shipmate. He had a sleek, nasty-looking gun in his hand and was taking aim on Arsobades. In a second he would have him.

Kayla brought the disruptor up and stared through the gunsight. She held her breath, squeezed the handgrip.

The shot missed him and dissipated harmlessly.

She squeezed the handgrip again and the weapon emitted a low buzzing sound.

The man stumbled, fell, and lay still.

The sense of contact, of hitting her target, was utterly satisfying. She savored it for a moment and the part of her that could smile in savage pleasure, close her teeth around the thrill of blood lust and taste it on her tongue, came to the fore. *Shoot again,* she thought. *Just one more time.* She took aim and . . .

A large hand closed about her forearm.

She turned, ready to kick and bite her way free, and saw Rab staring at her sternly.

"No fun shooting a dead target," he said. "We won the battle."

Iger popped up behind him, wide-eyed. "What do we do now?" he said. "Get out of port?"

"Worst thing we could do," Rab said. "If we leave, that makes it look like we're in the wrong. Nope. We stay and fill out the goddamned endless paperwork. Look, here come the port police. Great. Hi, guys. Nice to see you, now that the shooting's over."

* * *

The paperwork took hours. Tired, depleted, and dusty, the crew returned to the *Falstaff.*

For dinner, Kelso served up an uninspired vegetable stew that sat in the mouth like sawdust. Greer contributed a few bottles of harsh red wine, barely drinkable.

As she downed her second glass of the raw stuff, Kayla began to fume. What a day. She couldn't believe it. By the third glass of red, she could stand it no longer.

"Well, this is a fine way to celebrate my birthday," she announced to everybody and nobody in particular. "Today. Yes, that's right. My birthday! And what do I do for my birthday? What any other red-blooded girl would want do. Kill somebody." She forced herself to laugh.

Greer paused, her fork halfway to her mouth, and eyed her with mock concern. "How much have you had to drink?"

Arsobades' face was grave. "Is it really your birthday, Katie?"

She nodded a few times too many before she caught herself and stopped.

"Why in the nine heavens didn't you say something?" Rab said, half-amused, half-disgusted.

"I don't know." Kayla shrugged, starting to be sorry she had opened her mouth. "It seemed, well, childish."

"And this isn't?" Kelso muttered.

"Stow it," Arsobades told him. "Everybody deserves a birthday celebration. Katie's birthday party will begin in ten minutes. Now everybody scramble and get ready."

As Kayla watched, her crewmates scattered, leaving her alone with Third Child. The dalkoi gave an interrogative chirp and rubbed up against Kayla. She patted it tipsily.

"Nice dalkoi," she said. "No, I don't know where they all went. Who cares?" She poured herself another glass of wine, raised her cup to Third Child, and said, "To you and your lovely eyes."

The wine didn't seem quite as awful as before. In fact, it was really rather good. She had nearly emptied her glass when everybody returned, noisily settling around her, chuckling and nudging.

Arsobades came bounding into the room, his lute and a bag full of instruments slung over his shoulder. "Okay," he said. "Let the festivities begin. Here! Music-makers. Everybody grab one and no excuses. Genius that I am, I've composed an instant birthday tribute, and the chorus is easy, so sing along!" He strummed heavily and began singing,

"Katie has green eyes like emeralds.
Green eyes. Green eyes.
Katie has red lips. Lips like rubies.
Red lips.
Katie's my darling, my diamond,

my dear.
I'll drink to her health
and I'll drink to her wealth
Now that her birthday's here!
Yes, we'll drink to her health
her health and her wealth,
Now that her birthday's here."

What the group lacked in harmony they made up for
in volume, beating time with their sticks, drums, finger
cymbals, and tambourines. Arsobades made them sing
it five times through, until Kayla begged for mercy.

"Now," Arsobades said. "The gifts. With appropriate
accompaniment, of course." Strumming a sprightly
tune, he nodded madly at Salome.

She rose, curtsied elaborately as the others snick-
ered, handed Kayla a small pouch, and planted a
feather-light kiss on her cheek. "Next time, give us
more warning," she said, smiling. "We'll even manage
a cake."

Inside the bag were a pair of green crystal earrings
that Kayla had long admired. "I can't believe it,"
Kayla said. "Salome, your earrings. You didn't have to
do that!"

"Now we'll need to pierce your ears," the captain
said gaily. "Come see me tomorrow and we'll do it
first thing. Guaranteed painless."

"My turn," Rab said. "Here, squirt." To Kayla's delight, he tossed her his vid cube on astronomy. "And
don't worry, I made a copy for me."

Next, Morgan brought clippings of Katie's favorite
fire ivy, and wound the sparkling strands around her
neck and through her hair. "Red is good with your
eyes," she said. She made an odd pirouette, winked,
and sat down.

"Well," Kelso said, hands jammed in his pockets. "I
guess it's my turn. Don't suppose that dinner counts?"

"Not that dinner," Rab growled.

"Well, Katie, then how about if I balance your credit for you?"

Kayla eyed him dubiously. "I don't have any."

"No credit?" His long face got a trifle longer. "Hmmm. What the hell. I'll teach you how to juggle, okay?"

"Juggle?" Kayla said. "Sure."

To her amusement, Kelso shook her hand awkwardly and, nodding, backed away, obviously relieved.

Greer gave her a hand-scrawled IOU, good for a load of laundry, "As long as it's not hand-laundry," she said, smiling her flinty smile. "And as a bonus, I'll help you with your coiffure, upon request."

Kayla nodded. "Don't think I won't ask you."

Iger had watched the proceedings looking more and more uncomfortable. Obviously, he had found nothing to give and didn't like it. Suddenly he brightened and hurried out the door. A moment later, he was back with a purple bundle in his arms.

"Here," he said. "Happy-happy and all that. I remembered that I had it in my pack.

The bundle was a small, lovely bambera fur-tapestry which covered Kayla's lap. She stared down at its graceful interlocking lavender patterns and felt her throat tighten. It was so much like the one her parents had had. "It's beautiful," she said. "Iger, I can't take this. It's not right."

"Please," he said, blushing furiously. "I want you to have it. You can't say no. It's your birthday." He squeezed her hand and, leaning close, kissed her on one cheek, then the other. "That makes it official."

More drinking and singing followed. Kayla was dimly aware of Arsobades jigging with her as the others clapped, of Iger kissing her again, and of Greer and Salome dragging her off to bed and tucking her in. Her last thought that evening was that, even without flatcakes, this birthday had been eminently satisfactory.

* * *

Two weeks after Kayla's birthday, long past the last of the hangovers from her party, the *Falstaff* headed for Vorhays in the Novo Gabela System. They were halfway there when a brilliant red light began flashing on the comboard.

"Picking up a distress call," Kelso said.

Salome turned to him, brows raised. "Who is it?"'

"*Magellan's Luck.* A trader."

"I don't know them. Do you, Rab?"

"Nope."

She leaned over and pressed the com link. "Greer, do you know anybody on *Magellan's Luck?*"

"I'm pretty sure they're Free Traders," Greer said. "I don't know them personally, but they must be all right."

"There are Free Traders, and then there are Free Traders," Rab muttered.

"The ship's registered on Salabria IX," Kelso reported. "Of course, so are half the ships in the known galaxy."

"That tells us nothing," Salome said. "What's wrong with them?"

"It's a general distress call. No specifics. Requesting immediate assistance from any ship in the quadrant."

Arsobade's voice came over the com link. "Salome, something's wrong with their power levels. They keep fluctuating right up and down, all over the scale."

"I don't see how we can help them with that," Salome said.

"God's Eyes!" Greer said. "You're acting as though these are the Trade Police in disguise. They're on our side. Maybe they're just having engine trouble. Besides, we're required by law to respond to a distress call."

"I know," Salome said. "Damn it, Kelso, open a com link with them and see what's wrong."

"Yes'm." He leaned over the board, listening. "They request a medic. One crew member dead."

"What happened?"

"Explosion. Nonspecific."

Salome disentangled herself from the board. "Rab, we'd better go over there. Get Morgan and tell her to bring her kit."

"What if their distress signal brings the Trade Police?" Rab said.

"Have an escape course plotted, Katie. Subjump to Vorhays, and hope we won't need it."

"Right." Kayla punched in the coordinates on her navboard.

"I'll go, too," Greer said. "If it's Free Traders in trouble, I want to know about it."

Salome opened her mouth to disagree, then closed it. "I suppose I can't turn my back on Free Traders if they're in trouble," she said. "But we'll take along our laser pistols, yes? C'mon, Rab. Let's go see what's wrong. Kelso, you're in charge."

The *Falstaff* pod shuttle made the trip between the ships in minutes. An hour later, the shuttle was back, docking in its berth. But the suited figures that disembarked were short and stocky, swarthy asexual beings with the mark of Knathia's heavy gravity stamped upon their flat features. To Kayla they looked like tunnel rats, vicious and stupid.

"Where's our captain?" Kelso demanded. "Our crew?"

For answer, the lead Knathian pulled out a disruptor and pointed it at him. "We're taking this vessel," he said. "Step aside. Now."

Kelso held up his hand as though to ward off a blow. "Don't shoot, okay?"

He seemed completely undone by fear. But Kayla noticed that under cover of his quivering and shaking her crewmate had surreptitiously opened the allship com link so that the remaining crew could hear what was going on.

"Act right and we won't have any problems," said the Knathian. "Act wrong and . . ."

"No problems," Kelso said quickly, holding his hands up and smiling a broad false smile. "Aside from some creeps from deep-g and their guns. Right, Katie?"

"No problems," Kayla echoed. She made a quick mindsearch and found that, belowdecks, Arsobades and Iger had indeed heard them and were arming themselves. Next she took a farsense probe of the other ship and found, to her relief, that Salome, Rab, Morgan, and Greer, were still alive. One of them, Rab, was unconscious but he seemed unharmed, merely stunned.

The Knathians must have ambushed them, Kayla thought. *Otherwise, Salome and Rab would have raised hell over there and made certain that we knew about it. If only I could communicate with them now!*

What good was her being a tripath if she had to keep it to herself?

But the immediate problem was how to defeat these pirates. Aloud she said, "What's wrong with your ship?"

The Knathian didn't even bother to look at her. "We mixed it up with a trader. Lost our starboard stabilizers. Can't maneuver."

Kelso raised a skeptical eyebrow but said nothing.

The second Knathian shoved Kayla aside. "Show me how this board works," he said.

"Why? I can do it for you."

"Why should you."

"Because you have a disruptor pointed at me," Kayla said sweetly. She knew better than to surrender control of the navboard. "Where do you want to go?"

"Knathia Station. It's a three-jump." He stared at her. He was as short and lumpy as a stalagmite. "You'll show me how to use this."

Kayla smiled her nicest smile. *I'd like to show you a quick trip out the air lock,* she thought. Where was

Arsobades? What was taking him so long? Until he arrived, her options were limited. She could trigger a subspace distress call, and the Knathians might not notice. But the SOS could draw in other traders who would fall prey to them, and it would surely draw the Trade Police. The *Falstaff* had a false ID transmission which said they were a scout ship for the Haleran Corporation based on Salabria IV, but that would only hold up until the police boarded them.

She saw Kelso signaling her with his eyes. She took a quick nearsense probe and saw that he wanted her to distract the Knathians as much as possible. Great. What should she do, strip? They didn't seem to be interested in that. They were far more intrigued by the navboard. Maybe that was the gambit to use: tie them up in instructions about the navboard, engage and confuse them.

"Are you just deserting your ship and comrades?" she said.

"Don't be stupid," the Knathian said. "Once we learn your ship we'll leave you with ours."

Alive? Kayla very much doubted it. "Oh," she said. "Well, then you'll need to know how to cross-channel all routes to jump interfaces. Here, let me show you . . ." All three Knathians were intent upon her.

A suspicious scratching sound came out of the corridor beyond ops.

Scritchscratchscratch.

It grew louder.

Something much like uneasiness passed over the taciturn face of the Knathian leader. He tensed, looking around. "What's that noise?"

Scratchscratchscratch . . .

All three Knathians drew closer to the doorway, guns drawn.

Scratchscritchscratch.

Third Child toddled into the room dragging a length

of frayed insulation behind it, scratching and scraping against the floor.

"What in the name of the gods is that?" said the head pirate.

"Third Child," Kayla replied cheerfully. Any distraction bought them time. "A dalkoi."

"A what?"

The dalkoi toddled around the control room, seemingly oblivious to the men pointing disruptors at it.

Despite themselves, the three Knathians ringed the creature, staring in fascination.

"A dalkoi," said a sharp tenor voice. "Like she told you." Arsobades and Iger stood in the doorway, each holding a double disruptor in either hand. "Drop your guns."

The Knathians hesitated.

Arsobades drew a bead on the nearest pirate. "Duck, Katie. He might splatter on you."

The pirates' weapons went clattering to the floor, and Iger kicked the weapons into the far corner of the room.

"Now we're going to have a little chat," Arsobades said. "Ship to ship. Call 'em. We want our companions sent back here, pronto." His face was bright red. Kayla had never seen him so angry. "Move it, you flat-faced toads!"

Iger tossed one of his pistols to Kayla. "Here. Help me cover them."

The gun was heavy in her hand. She held it carefully, propping her wrist with her other arm.

Arsobades prodded the lead Knathian, not gently, to the comboard. "Get busy," he said. "Kels, open a channel to the other ship."

"Open and waiting," Kelso replied.

"Well?" Arsobades said.

The pirate crossed his arms. "You want to talk to them? Then talk. Or shoot me."

"How about if I shoot one of your friends here?"

The minstrel swung his pistol to aim it at the other two Knathians. None of them reacted. They didn't seem to care if they lived or died.

"Gods," Kelso said. He leaned over the comboard and said, "*Magellan's Luck,* this is the *Falstaff.* Your boarding party has been captured. We propose a hostage swap."

There was no response.

"Tell them again," Arsobades said.

Kelso repeated his message.

"What's taking so long?" Kayla said.

"Maybe you should put up the shields," Arsobades said. "Just to be safe."

Kelso shook his head. "It'll interfere with communications."

Kayla tried a farsense probe, but there were too many minds at work over on *Magellan's Luck.* She couldn't sort everybody out. She did get a sense of great confusion, with an undercurrent of menace that she didn't like.

"Incoming fire," Kelso said. "Dammit, Arsobades, you were right. They don't give a damn about their friends here. Brace yourselves."

The ship shook as though a giant hand grabbed the outer hull and was tipping it back and forth. The Knathians maintained their balance and looked surprisingly composed, even unconcerned. But Arsobades had turned pale behind his fiery beard.

Kayla grabbed hold of the navboard to keep herself upright. "What do we do?" she shouted above the blare of alarms. "We can't return fire with half of our crew over there!"

"Sit tight," Arsobades said. "If Salome and Rab can't get themselves out of there, we'll know it soon enough. And for God's sake, get those shields up!"

Iger hurried to the ops board and punched up the main deflectors just as another shot came at them. The *Falstaff* rocked like a mad cradle and red emergency lights began flashing all over Salome's ops board. As Kayla watched them with growing dismay, Iger peered at the readout.

"I think we took some damage on that hit," he said. "The screens weren't all solid yet."

Kelso glanced away from his own board and frowned. "Must be the directionals," he said. "Hard to keep them properly shielded. That should screw up communications for us but good."

"I could pull us out of firing range," Kayla said. "But that would make it almost impossible for another shuttle to reach us."

"Why don't you pull us a little farther out?" Arsobades said. "Make it a little tougher for those shots to reach us."

"What are their power levels?" Kayla said.

"Pretty low," Kelso said. "Actually, I'm surprised they could get those shots off. That last round seems to have depleted their weapons banks. Maybe they can't recharge."

A half-hour went by, minutes crawling as Kayla tensed and waited for further attack.

"Hey," Kelso yelled. "A shuttle's disembarking, coming toward us."

Kayla looked over his shoulder at the board. "Who's on it? Is it ours?"

He shook his head. "Dunno. I've tried hailing them, but there's no answer. We'd better assume the worst. Let's prepare for 'em."

"We'll get down to the shuttle lock," Arsobades said. "C'mon, Iger. Kayla, you play host to our guests."

"I'll get us on autopilot," Kayla said. "At least we won't hit anything. Not that there's much out here to hit."

Kelso pulled a disruptor from the wall holder and checked its power levels. He nodded grimly. Kayla motioned the Knathians against the far wall.

Metal clunked and chittered in the distance as the shuttle docked.

Footsteps sounded in the corridor, louder and louder, nearer and nearer.

Agonizing moments went by before Salome and Rab appeared in the control room. Salome's face looked bruised and puffy. Rab had a cut over his right eye that was oozing blood. Right behind them came Morgan, silent as usual, with a grim-faced Greer bringing up the rear.

"What about the Knathians?" Kayla said.

"We fixed those bastards," Salome said.

"Yep," said Rab. "Made them think we were all frightened shitless and then jumped them when their guard was down. Left 'em trussed up in their ship with the distress signal on automatic. Either they'll starve or the Trade Police will find them."

"Have found them is more like it," Kelso said sourly. "Police cruiser coming up fast on port side."

"Let them come," Salome said. "We're running empty. Nothing to hide."

"Gods!" Greer ducked out the door.

Rab shouted after her, "If you've got your Free Trade crap sitting around just waiting for the cops to find it, I'll wring your skinny neck."

"Easy," Arsobades said. "Take it easy."

"You take it easy," Rab said. "Who needs her? God-damned troublemaker, telling us that any Free Trader is an ally, and none of us with enough brains to question that." He leaned out the door to shout after Greer. "Free Trade! I'll set you free, lady. Right out the nearest air lock!"

"Prepared to be boarded," came a metallic voice from the comboard. Kelso shrugged helplessly.

Three representatives of the Trade Police arrived, clad in black uniforms piped with silver. They were cool, efficient, and cynical.

One officer, dark-skinned and steely-eyed, stood

guard by the door while the other two, a blonde woman and gray-haired man, checked their records for information on the *Falstaff*'s crew and the Knathian hostages.

The blonde read from her portascreen: "Class-C merchant ship *Falstaff*. Owner, Salome Fiesco. Inherited vessel from Fin Fiesco."

"Father?" said the gray-haired cop.

"Uncle."

They exchanged knowing, suspicious looks.

"Fin Fiesco was quite the smuggler," said the blonde. "Think it runs in the family?" She kept reading. "Barabbas Purkinje, first mate. One prior. Running illegal medicines to a plague ship."

They closed on Rab and he faced them down. "I was acquitted," he said proudly. "Nothing was proved. And while you waste your time chasing phantoms over here there's a shipload of real pirates next door just waiting to be plucked. And a couple of goons right here for the taking."

"Why didn't you report them as soon as you saw them?"

"Are we supposed to handle all your work for you?"

"Watch it," the blonde officer snapped. "Another smart remark like that and we might just decide to bring you down to base and have a little talk. Or find it necessary to impound this ship."

"On what ground?" Salome demanded.

"Suspicion of smuggling."

"What's your proof?" She looked completely fearless. Watching her, Kayla was proud to be part of her crew.

"That the first mate needs to learn some respect," said the blonde, who seemed to be their leader. She pulled out a long metallic baton from a holster at her waist and pressed the handle. Coruscating yellow sparks swarmed up and down the length of the baton. "Let's see just how witty you feel now."

Rab glowered, obviously ready to jump all three of them.

Kayla knew somebody had to stop him before this escalated. But nearsense wouldn't work on this many people. She couldn't use a shadowfield on them all, either, it wouldn't hold together.

Quickly, she used a farsense probe to scan the police cruiser until she found an extremely receptive, pliable mind. There. Work on him for a while. Convince him that he's just received a message, an important one.

—Smugglers operating nearby. Call back the boarding party. Take Magellan's Luck *in tow. Hurry, there's no time to lose.*

Kayla put everything she had into the mindlink. The sense of urgency, the need to recall the boarding party. It was harder than she thought, almost as though she were forcing her way through some sort of obstacle, some shield. She pushed harder. Harder.

A yellow light at the lead policeman's wrist began blinking. He stared down at it. "Yellow alert," he said. The other two officers stirred uneasily.

"That calls for immediate return," said the blonde. "Let's move it." She glared at the Knathians. "You three slugs come with us." When they hesitated she tapped her baton. "I mean, now."

The Knathians straggled out of ops with the Trade Police right behind them. The blonde turned at the door. "Keep it clean, *Falstaff*. We'll be watching for you."

Kayla hung on to the mindlink, but she was weakening fast. Dizziness sent her senses whirling. She felt giddy, too light on her feet. And that strange interference, as though someone nearby was jamming her mental signal, was getting stronger. Despite the increasing throbbing in her head, she forced herself to keep at it.

—Urgent. Hurry. Smugglers. Catch them. Go!

The police cruiser shimmered as it went into

jumpspace and was gone, taking *Magellan's Luck* with it.

Kayla sagged down into her chair, hoping that no one noticed.

Greer scowled at the screen. "Good riddance, police scum."

Rab rounded on her as though she had stuck a knife into him. "This is all your fault," he thundered. "I don't understand why the hell we listened to you in the first place."

"I told you I had it under control," Greer said. "But you panicked."

"Yeah, great. You go in there shaking hands like we're all old friends. Why didn't you give them the secret code word while you were at it? Maybe open the *Falstaff*'s vaults."

Greer pulled away from the angry giant. "Ratch off, Rab. You're just peeved that the Knathian captain slapped Salome."

"Oh, you think that's funny?" Rab's voice got even louder. "You think that when somebody hits Salome, it's some sort of a joke? And if they had shot her instead? That would have been even funnier, wouldn't it? A real riot."

"Rab," Arsobades said. "Hey, come on."

Rab ignored him, advancing as Greer retreated. "You and your damned political games. You were so eager to greet these unknown comrades of yours that you nearly got us killed—or imprisoned."

"You're so full of it," Greer said. "Great, big, brave Barabbas." She made a face. "You know what you are? A dilettante. You talk the talk, but all you really care about is your ass and Salome's. You don't give half a damn about what's happening to the Trade Alliance."

"Damn straight." Rab's mouth quirked in a half-smile, but Greer would not be gentled.

"You saw those police," she said. "They're getting worse and worse. And Karlson encourages it. Meanwhile, the entire system's going to hell. The smaller traders suffer and fail. Nobody cares. Only Karlson's getting richer and richer. But you just give lip service to the cause. Bravo, hero. At least I try to do something."

Kayla expected Rab to explode and lash out at her roommate. Instead he seemed completely and suddenly calm, his temper blown over and gone. "Look, I don't like Karlson any better than you do. The major difference is that I haven't let it drive me nuts."

Greer gave him a look of contempt laced with sarcasm. "You think I'm crazy?"

He crossed his arms and leaned back against the wall. "You got it."

"Good. Why should I care what you think? I'll tell you a little secret, Rab. The whole damned galaxy could think I was crazy. But that wouldn't mean I was wrong." Greer's eyes burned into him. Without another word she was out the door.

Kayla stared after her roommate. She was beginning to think that Rab was right: Greer seemed to be out of her mind.

Kelso gave a low whistle and rolled his eyes.

"Let's get out of here," Salome said crisply. "Everybody to their stations."

Chapter Twelve

They made good time to Vorhays. Nobody spoke much, just did their work, concentrating on putting space between them and where they had just been.

Since they were traveling at subjump speeds, Kayla bounced casually around the canyons and mountains of cyberspace until the first ringed satellite of Vorhays Station appeared, doorkeeper to the port, growing larger, looming in their vid screens.

She pulled easily into the berth assigned to them by the stationmaster. Once the *Falstaff* was safely parked and supply lines had been connected by the port crew, Kayla set her board on power-down and locked it. A private message was waiting for her from Iger, asking her to come explore the port with him.

"Meet you in fifteen minutes," she told him, and raced down to her room to pick up a sack and jacket. She got there just in time to see something hit her pillow and bounce.

Kayla's heart thudded in her chest. It was the bag of precious mindstones that she had so carefully hidden!

Chirp!

Her fear changed to annoyance as Third Child appeared from out of the depths of her closet and leaped onto the bed. The dalkoi bounced twice and craned its skinny neck toward the mindstone sack.

Kayla snatched the bag out of Third Child's reach. "What are you doing? Didn't Iger teach you to stay out of other people's things?"

The dalkoi chirped again, blinked, and extended its neck to be scratched.

"No, I'm not going to pet you. This is my room. Get out, go snoop through somebody else's belongings."

Third Child chirped again.

"Don't pretend you don't understand me. I know that you do." *Oh,* she thought, *if only I could make a direct mindlink with the thing!* But she had discovered that probing the dalkoi was a waste of time: it only gave her a headache. They were wired so differently from Homo sapiens that any readings she came away with would be hopelessly confusing. Instead, she simply flapped her arms until the dalkoi retreated out the door, chirruping reproachfully.

When it was gone, Kayla checked the bag. To her relief, every faceted ruby-blue stone was there, rubbing against its neighbor with a faint musical clink. Perhaps Third Child had been attracted by its sound or maybe it gave off an aura that only a dalkoi could see. But why was Third Child in her room to begin with? How had it homed in on the sack?

The intercom buzzed. "Kayla, where are you?" Iger, called, impatient and waiting. "I'm at the air lock. Come on."

Kayla shrugged, tucked the bag away along with her questions, and hurried down to meet him.

* * *

The town of Vorhays Junction was dominated by trade and the diversion of those who traded. A null-g floating rink was set in the center of the main boulevard, framed by an old-fashioned towline rather than a magnetic slidewalk. The buildings resembled giant beehives, round and golden brown with domed roofs tiled in strange patterns: yellow squiggles, purple dots, green ellipses. They were filled with shops, bars, sports clubs, and sex parlors.

After a brief tour of the cyberarcades, Kayla and Iger settled in at the curving main bar of Peg's Big

Toe. It was a favorite spacer haunt, shaped like a huge teacup, spinning slowly so that none of the patrons developed airsickness as they slid along its slick black walls on the continuous floating banquette.

The ceiling was covered in holoplas which mirrored the action below in neon 3-D. By midnight, a genial crowd had gathered along the walls, and at their center sat Arsobades, resplendent in an embroidered black tunic, his red hair glowing in the hololight.

Quietly he strummed his mechlute, allowing the chords to gather into a plaintive refrain which grew sadder, more poignant with each string he plucked. The song had no words and by the time he had finished, the minstrel's face was wet with tears.

"It's for his wife," somebody whispered. "Must be."

"The one who died?"

"Yeah, killed herself. It's been five years and he's still not over it."

Kayla's heart ached for her crewmate. Did everybody have some secret sorrow? As she watched, Arsobades rallied, and his strumming took on added vigor. Now he was striking chords with one hand while he beckoned with the other for people to join him in song. The crowd responded by calling out requests.

"Do 'The Great Up and Out,' Arsobades!"

"Sing us 'The Bambera's Revenge.' "

" 'Ode to Odin,' "

"No! I want to hear 'McGavin's Lament' first."

The minstrel complied with gusto. Soon everyone was singing, drinking, and calling good-natured insults to one another. Again and again they toasted the bartender, tiny, gap-toothed Hanno, and his Junoesque wife and chief bouncer, Hermione. But when Arsobades began to sing one particular song, all fell silent as his light, clear tenor voice filled the room.

"Through space and time and middle years,
We stay away from Karlson's ears.

We ply the space lanes neat and slick.
We pick up cargo, sell it quick,
And never pay the taxman, no.
We'll never pay the damn taxman!
Karlson can go to hell and wait,
Our taxes will be a trifle late.
Accounts are always in arrears,
So stay away from Karlson's ears.
Free Trade, forever. Free Traders, free.
Free Trade forever, Free Traders, free."

Arsobades repeated the chorus twice, and the room
rang as all there joined in.

Hanno pounded on the bar. "Drinks on the house if
you'll sing it again, Arsobades."

"How about a drink first?" the minstrel countered.

Everybody began clapping and stomping. Arsobades
held up his hands in defeat, picked up his lute, and led
them through the chorus one more time.

In the crush, Kayla felt Iger press up against her and
a flood of warmth cascaded from her neck all the way
down to her knees. She wanted to pull away and draw
closer to him at the same time. When he put his arm
around her shoulder, she leaned back against him.
Soon she was cuddled, back to his front. She had never
been so exquisitely aware of her vertebrae before. As
each one came into almost direct contact with Iger's
chest, it took on immense sensory importance.

"Once more, Arsobades!"

"I'm sung out," Arsobades said. "Time for a drink
and another choba roll, Hanno. Then maybe we'll do
another chorus." He walked up to the bar and people
gave way, clearing a space right next to Kayla. He settled in before he noticed her with Iger.

"Hey, I hope you folks were singing."

"Humming is more like it," Iger said.

Kayla nodded. "I didn't exactly know the words."

"No problem." Hanno winked. "If you spend enough

time with this gent, you'll know all the words, and more."

The balladeer stuffed a steaming roll into his mouth and reached for another. "So, Hanno. What do you hear?" he asked, chewing noisily.

Hanno's wizened face grew guarded. "That damned mindsalt is getting everywhere, making zombies all over the galaxy. Damned addicts."

Arsobades grunted and wolfed down another roll. "Spread fast, didn't it? In less than a year, and cheaper than mindstones."

"Addicts?" Kayla said. "To mindsalt?" An unwelcome memory swam before her eyes, of the council chamber on Styx and a heated discussion over the burgeoning mindsalt trade.

"Sure," Hanno said. "People are pouring all of their cash, hard or soft, into shipments. Say they can't live without it. Rudgear over there lost his ship, his crew, everything, because of his habit. Hermione finally took him on as assistant bouncer so long as he doesn't use that filthy stuff around here."

Kayla thought of Beatrice Keller. No need to wonder who was selling the mindsalt. She was making huge profits while users destroyed themselves and died.

Arsobades gestured for Hanno to refill his glass. "How's your son, Denys?"

"Recovering. Those Trade Police treated him pretty roughly. Found a shipment of laser cannons aboard his rig and set their empaths to work on him."

Arsobades shuddered. "Damn."

Kayla listened in disbelief until she remembered that fleeting impression she had received from the police cruiser: an empath on board. Unmistakable.

"He's lost half of his memory," Hanno continued. "Thinks his wife is his mother, his kids are his brothers." The little man shook his head more in sorrow than anger. "It's a dirty shame what they did to my

boy. Somebody ought to do something about those police bastards and their damned mind spies."

A tall, well-dressed couple entered the bar, the man
sleek and handsome, the woman blonde and solidly-
built. Together they made their way over to Hanno.
"Two red jacks," said the man.

Hanno paid close attention to the bar surface as he
swabbed it with a dirty rag. "Sorry, bar's closed."

"Is that so?" the man said heatedly. "Then why
doesn't anybody else here seem to know it?"

"Bar's always closed to you, Fichu. You, too,
Raintree. What are you doing here, anyway? I thought
you graduated from beat work. Get busted?"

The man's face grew red. He started to say something,
but his companion touched his shoulder commandingly.
"Come on, Robard."

They stalked out.

"Damn spies," Hanno said. "Sniffing around, looking for something that'll get 'em a promotion. I remember them when they weren't so high or mighty."
He polished the spigots with fresh, angry energy, and a
black starburst tattoo on his upper arm peeked out
from under the cuff of his short-sleeved tunic. Kayla
watched out of the corner of her eye. So Hanno was
part of the Free Trade movement, too. And so, probably, was everybody else in the bar. She had thought
that Arsobades' ditty was just a rousing drinking song.
But maybe it was more, much more. A call to action,
but of what sort?

She looked around and saw a room full of hearty
weathered folk who were probably all smugglers and
outlaws. Salome and Rab were sitting, laughing with
some friends against the far wall. Greer and Kelso
shared beers with their counterparts from another
cruiser. It looked like a roomful of friends. Were they
all united in one cause, tied together by hatred of
Prime Minister Karlson and fear of his Trade Police?

Pondering, she took another sip from her cup and wondered if she should ask Hanno for a refill.

Iger pressed against her and his breath was warm on her neck. "Want to go someplace less noisy?"

It was warm where he touched her and she leaned into that warmth greedily. Suddenly she wanted to be alone with him, alone in a dark and private place with just enough room for the two of them.

"Yes," she said. "Yes."

Arsobades was still listening to Hanno mutter darkly about the Trade Police. No one in Peg's Big Toe seemed to take any notice of her or Iger as, hand-in-hand, they slipped out, into the night.

The air was gray with mist and the glow lamps that hung from each building were haloed with pinkish rings. Iger paused in the shadows of a doorway, pulled Kayla close, kissed her, then kissed her again. His lips were soft, very soft.

"You don't know how long I've wanted to do that," he whispered.

Kayla's heart pounded even as she lifted her mouth to his once more. Where were they going? What were they doing? It didn't matter, so long as it didn't stop.

They clung together in that doorway for what seemed like ages, kissing and rubbing against one another. But when Iger began to fumble at the neck of her tunic, she stopped him.

"Not here," she said, and paused, wondering. Where could they go? Back to the ship? She didn't want to take the time, to pretend that her breathing was normal and her eyes clear as they passed the port authorities. No. She wanted him, right now.

They drifted down a tiny alley and found shelter behind a pile of crates on a stack of baled grass. The scent of the dry grass was all around them, sweet, almost intoxicating. Kayla was immersed in a myriad of sensations. She wasn't thinking, wasn't aware of anything save the quick pounding of the blood in her

veins, the feel of his skin, and the touch of him against
her. She felt as though she were running up a very
steep hill, heart pumping, lungs gasping for breath.
When she reached the top, she took one deep breath
and jumped, plunging down and down through molten
sensation on a wild cataclysmic ride that she hoped
would never end.

* * *

In the dark, after love, tangled and sweaty, they
talked.

Kayla traced the line of Iger's jaw with her fingers,
marveling at the silky feel of his skin. "Why did you
leave?" she said. "Why did you leave Liage? At least
you had a home, people who cared about you, a place
where you belonged."

He shrugged, so careless, so unconcerned about his
past. "I didn't want that. I couldn't stand the thought of
nothing more than herding bambera, day in, day out,
until I bleached out like my father, burned empty by
the sun. I hate bambera, they're so stupid. All they do
is eat and crap. It's purple crap, you know."

"And what about the dalkoi?"

"I found it in a field near the grazing lands."

"All alone?"

"Yeah. It seemed, I don't know, lost. Sad. It followed me."

"What happened to its family?"

"Gone. I don't know. I've heard crazy stories: the
dalkois are being kidnapped and sold to rich people's
zoos, they're being killed and processed for bambera
feed. I don't know. Maybe they just fell into a dust
pit."

"Is somebody really stealing the dalkois?"

"Liage is a big place. We don't monitor the coming
and goings of people or animals. The only thing we
keep track of is bambera, because that's trade."

"So you found Third Child ..."

"Yeah, we sort of bonded."

"Is that usual?"

"No. Not at all. Dalkoi stay away from humans. At least, they always have before. But when I left Liage, Third Child came with me, simple as that."

Simple? Kayla thought. Nothing about the dalkoi was simple. But she let it slide. Iger had thrown away what she most wanted: family, place, connection. Some people didn't know how rich they really were.

She sat up abruptly and began to pull her clothing on. She didn't want to think about what she had lost, and what others had thrown away. She didn't want to be close to anyone or to feel anything. Iger was getting too close. She had to be careful. "Let's get back to the ship."

*   *   *

Iger left her at her bunk with one last lingering kiss. "See you tomorrow." It was a statement of possession, not a question, but Kayla was too tired to dispute it.

"Tomorrow." She tingled with pleasant exhaustion, and fell into bed, into a deep, dreamless sleep.

Sometime in the night she awoke to hear someone stirring. Half-awake, she called out, "Greer?"

"Yes."

She turned on her side as her roommate switched on a dim light, and sat up, staring. "What in hell?"

The figure that stood by her bed was a tall, shapely woman with a long mane of golden hair who looked nothing like her roommate.

"Relax." The voice was definitely Greer's, definitely amused.

"Why the getup? A masquerade party?"

Greer laughed her sharp, short laugh. "Hardly. Business." She yanked off her wig and dropped it on the bed. "Business which, come to think of it, you might find interesting. It's time you grew up a bit, learned what's what."

Kayla watched her sleepily and wished that her head

was clearer. "Yeah? Is this more of that Free Trade stuff?"

"Let's just say it's business."

"Is that the business you were on tonight? Why did you need a disguise? I thought that Free Traders were all over Vorhays Junction. Everybody in the bar—"

"Was a Free Trader? Sure. But that doesn't mean the entire station is sympathetic. And there are plenty of Karlson's Trade Alliance spies here, looking for me and people like me."

Kayla shook her head. She remembered Rab's warning: *stay clear of Greer's politics.* But she liked Greer, and she wanted to help her. "What's there to learn about Free Trade? No tariffs. Stay away from the Trade Police. Simple."

Greer smiled. "There's a bit more to it than that. But this isn't the time for it. Get some sleep. We'll talk tomorrow." She turned out the lights.

Kayla lay awake for some time, trying to imagine what secret rituals Greer would show her. When she fell asleep, she dreamed that she was falling from a great height into the blue-green depths of a pool whose bottom she couldn't see.

* * *

When Kayla awoke, she found Greer's bed empty and seemingly unslept in.

Strange, she thought, remembering her conversation with her roommate. Greer usually liked to sleep in when she could. Where was she?

Kayla bathed, dressed, and reached into her locker for a sash. Her few possessions were sitting neatly in a corner of the strongbox. But something was wrong. Something was missing.

Her mindstones. Her mindstone sack was gone.

No, it can't be.

Frantically she tore through the locker, to no avail. She searched every nook, every crawl space in the small room. The bag was nowhere to be found.

What should I do? she thought. *I can't accuse any-body without revealing who I am. But whoever stole it must realize that I'm connected to the miners on Styx, and probably an empath. Dammit, why isn't Greer here?*

A sudden sickening conviction filled her.

Greer had taken them. Who else had access? And wasn't she capable of doing anything, anything at all if she saw a good political reason for it?

No. It was too obvious. Greer feared Kayla's em-pathic powers too much to risk starting a quarrel with her. Besides, Kayla would have heard her roommate fumbling around with her strongbox. No, it wasn't Greer or anybody else who had been visiting port last night. It had to be someone who had remained with the ship.

Morgan.

Kayla turned icy cold. The ship's medic. Of course. She hardly ever spoke. Never mixed with anyone. And didn't go on shore leave, which gave her all night to dig around the ship, stealing from her crewmates.

Furious, Kayla stumbled out of her room and into the corridor, nearly colliding with Pooka, who hissed twice and ran.

And right back to you, Kayla thought. She steamed down the hallway toward Morgan's room, nearly col-liding with Iger.

"Katie," he said, smiling.

"Not now." She marched past him.

"Hey, Katie!"

"I said, not now." She shook him off and continued along the corridor and around a corner. She didn't have any clear plan of what she would do when she found Morgan. Maybe just bust in and start digging through her clothing, or punch her, or, better yet, borrow Rab's laser pistol and . . . No. Better to wait and see what Morgan had to say—if she said anything at all. Then she'd get the laser pistol.

Morgan's door was closed. Kayla pounded on it, but no one answered.

"Morgan! Open up!"

Still no answer.

Kayla tried the palm plate. Locked. "Morgan!"

Rab loomed up behind her. "What's going on? Morgan's not here, Katie."

"Where is she?"

"Do you feel all right?" Rab's voice contained a touch of annoyance. "You look mighty agitated to me, lady."

"It's nothing. Nothing, I just ... where is she?"

"Take it easy, Katie. She's at an ashram on Levity Point, the next town over from Vorhays Junction. Goes there whenever we make port here. Morgan's been there since landfall yesterday."

"She has?" Kayla paused, considering what he had said. "Then who was on watch last night when everybody else was in town?"

"Nobody. Salome set *Falstaff* on autowatch. She's done it plenty of times with no problem."

Kayla was stunned. "No one was here?"

"Well, if you count the dalkoi as someone, Third Child was."

Third Child. Kayla remembered the dalkoi poking the sack of mindstones with its toes. "Maybe I do," she said. "Maybe I absolutely, positively do. Thanks, Rab."

"Hey, are you sure that you feel okay?"

"Great. Fine. Bye." She took off at a run back the way she had come and found Iger standing in front of the mess. He gave her a hurt, angry look and turned away.

"Iger, wait." Kayla grabbed his hand. "Oh, don't sulk!"

He pulled free. "Sure, now you're talking to me," he said. "But maybe I don't feel like talking to you."

"I'm sorry! Iger, I was in a hurry. I didn't mean anything by it. Really. Forgive me."

"You were rude, Katie."

"I know. I'm sorry."

"Really?"

She pressed close against him. "Absolutely."

"Well, that's better." He began to embrace her.

"Oh, Iger, not right now."

Iger frowned but released her.

Taking a step back, she said, "What I mean is, first I want to see Third Child. Where is he?"

"Where is *it*."

"Whatever."

"Third Child is watching a vid cube in the rec bay. Do you really need to see it that badly right now?" Iger's voice was filled with reproach and disbelief.

She smiled her brightest smile. "Yes. It'll only take a minute. Why don't you wait for me in the mess?"

That seemed to pacify him. "Okay. But hurry up. We've got a lot to do today."

Men, she thought. *You sleep with them once and they think that they own you.* She waved and hurried toward the rec bay.

Third Child was sitting on a floatchair and staring at a cube on which herds of bambera pounded across a dusty plain. Occasionally the dalkoi squeaked as though it recognized one of the animals.

"Third Child?"

The dalkoi saw her, uttered a series of fluid chirps, and began to rub its pointed head against her shoulder.

"Nice Third Child. Good dalkoi. Show me where you put the mindstones. Come on. Show Katie."

Third Child didn't seem interested in showing her anything. Third Child wanted its neck rubbed right away.

Kayla rubbed its neck and as she did so, she tried to project a nearsense image of the mindstone sack at the dalkoi.

"The mindstones," she said. "You took them, didn't you? Where are they? What did you do with them?"

Third Child sat up and blinked. Kayla got a strong negative thought-impression, as though the dalkoi had understood and was telling her no, it hadn't taken the stones, but she couldn't be sure. It was so difficult to read this dalkoi.

"Come on, Third Child. Don't lie to me!"

Again, a wave of negative thought-impression, stronger than before.

"Okay," she said, slowly. "Okay. Somehow, I believe you. But if you don't have them, who does?"

Third Child chirped softly.

Kayla stared in anger at the purple animal. "Oh, why am I asking you? You can't tell me even if you do know."

The dalkoi chirped once again and turned back to its vid cube.

She was flat out of suspects, and she couldn't exactly ask her crewmates if they had seen her mindstones. That would raise too many questions.

Maybe Iger took them, she thought. *But he was with me the entire time, and I can't believe it was him. Rab, then? No. Arsobades? No. No. No. I can't believe it. I can't believe it was any of them. But I'll have to try and scan them all and hope that nobody besides Salome is probe-sensitive.*

But that was the least of her worries. Whoever had taken the mindstones knew at least part of her secret, and had a key to her past. What would they do about it? With her stomach churning and her thoughts in disarray, Kayla reluctantly went to meet Iger as she had promised.

Greer intercepted her just outside the mess. "Katie, I need to talk to you." The mindstone hanging from her ear glittered ruby-blue in the light.

Kayla's suspicions flared yet again. Greer could have stolen the sack. Look at that earring. And who had more access? "Greer, have you been in my locker lately?" She focused a tight nearsense probe on her roommate.

"Your locker?" Greer looked at her in surprise. "Why would I go in there?" Her mind was open to Kayla, and it was obvious that, whoever had taken the mindstones, it wasn't Greer.

"Look," she said desperately. "Somebody stole something from me. Something important."

"What was it?"

"You have to promise you won't tell anybody."

"All right. What did you lose?"

"Mindstones. A sack of them."

The expression on Greer's face was frankly disbelieving. "Mindstones? Where would you get mindstones?"

"Where do you think? My father. He left them to me." Kayla's voice began to crack. "They're all I have left from him."

Greer's mouth was a hard line. "Your father's last gift, huh? And some bastard took them? You think it was somebody on the *Falstaff?*"

"Had to be. Who else could have done it?"

"How would they know what you had?"

"No idea."

"Did you ask Iger?"

"I'm sure he didn't do it."

"Oh, come on, Katie. At least use your power to check him out, x-ray him, whatever. Maybe he took 'em. How well do you really know him?"

How well do I really know anyone? Aloud, she said, "I can't believe Iger would take them. He didn't even know about them. And are you actually suggesting I probe him? You hate that kind of thing."

"Maybe I've had a change of heart about your skills, Katie." Greer tugged her by the arm. "Come on. We need to talk."

"Where are we going?"

"Come on," Greer said impatiently. "You've got to change. We're going into port."

"But—"

"I'll help you find your mindstones. I swear it. But you've got to help me, too. So let's go."

"Okay." Kayla said. *This will really tear things with Iger,* she thought.

Once in their room, Greer closed the door and handed her a neat green stretchsuit with the Vorhays Station exec insignia attached at throat and shoulder. "Put it on."

"Why?"

"Just do it and stop wasting time."

Kayla shrugged into it. The uniform fit her fairly well, a little baggy in the rump and knees.

"Here." Greer gave her a short curly auburn wig and a head wrap.

Kayla eyed it skeptically. "Are you sure this is really necessary?"

"Humor me." Greer dropped the wig over her head and gave her an approving pat. "Katie, y'know, that color suits you."

"I'm thrilled."

"Now I want you to carry this sack all the time. Don't put it down even if you have to go to the bathroom."

"What's in it?"

"Bread."

"Oh, come on, how stupid do you think I am?"

"I'm being honest with you."

"Sure you are." Kayla knew she could always mindprobe Greer again. But she didn't really care. If her roommate was so determined to withhold the truth, maybe ignorance was best. She shrugged. "Fine. Bread it is. Whatever you say."

"Good," Greer said. "Now you're going to hop the monoline to Vorhays City."

It was Kayla's turn to stare in surprise. "Vorhays

City? But that's practically on the other side of the station!"

"Right. A place where I can't set foot without fear of arrest. Or worse."

"Great. Must be a hotbed of bread-snatchers."

Greer ignored her. "I want you to signal me when you're back. I'll be waiting on the ship."

"And if I get into trouble?"

"You won't. Don't look at me that way. Free Traders trust one another."

"Greer!"

"All right, if it sets your mind at ease, if anything happens, leave word for me at Peg's Big Toe."

The thought of Hanno and his wife calmed her. "And this is going to help me get back my mindstones?"

"Let's just say it's the first step to meeting the people who might be able to help you, and to keeping your possessions safe from now on."

That was good enough. Kayla was suddenly anxious to be off on her mission, to do whatever it took to help her get back her mindstones and punish whoever took them.

The monorail depot was near the null-g rink, and filled with trading folk in silks and homespun, furs and loincloths. They chattered noisily, ate choba chips and nogales, sipped huge swirling, multicolored drinks, and behaved in general as if they were on some grand holiday. Laughing and shouting, they bought tickets at the station kiosk and queued up to wait for their transport.

The kiosk header listed the fares to different locations around the huge ringed space station. Kayla pushed her way to the head of a ticket line and counted out credits for a round-trip passage to Vorhays City.

Her half-empty train was a gleaming silver tube with pink padded airseats. It made a high, bleating sound as it slid through the station tunnels. Mandalay. Hitgars. Nuova Mensa. Vorhays City.

Kayla got off the train, paused, looked right, left, and all around her. Her right hand was on her vibroblade, concealed in her tunic. Just in case.

The train station was clean, much cleaner than the one at Vorhays Junction had been. And nearly deserted, which made her feel even more conspicuous. She exited the shining hallways quickly and found herself at the mouth of a neat, broad boulevard lined by green mats. When she got closer, she realized that the mats were actual plants. They didn't even seem to be hydroponics. Were they growing right there in the ground? How strange.

Don't stare, she told herself, and stepped onto a slidewalk. It took her down the street at a good clip, past tidy shopfronts and colorful cafes. Everybody around her was well dressed, well groomed, and serene. Gray-haired men and women walked arm-in-arm. Mothers pushed toddlers in null-g strollers. At the edge of one greensward a vendor was selling glow sticks which tinkled and changed color whenever he swept them through the air. Where were all the criminals and desperadoes?

The address Greer had given her was on a side street off the main boulevard. It was a cul-de-sac filled with tubs of blue and green flowers and paved with iridescent purple stones. The door she stopped at was white and looked freshly painted. She pressed the doorpad.

A pleasant-looking woman with neat black hair swept back into twin loops opened the door. "Yes?"

Kayla spoke the lines she had rehearsed with Greer. "I'm Katie. Mother sent me with some fresh bread for the family."

The brunette broke into a wide smile. "Lovely! Come in, won't you?"

Kayla hesitated. Should she? The woman looked harmless. Greer hadn't said anything about going in.

She would have to improvise. And besides, to refuse would be rude. Kayla stepped into the house and saw that it was a small brightly-lit space filled with flowers and tinkling music.

"Please wait here," the woman said. She vanished through a curtained doorway.

Who would ever suspect anyone in this pretty place of nefarious undercover dealings? Kayla wondered what allure the Free Trade movement could have for such prosperous folk. She could hardly imagine.

The house was overflowing with all the niceties of civilized living—vid cubes and padded visors, thick rugs and cushions. The walls were covered in tapestry cloth whose patterns flickered and changed in the light of the glow globes.

A gray-haired, blue-eyed woman walked in and glanced at Kayla. "So. Bread from Mother? Let's have a taste, shall we?"

Kayla handed the sack to her and was more than a little surprised when its contents were revealed to be a loaf of bread. What was Greer doing?

The woman broke off a piece and took a bite. She chewed thoughtfully for a moment, then offered a hunk of it to Kayla.

The others waited while she bit into it. The crust was light brown and chewy, the inner bread mottled white and tan, meltingly sweet. It really was bread, the kind that traders might eat at breakfast.

Kayla chewed with care, not knowing what to expect next. She swallowed heavily. The two women across from her smiled.

"How is Mother?" the older one said.

"Fine. She sends her very best love."

"Well, that's splendid." The gray-haired woman stared at her for a moment, seeming to measure her from top to bottom. Then she nodded. "And please convey ours to her. Make sure you thank Mother for the bread." She stood, obviously dismissing Kayla.

Was that it? Wasn't there going to be some sort of return transaction? Secret documents? A severed head? Apparently not. And how would these people help her recover her missing gems? Greer would have to explain. Kayla smiled. "I'll be going, then."

"Safe trip." Was that a flicker of something odd behind the older woman's eyes? Something ferocious peering out of the benign blue and just as quickly gone, hidden once again? Kayla couldn't be sure. Suddenly she wanted very badly to be out of that lovely house and far from these oh-so-nice people, someplace where things made sense.

She forced herself to get up slowly, wished them farewell, and proceeded calmly to the door. Not until she was up the street and well along the main boulevard, moving at a good clip along the slidewalk, did she draw a full breath.

What was that all about? Who were they?

She had perhaps a minute's wait for the monoline back to Vorhays Junction. Gladly she boarded, putting the train's solid doors between her and the spotless deserted station, the awful clean and cheery boulevard.

At Vorhays Junction she took a deep thankful breath of musty air. People bustled past her. Papers and food wrappers spilled out of containers and across the floor. What of it? At least this felt like a living, breathing place. Not some carefully mummified paradise.

She buzzed the *Falstaff* from a station kiosk. "Mother? Bread delivered. They said thank you."

"Good girl," Greer said. "Come home soon." She broke the connection.

Yes, ma'am, Kayla thought. *Good little courier, that's me. Just do as you're told. Don't ask any questions. Eat your bread. Just so long as I get back my mindstones.*

She passed a mirrored panel and stopped short, staring in horror at the red-haired reflection, that familiar-yet-strange face. That was Kayla John Reed, tripath, daughter of Redmond and Teresa, wanted by the Trade Police for questioning. The wig! She had forgotten all about it. Without realizing it, Greer had disguised her as she really looked.

It's a good thing we're light-years from the Cavinas System and any bounty hunters, Kayla thought. *But I've got to ditch that wig right away.*

She scanned the hallway. A bathroom, there. She plunged through the door, stopped to make certain that the room was deserted. She pulled off the wig and stuffed it into her sack. There! Much better. That was Katie, the navigator of the *Falstaff*. The woman without a past, without a shadow.

Out on the street she swung along, light on her feet, relieved to be done with her secret mission. Even the thought of her missing mindstones couldn't bring down her spirits. Perhaps she would try out the null-g rink, she thought. A dozen people were already on the rink, floating and tumbling over one another, laughing giddily. It looked like fun.

"Want to give it a whirl?" asked a familiar voice.

Arsobades was leaning against the side of the rink watching the action. He grinned at her. "Come on, Katie. Let's see how well two seasoned spacers do out there."

They bought their tickets and strapped on the rental null-g units. The octagonal devices made an odd buzzing sound. For a moment nothing happened. Then gravity evaporated.

Kayla fought to keep her stomach under control, clinging to a guardrail. This didn't feel anything like being in space.

Little by little her equilibrium returned and the nausea abated until she was floating easily. Arsobades beckoned for her to follow. She caught a towline and breezed along behind him, legs dangling.

They floated up, they floated down, they floated all around, grinning and giggling. The hefty minstrel even managed a somersault that almost bowled down a man with three children.

"Hey," the father called. "Watch it!"

Kayla grabbed Arsobades by the shoulder and they retreated, laughing mischievously.

"C'mon," he said. "I'll buy you a drink. Iger won't get angry, will he?"

"Iger doesn't own me," Kayla said. She felt a pang as she remembered her promise to meet him. Well, it was too late now. He would just have to understand.

They turned in their rental packs and Arsobades gave her a mock ferocious look. "Pardon me. I stand corrected. So what's your pleasure?"

"A degli shake."

The minstrel shuddered. "Oooh, too sweet. And I just happen to know a place that makes 'em in double containers. If that doesn't make you sick, nothing will. Come on, I dare you to drink one."

* * *

The Oort Cloud was cool and lit by nests of blue globes that gave Kayla the sense of being underwater. She settled back against her padded chair and contentedly sipped the frothy alcoholic concoction in front of her.

Arsobades sat next to her, plugging away at a beer. "I don't see how you can drink that," he said. "Gives me the chills just to watch."

"Then don't."

"Brrr." He took a hearty sip. "Tough lady. So how do you like the Free Trader life?"

"I like it fine." Kayla gulped down the last of her drink. "The pay is okay and the company's not bad."

"Glad to hear it. And how are you and Greer getting along?"

Kayla felt a cold prickle of suspicion. Her voice was deliberately casual. "Greer? Fine, I guess. Why?"

"Just curious. She's got some wild ideas."

"I think she saw a lot of ugly stuff close-up," Kayla

said. "She was on St. Ilban, you know. She was even at the Trade Congress."

"Yeah. It was the worst thing that could ever have happened to her. Sent her right around the bend."

"So you think Greer is crazy, too?"

"Let's just say I wouldn't vouch for her sense of perspective. And I hope you won't let her drag you into any of her weird political intrigues."

Kayla's throat felt oddly congested. "What do you mean?"

"Simple. Greer has a way of trying to get everybody involved in her personal concerns. Which is okay to a point. But I'd hate to see anybody else take the rap for her if it comes to mixing it up with the police."

"You're saying that she would desert her friends?"

"I'm just saying that she would do whatever she thought was necessary to further her Free Trade goals. Even if it meant hurting her friends."

He paused, staring meaningfully at her, then went back to his drink.

Kayla knew that Arsobades really cared about what happened to her, but she wished that he would stop treating her like a child. She also wished that she could ask him about who he thought had taken her mindstones, but she knew better. *Perhaps a small mindprobe,* she thought. *Just to see if he can give me any clues. He knows everybody on the ship much better than I do.*

She waited until he began to hector the bartender about the amount of the bill. Then she slipped a tiny probe in and looked around.

To her surprise the minstrel's mind was surprisingly well defended, almost as though he had received post-hypnotic shields. There were few facts for her to glean. She touched gently upon the subject of mindstones and felt the delicate mechanisms of an internal alarm system begin to quiver.

Had Arsobades taken the mindstones? Was he on guard against probes because of his guilt?

Too late, Kayla remembered that his wife had died of drug addiction. Any drug, anything that affected people with potentially addictive results, was a sore point with him. And that included mindstones.

Arsobades wasn't protecting himself because he was guilty: he was protecting himself from memory's pain. And her muddling around might produce a terrible reaction, even a seizure. This was too dangerous, too sensitive a topic even to probe for.

She got out of his mind in a hurry, her insides curdling from guilt and degli shake. The outer world whirled back into being and she felt the padded cushion of the chair against her spine. The scent of stale beer perfumed the air. Next to her Arsobades was scowling and looking around the room.

"Is it hot in here?" he said.

Kayla nodded quickly. "Yeah, awful."

"Time to go." He emptied his glass and put it down on the bar.

Smiling, Kayla stood up and prepared to leave, swearing never again to intrude on her friends' secrets.

Chapter Thirteen

Greer shook Kayla awake. "Let's get moving."

"What time is it?" She sat up, squinted at the clock. "Gods." Early. Very early. "What's up?"

"You want to get your stones back? Hit the floor."

They set off into the morning bustle on the main boulevard of Vorhays Junction. Kayla was soon lost in the maze of shortcuts and alleys that Greer led her down. "Where are we going?"

Greer glanced back at her. "Yesterday was step one. You passed your first inspection. Today, step two."

They came to a broad building that looked like a warehouse.

Greer knocked once, paused, knocked twice.

"Who's there?"

"Mother."

The door slid open just enough to admit them and slammed as soon as they had stepped through. They were in a long room filled with echoes and shadows, its floor partially padded by stained mats. It was empty save for a lone figure by the far wall. As Kayla drew near, she saw the gray-haired woman to whom she had delivered bread the day before.

"Here," Greer said. She handed Kayla a springy cloth bundle. "Put this on."

Unrolled, the bundle was a plain black stretchsuit.

"What's this for?"

"So you can learn to take back anything that is ever taken from you."

Intriguing words. Kayla felt her excitement build. "When do we start?"

The gray-haired woman flashed a quick approving look in her direction. "I see you brought our young friend, Greer. Welcome to training. This morning you'll learn how to defend yourself, maybe even how to save your life, and the lives of other Free Traders like you."

There was a toughness and self-assurance about the woman that was fascinating. Gone was the genteel demeanor, the housewife's facade. Kayla said, "You mean hand-to-hand combat?"

"Exactly. It's something every one of us should know."

"Great." Eagerly she followed Greer's pointing finger to a small room that smelled of sweat and disinfectant and dust. Three women were already in there, changing, all of them young—one looked barely past thirteen. Were the Free Traders so hungry for members that they were recruiting children? When the girl straightened up, she glanced at Kayla and the expression in her pale gray eyes was angry and ancient. Kayla didn't need to use a mindprobe to know that while the girl might appear youthful those eyes had seen a hundred years of sadness and trouble.

They nodded warily, sizing each other up.

"I'm Katie."

"N'gera."

"Let's get going," a loud female voice said.

They trailed out to join the others: Kayla estimated the group at nearly twenty people, swelled by several older folks and teenage boys ranging between thirteen and eighteen.

The gray-haired woman who had greeted them was standing in the center of the room. Obviously, she was the head trainer. "My name is Purshil," she said, and her eyes flashed. "In the next couple of hours I'm going to teach you how to stay alive. After that, it's up to you."

First she had them move through a series of stretching exercises. Then she showed them different postures for self-defense. Eventually Purshil divided them into groups for wrestling practice. Kayla found herself paired with thin, wiry N'gera against two women who appeared to be sisters: both were fleshy brunettes, one taller than the other.

"Ever done this before?" Kayla asked her teammate.

"Sure," the girl said. "This is too easy. Just grab their throats or go for their eyes. If all else fails, punch 'em—hard—in the boobs." N'gera offered the advice as casually as she might give directions to someone who was lost.

Kayla gave her a quick, astonished look. What hell had grown this child?

They repelled the first onslaught with ease: Kayla merely applied the simple moves she had been shown and knocked her opponent—the larger sister—to the ground. N'gera tussled a bit longer before forcing the smaller sister down. When she straightened up, she was grinning with feral pleasure.

"Good," Purshil said. "Now we'll speed things up a bit."

She sent groups of trainees racing across the floor at one another, barely pausing to allow them to regain their feet before she ordered them back on the attack. Kayla got bruised in a dozen places and twice fell on her face, but she kept at it gamely, noting which moves helped her elude pursuers and which were best to use when she had to stand and fight.

Despite N'gera's helpful advice, she found that a punch to the throat was most effective for dropping her antagonist. Grappling just led to more bruises.

"Come on," Purshil shouted. "I want to see some spirit here. Do it as if you meant it!"

An elbow slammed into Kayla's head and sent her

reeling, red sparks flashing before her eyes. She fell back, caught her breath, and launched herself back into the melee. An exposed face. She kneed it, and felt wild jubilation as the face vanished.

Over there, a leg. She kicked at it, misjudged the distance, overbalanced, and fell. The mats were cold and not much softer than the stone floor.

GET UP. GET UP!

She got to her knees, ducked as a body flew past, and bounced back up onto her feet. She pivoted, ready for the attack, but things had quieted down and everybody was huddled on the mats, nursing their bruises.

Kayla sighed with relief. *Okay,* she thought, *at least that fight is done.*

But it wasn't over.

Kayla saw Purshil's eyes fix on something behind her. The trainer was frowning. Kayla turned to see N'gera holding an opponent in a grip that seemed to be strangling her.

"Enough, N'gera," Kayla said. "Leave off."

The girl had that fixed feral grin on her face. She was beyond hearing.

Kayla probed her and recoiled at what she found. Blood rage. N'gera wanted to kill, badly.

—No!

A nearsense probe arrowed into N'gera's motor control center. The girl gave a surprised cry and crumpled, releasing her opponent.

There was a sudden hush in the building. Kayla glanced up. Greer was staring at her with an odd expression on her face. Did she suspect the truth? Kayla hoped that her crewmate wouldn't ask her any direct questions.

The woman whose life Kayla had just saved came bounding toward her.

Kayla smiled and held out her hand.

The woman ignored the proffered grip and grabbed her around the throat.

"Dammit, let go!" Kayla wheezed. "It's over."

Her opponent just laughed.

"Are you all crazy?" Why wasn't Purshil stopping this?

Kayla remembered what the trainer had said. "Visualize your worst enemy and defeat him." Who was her worst? Beatrice Keller? The faceless person who had stolen her mindstones? Suddenly she saw Yates Keller leering, crouching on a shelf of rock and hurling jagged boulders at her. Bastard. She wanted to smash his handsome arrogant face.

Twisting, she broke the woman's grip, turned, and hammered her fists into her stomach, her neck, her head, beating her to the ground. Then, breath coming in gasps, she stared defiantly at Purshil. "Anyone else you'd like me to fight?"

The blue eyes took her full measure. Purshil smiled a wintry smile. "That's enough," she said. "Well done, Katie. You're dismissed. We'll resume tomorrow."

As the red haze in her vision cleared, Kayla felt relieved, even pleased. She had enjoyed winning that fight.

And why not?

She rubbed a wet spot on her lip and her fingers came away bloody. For a moment, an odd mixture of exaltation and revulsion warred within her but she shoved it away. Shrugging, she wiped her hand on her stretchsuit and went to change back to her street clothes.

* * *

"So," Greer said to Kayla. "How does it feel to be a warrior?"

They were sitting with the rest of the crew along the curving wall of Peg's Big Toe.

"Terrific." Kayla raised her glass gleefully and took a self-congratulatory sip of red jack.

Arsobades made a disgusted sound and glared at

both of them. "That's just great," he said. "Congratulations, Greer. Another convert or, should I say, victim?"

Greer eyed her crewmate coldly. "What the hell is bothering you? Katie enjoyed it, didn't you, Kate?"

Kayla shrugged. "It was exciting."

"Enough of this Free Trade crap," Salome said. "I want to talk business."

Her shipmates drew closer.

"I've gotten a line on a load of orbital N-ware. Old stuff. We can pick it up for practically nothing. And deliver it to Osaay IX for a very nice fee."

"To the rebels?" Kelso asked.

Salome nodded.

"Hey, boss lady," Rab said sharply. "I thought we had an agreement against running old-style nuclear armaments. Isn't it just a bit risky? And don't forget the Admanan Prohibitions: get caught and it could be our lives."

Salome gave him an impatient look. "Nobody's been prosecuted over that in years. And we won't get caught. I tell you, this deal is too good to pass up."

"Another thing," Rab said. "Just a technicality, of course. But we don't support that rebellion. Those guys are bloodthirsty maniacs."

Greer leaned forward, her face tight as a closed fist. "We should," she said. "They're against Prime Minister Karlson and his crowd."

"Oh, sure. Any enemy of Karlson's is a friend of yours."

Greer's glance was icy. "We should help them out and bring them into the Free Trade movement."

"Yeah," Kelso said. "Besides, it's good for business."

"Bambera crap," Rab said. "No business is that good. I don't like running guns into an active engagement. And I'm not a recruiter for the Free Traders like you, Greer. I'm no agitator."

Arsobades nodded. "Agreed. Things *might* get messy, and I'm kind of attached to my life."

"Nothing will get messy," Salome said. "I tell you, we can do it and get out."

"Hsst! Heads up," Rab said. "It's Morant and his crew."

Shaum Morant, rival trader, was an old enemy of the *Falstaff* and its crew. Kayla had heard Salome speak of him, always with contempt. Curious, she looked up to see a tall thin man with a hawklike face, dressed in black. The rest of his crew were gathered around him like a vulture's chicks, and in their midst was a familiar face. N'gera, the feral girl from Free Trader training camp.

N'gera caught Kayla's eye and grinned nastily. Kayla held her gaze for a moment, then looked away.

The mechband started up, and couples moved out onto the dance floor. Iger was in front of Kayla, his hand on her arm.

"Want to dance?"

They moved together easily in time to the beat. Kayla enjoyed the feel of his arms around her and rested her head against his shoulder. She closed her eyes and let herself relax, enjoying the music and Iger's closeness. She was thinking about going back to the ship with Iger when she felt somebody poking her in the back.

It was N'gera, cutting in.

Iger seemed momentarily surprised, then irritated. Kayla got a hint of something coming from N'gera that she didn't like, a malicious spark in her pale eyes. The girl didn't really want to dance with Iger, she only wanted to antagonize Kayla.

"Ratch off, N'gera."

The girl ignored her and spoke directly to Iger. "What's the matter? Afraid that your girlfriend will yell at you?"

Iger frowned. "Lose yourself."

N'gera smiled pleasantly and kicked him in the knee, hard.

Gasping in pain, Iger went down.

Kayla whirled to confront the girl. "You little bitch! What did you do that for?"

N'gera was still smiling, but her eyes had an unfocused craziness to them that was frightening to see. "What are you going to do about it?" she said, laughing.

The music was still playing, but all other action had stopped. A crowd was gathering around them, and Hanno was peering over the bar, a look of disgust on his face.

Kayla stared at N'gera and knew she would have to fight her. There was no other way. More disturbing still, a part of her *wanted* to fight, longed to take the crazy girl apart.

Somebody pressed something sharp into her palm. Out of the corner of her eye she saw a flash of gold and brown: Salome stepping back into the crowd. Kayla felt the icy length of a supple blade in her hand and flashed her captain a quick look of gratitude.

"Hey, wait—" Iger said.

She silenced him with a glance. It was between her and N'gera, now.

Without hesitation the feral girl launched herself at Kayla and landed a punishing blow to the side of her face.

Kayla's head rocked back. She grunted as N'gera struck at her again, a savage lashing at her neck. She fell to her knees. N'gera's hands closed around her throat, cutting off her air supply.

Salome's blade. Use it.

She slashed up in a wide arc, catching N'gera's cheek. Blood sprayed out, staining her arm with red droplets. N'gera screamed and clutched her face. Kayla knew she could knife her again—even kill her . . . No. No. She fought the blood lust and its seductive reasoning. This girl had done nothing more than challenge her. That surely wasn't a killing offense. But this duel might end in death if she didn't find a way to stop it, right now.

Kayla took a deep breath and reached deep within, summoning her internal forces. She sent a mindbolt sizzling toward N'gera, taking care that at the instant it connected N'gera hit the ground, seemingly knocking herself out.

N'gera fell hard and stayed down.

There was a brief murmur from the watchers, almost a sign of disappointment that the spectacle had ended so quickly. The crowd began to disperse. Kayla caught Arsobades' eye and received a strange, disappointed look from the minstrel before he turned back to his drink. Iger loomed suddenly, reaching for her hand but she shook him off.

Salome stood near the door, grim approval on her face. "Nice going."

Kayla grinned, wiped the knife on her leg, and handed it to her. "Thanks."

Rab looked disgusted. "Women. Always fighting."

Greer came striding over. "Good move," she said and clapped her on the back. "Maybe you can demonstrate that tomorrow at training.

That irked her. Kayla was getting a little tired of Greer telling her what to do. Icily, she said, "I don't think I need any more training lessons right now," and before anyone else could add a word, she had stepped past friends and strangers alike, out into the welcome darkness.

Footsteps pursued her. "Hey, Kayla!"

Iger.

She turned. "What do you want?"

"What do you mean, what do I want? You could have been killed in there! What do you think you were doing?"

"What did it look like?" She kept walking. Suddenly

she hated everybody and everything that she had been
feeling. Enjoying a fight? God's Eyes!

"Hey, know something, Katie? You're a real bitch."

That stopped her.

Slowly she turned to meet his blue gaze. "Yeah," she
said slowly. "I guess so. I suppose that's the way it
must look." She made a gesture, palm open, half-
apology.

"Well, just so long as you know it." His quick smile,
so appealing. "Gods, you are the hardest woman to get
to know." He moved toward her. "Why won't you open
up, Katie? I want to get closer, but you won't let me.
Always pushing me away."

His words pricked her soul. *Oh, Iger,* she thought. *I
want to let you in, really I do. But I can't, I just can't.*
Aloud, she said, "Sorry, it's not my style."

"Oh, but fighting is?"

"No!" She wanted to tell him that she didn't really
know who she was any longer, or what she was becoming. A trained fighter? A killer? Spacer, outlaw, thief?
Free Trader? Empathic freak? "Look," she said, her
voice shaking. "I'm a fugitive. There's a price on my
head, all right? That's why I left Styx."

Iger said nothing, merely stared. Somehow that only
infuriated her. "I didn't have a mama and papa who
wanted me to stay with them, understand? I didn't have
anybody! They were dead. And a bunch of people
wanted to take the little bit that was left to me. I made
a mistake, panicked, and for that they wanted to lock
me up for the rest of my life.

"So the galaxy isn't some big funhouse to me. It's
not a place to go on a joyride because home was too
tame and the bambera were too stupid. I'm here because I've got nowhere else to be, and I don't know
what else to do. And the people I'm with would kill me
if they knew who I really was." Tears flooded her eyes.
She turned her back on him, determined that he not see
her cry.

"Kill you?" Iger's tone was so gentle it brought stinging tears to her eyes. "Katie, what are you talking about?"

"You idiot! I'm an empath. And everybody on the *Falstaff* hates empaths."

His stunned look told her all she needed to know.

"And you do, too, don't you?" She gathered up the shreds of her dignity and pulled away from him. "Excuse me."

"Wait a minute. I said, wait, dammit! You're always in such a goddamned hurry. Katie, hold on." He grabbed her arm and pulled her back roughly. She flailed, tried to punch him, tried to kick him, and ended up with her nose on the ground and Iger sitting on her back. "Now will you listen?" He sounded completely disgusted.

She turned her head and spit out a mouthful of dirt. "Listen to what?"

"I don't know whether to believe you or not. But I won't let you up unless you promise not to run away."

She didn't want to risk attachment, to let anybody get too close. But his weight was crushing the wind out of her. "All right."

"Promise?"

"I promise, cross my heart. Just get the hell off!"

"Sorry." He rolled to the side. "Now, talk to me."

She sat up and, after a few deep breaths, began her tale. When she was done, he had his arms around her. Sighing, she wiped tears off her face and onto his sleeve.

"Quite a story." He hugged her even tighter.

"Wait," she said, sniffing shamelessly. "There's more."

"More?"

"I've got some sort of jump sickness."

"What's that?"

"Whenever we go into jump, I get all wonky. Can't move. If Salome finds out, she'll probably kick me off the ship. And I don't blame her, really. But the *Falstaff*'s all I've got." Her voice cracked and she felt Iger's hand on her hair, stroking gently.

"We won't let that happen," he said, kissing her cheek. "There's got to be some way to beat it. We'll find it."

We.

It was a good word, one, of late, she had heard too rarely. It got in through a chink in her defenses and glowed in a small, friendly way. *We.* She sat up a bit straighter and filled her lungs with air. "Okay," she said, and smiled weakly. "Okay, we will."

Chapter Fourteen

In the middle of the night, the *Falstaff* took on the contraband load of N-ware, just as Salome had decreed. And the next morning, Kayla plotted a course to Osaay IX.

She was deep in the cyberspace of the navigation board when, unexpectedly, the jump engines came on.

At first they registered on her consciousness as a group of strange orange flapping things—hinged vees—flying in formation down the wide canyon in front of her. But the formation parted, rolled, and began swirling around her in hypnotic patterns, fluttering iridescent feathers.

Kayla's stomach went sideways and tried to turn over. Her lungs hurt, her head pounded, and she couldn't breath. It felt as though a vise had been slapped around her chest and tightened.

The engines were stuck, caught in a jump-loop, and the *Falstaff was* warping from point to point across the galaxy.

Somewhere the knowbot was shrilling: *Warning! Abort jump! Warning! Stop!*

If only I could, she thought. If only Iger were on the board instead of down in auxiliary ops.

She desperately wanted to shut down the engines, but she couldn't move. It was as thought she were encased in a block of ice. She had no control of the ship. Worse yet, wherever they were, they weren't alone.

A huge dark hulk grew larger and larger on their radar screen. It looked like a small asteroid, but the computer identified it as a dead, abandoned worldship looming in front of them. And the *Falstaff* was caught in jump stasis, heading right for the derelict, its cargo hold filled with obsolete but still-deadly nuclear weapons.

"Impact in thirty-eight seconds," the knowbot announced flatly. "Immediate evasive action recommended."

They would hit the ghost ship, explode, and everyone on board would die. The N-ware would detonate and set off a nuclear reaction on a nearby sun or destroy a planet or two, killing how many millions?

There was nothing Kayla could do. The band across her chest was suffocating her. She couldn't move, couldn't breath, much less warn anybody.

"Impact in thirty-five seconds."

Nearsense, she thought desperately. —*Iger, can you hear me?*

"Thirty seconds."

The jump engines were overloading *Falstaff*'s systems. Lights flashed, buzzers became alarms.

Kayla reached out in search of Iger's mind signature, but her nearsense wasn't working. He was inches behind her, jacked into the same board, but he might as well be on another ship.

"Twenty-five seconds."

As Kayla reeled, overwhelmed by dizziness and nausea, she felt something creep up and envelop her, a comforting presence, oddly familiar, wordless yet somehow reassuring. A calming radiance surrounded her as she gently shifted into a neutral glowing space, insulated and protected. The pressure on her rib cage eased and was gone. She could breath once again. The paralysis lifted, she could move. The navboard was once more within reach.

She grabbed for it, punched in coordinates, and prayed.

The walls rattled as the engines whined and sputtered. The ship responded sluggishly, stalling, bucking.

Come on!

Kayla diverted additional power from life support, climate, and gravity control.

The engines roared as the *Falstaff* suddenly came to life and surged forward, skimming close to the worldship, then eeling past it. In a moment the derelict was a black dot on the navscreen, receding to invisibility behind them.

Close. Too bloody close. Kayla blew the accumulated air out of her lungs in relief and shut down the engines, taking the ship out of jumpspace. The galaxy winked into being all around them, the steady cold light of stars like beacons in the dark.

Engines whined to a halt as the *Falstaff* hung dead in the vacuum, all energy levels at bare minimum.

Salome's voice cut into Kayla's headset. "Katie, what the hell was that?"

"Power surge," said the knowbot. "Defective jump triggered by malfunction of navboard."

"Why didn't you get us out of their faster?"

"I couldn't move," Kayla said. "It was like I was frozen in place." The memory of it chilled her. The only thing that had saved her was that odd radiance—the energy field that had gotten between her and jumpspace.

"What?"

"I've never experienced anything like it." Would Salome probe more deeply? Kick her off the board? Kayla held her breath, waiting. But the *Falstaff*'s captain was distracted by other concerns.

"Where are we?" Salome demanded.

"I don't know." Kayla punched in the cartographic system.

"Memnon System," said the knowbot.

"Great," Salome said. "The ass-end of nowhere." She slammed back down into her seat and her hands flew over the board. Red lights made a connect-the-dot pattern from left to right. "Dammit," she said. "Double and triple dammit!"

Rab peered over her shoulder. "How bad?"

"No jump capacity whatsoever. We're barely operational."

"Life support?"

Kayla stared at her monitor. "Low but still functioning."

"Can we dump cargo and get rid of the bloody N-ware?" Rab asked.

"No, we don't have enough power," Salome said. "Besides, the stuff will just float around outside our hull, and I, for one, don't want to look at it."

Something moved to Kayla's left, just on the periphery of her vision. She turned to find Third Child standing behind her. How had the dalkoi gotten into the control room?

It chirped softly and rubbed up against her. She felt a familiar empathic presence, and suddenly a wild hunch began gnawing at her. Was it possible? Maybe, just maybe. She might be crazy, but she had a sudden certainty that, somehow, Third Child had rescued her from jumpspace. In some strange way it had sensed her peril, penetrated the jump interface, and shielded her.

Feeling a mixture of awe and disbelief, Kayla patted the dalkoi's head. Beside her, Salome cursed quietly as she surveyed her screen. "Bad and worse. Dammit, we need a tow, Rab."

He peered down at her. "Is there anybody else we can trust in this quadrant?"

"Who the hell knows? Kels, put out a distress signal on the Free Trade frequency. Let's hope somebody hears it before the Trade Police come by."

Or we run out of power, Kayla thought. *Or air.*

They drifted, pulled this way and that by various eddies of gravity between stars. Finally, after what seemed like hours, Salome said, "This is no good."

Rab nodded vigorously. "I second that emotion. But what are we going to do about it?"

"Put out an all-channels distress call."

"Great. That should attract the Trade Police. What happens when they notice that we've got an illegal shipment of nuclears?"

"Better to just float along like this until we run out of power and suffocate?"

Rab snorted. "Greer might say death before dishonor. Me, I'd just like to avoid death by stupidity."

"Put a plug in it, Rab. And give it another hour."

The message board crackled. "*Falstaff?* This is *Sedona.* Sure didn't expect to find you way the hell out here. What's wrong? We're getting such low energy readings on you we can hardly make a fix on your location. Can you boost your signal at all?"

"That's Ivan Wender's ship," Salome said. "Thank the gods and demons. Rab, is there anything else we can do to put some power into that signal?"

"We could cut gravity. You won't like it and I know that I won't, but as long as we're webbed in, it won't hurt us. Not much, anyway."

"Do it."

Kayla felt a surge of panic. No gravity?

Rab hit the intercom. "Get your webs on, everybody. Null-g in ten seconds."

"Knowbot," Salome said. "Countdown to null-g."

"Nine, eight, seven . . ."

Kayla pulled the belt webbing of her seat across her lap and secured it on either side as Salome and Rab did the same.

"Four, three, two . . ."

Belatedly, she remembered Third Child. "Wait," she said. "The dalkoi—"

"No time," said Salome.

Kayla sent a mental warning just in case Third Child could understand her.

—Hold on! We're losing gravity.

"Diverting power from gravity control to signal. Null-g in effect. Repeat, null-g conditions."

Kayla felt her feet come off the deck. Her hair drifted up lazily as though she were underwater. Her legs and arms felt oddly numb and her stomach complained loudly. Equilibrium vanished and in its place was a vague, nagging nausea. This wasn't the same as tumbling around the null-g rink at Vorhays Station, not at all.

Salome's long golden hair floated high above her head, giving her the eerie aspect of a human candle.

"Crap!" Rab's beard was covering his face, nearly blinding him. Kayla bit her lip to keep from laughing.

"Djeeeep!" With a loud chirp verging on a squeal, the dalkoi began to float up, up, up toward the ceiling. At the last moment it reached out its right foot and snagged the wall webbing with one of its multi-knuckled toes. It held on, hanging upside down like a light blue bat.

A distant clang announced the arrival of the *Sedona* and its traction beam. Kayla bounced in slow motion as the *Falstaff* came under tow.

"Twelve hours to Mammoth Station," Salome said.

Kayla's eyelids felt heavy, and her body ached from the effects of the jump sickness. Twelve hours of this? Her body cried out for relief, a muscle relaxant and a good stretch, but there didn't seem to be much of anything she could do about it. She wanted to talk to Iger, to consider how she and the dalkoi might be linked in some sort of telepathic loop. There was so much to think about. But she was tired, so very tired. She leaned back and told herself she was comfortable. As Third Child chirruped softly in the background, she fell asleep. And dreamed.

* * *

She was in a nest of purple fur and soft grasses. Her nestmates chirped and whistled around her, making comfortable noise. Some of them had already lost their early coloration and were turning tawny and golden. It was warm and safe here. Soon, food would arrive.

* * *

The nest was gone. She was walking through fields of lavender grass under a green sky. The sun, red and angry, burned her skin until it was dark and leathery. Her hair bleached to white. All day she walked the veldt, watching for stray bamberas.

* * *

Space was deep and velvety, lit by a hundred thousand cold lights, a mystery to be penetrated. She strode the deck of her new vessel, lithe, blonde, dark-skinned, completely in command, and waited to meet the candidate for first mate. He walked up, towered over her, smiled down. "Name's Barabbas," he said. There was something insolent and inviting in that grin, something she liked.

"You're hired."

* * *

Nighttime. Quiet corridors, silent rooms. Quick footsteps from door to door. Each locker gives so easily, but the contents are always the same, slim to nil pickings . . . but wait, what's this in the new girl's stuff? A bag of . . . can it be? Beautiful mindstones, the finest quality. Fetch a fortune on the market. Thanks, Katie. Thanks very much.

* * *

As the *Falstaff* rode upon its tractor beams on the long journey to Mammoth Station, Kayla's mind cycled into deeper sleep and away from the minds of her crewmates.

* * *

Mammoth Station was a typical shipyard: noisy, dirty, and expensive. Very expensive.

Salome vanished to confer with the yardmaster and when she returned, Kayla knew from one look at her grim expression that the news about the *Falstaff* was not good, not even remotely.

The *Falstaff*'s captain gathered her crew around her. "That hit we took on the way to Vorhays did more damage than we thought. Two engines need overhauling and one has to be completely rebuilt. Our shielding got torn to pieces." Salome closed her eyes as if she hoped this were a bad dream and she would awaken to something better. "Which means we're out of commission, folks. At least a month. Maybe two."

The crew buzzed quietly with the news.

"How are we going to pay for this?" Kelso asked, his long face growing longer by the moment.

"We're out of money."

Everybody groaned.

"The good news is, the yardmaster has agreed to continue work on *Falstaff*."

"That's big of her," Rab said. "What's the catch?"

"We can work off our account if we agree to ship out as crew for a merchant run."

"What?" He stared at her as though he had never seen her before.

"We'll be on the *Corazon*, the escort ship to the *Cabeza*, a deep space freighter."

"And abandon the *Falstaff*?" Rab said. "Just like that?"

"One of us could stay . . . no, not you, Rab." Salome frowned. "Morgan, you probably wouldn't mind, would you? Besides, Ivan Wender will be in dock for a while. He offered to keep an eye on the repairs while we're gone."

Arsobades said, "How long's the run? And where to?"

"A month. The Cavinas System."

Kayla's heart began beating a little faster at the mention of her home system. What if they were going to Styx? What would she do? What would she say?

Rab wasn't satisfied. "And why do they need an escort ship, pray tell?"

"They didn't mention that."

"And you didn't ask? When our tails are being put on the line? Sweetlips, where did you park your brain?"

Salome swung around to confront her lover with a warning glance. "When you're being offered what amounts to charity, you try to be grateful."

"So when we do leave?" Greer asked.

"Tomorrow."

"I'm for it," Arsobades said. "It beats cooling our heels in this backwater. Besides, how dangerous could it be?"

"Famous last words," said Rab.

Kelso shrugged. "No pay if I don't play, so count me in."

"And me," Iger said.

"Okay, okay," Rab said. "If you're all going, I guess I'm going, too. Somebody's got to keep an eye on you assholes."

Salome smiled and reached for his hand.

"Hey," Arsobades said. "Maybe we could trade our cargo to your pals. Would they have any use for outdated N-ware?"

"Don't be ridiculous," Greer said. "They'll confiscate it and turn us in, or blackmail us. You know Mammoth Enterprises. They're almost as corrupt as Karlson's government."

Rab scowled at her. "Got a better idea?"

"Yeah, let me see what I can do in town—maybe find some traders," Greer said.

"You?" Salome raised an eyebrow in surprise.

Greer shrugged. "I've got some contacts here that might be useful."

"All right," Salome said. "See if you can get rid of it."

"Yas'm." Greer gave a mock salute and stood up.

Rab stepped in front of her. "Remember, Greer, this is neutral territory."

Her eyes went wide with exaggerated innocence. "I

know that. I just want to get rid of our cargo, as per the captain's instructions."

"And maybe stir up a little Free Trader action?"

Greer smiled dryly. "Only if it can't be avoided."

"You know the stationmasters don't like to have agitators on dock. Get labeled as one and you're on your own. If you get picked up you'll rot in their jail."

"Gee, thanks, Rab. It touches my heart the way you don't seem worried about my dumping our illegal and dangerous cargo but you're in a sweat over liability. Maybe you should have been a lawyer."

His dark eyes flashed. "I mean it, Greer. We need these repairs, and we need the goodwill of the folks here. Stay out of trouble."

Greer met his glare. "Get out of my way."

"Promise me, Greer."

"Okay. I promise." She pushed past the bearded giant. "Katie, why don't you join me? You might learn something." It wasn't a request.

"Give me five minutes," Kayla said.

"Meet me at the air lock." Greer vanished.

Rab shook his head. "Damned politics. She'd love to drag us all right into a trade revolt."

Kayla paused in the doorway. She didn't like the way he was talking. What was so wrong with the Free Traders, after all. "I thought that you all supported her movement."

"Aren't you the good little foot soldier?" Kelso said.

"Shut up, Kels." Rab gave Kayla a long, hard look. "Listen, Katie. Only a fool would think that Prime Minister Karlson's tariff system works. Or like it. But there's a difference between disagreement and armed conflict. I don't believe in asking for trouble. And your roomie does."

"She really wants to see a better, fairer system of trade," Kayla said. "I know you think she's crazy. But I understand her, sort of."

Rab rolled his eyes. "Don't follow in her footsteps too closely, okay? She likes to stir things up."

"Don't be such a spoilsport," Kelso said. "Greer just likes lively talk."

"Are you're kidding yourself. The woman is a born troublemaker. She sees something that isn't broken and she can't stand it."

Salome nodded grimly. "She does have a strange ability to screw things up. Katie, be careful."

"Won't Iger miss you?" Arsobades said, teasingly.

Kayla shrugged. "Tell Iger I'll see him at dinner."

"It's your romance," Arsobades called after her.

Chapter Fifteen

Kayla and Greer stepped out of the *Falstaff* and onto a moving slidewalk which whisked them away down a long, noisy pier. Two women whipped past going the other way, fashionably dressed in tunics made from contrasting strips of orange and green cloth. Their eyes were closed as though they were meditating, and it took Kayla a moment to notice the red-blue glow of gems set into necklaces. Mindstones, and the women were trancing with them.

"Zombies," Greer muttered.

The sight of the stones gave Kayla a pang of sadness for her own lost hoard. On the heels of that she remembered a piece of a nearly-forgotten dream. Somebody on the *Falstaff* had been rifling through her locker, had found her stones. She could almost recall the flavor of the mind signature.

"Greer, I'm sure that a crew member took my mindstones," she said. "I had some sort of dream or vision."

"Are you going mystic on me?"

"No."

"Well, be patient. We'll find those stones, somehow."

They slid past the various repair bays and parts concessions until they came to an intersection: five sidewalks met and crossed. A holosign in the form of a giant red hand pointed toward the wide-open tariff-free district where anything, anything at all, was for sale.

"This way." Greer led her toward a row of garishly lit bars.

THE PINK LADY AND HER MAN
AZTEC REVENGE
WORMHOLE

"This looks promising." They peered in the last: dark, tired, and not very clean. To Kayla it looked like exactly the kind of place where a bunch of revolutionaries would gather to drink and plot strategy and buy old nuclears. But the tavern was empty. Only a fat barmaid was inside, swabbing tables, and she didn't even bother to look up.

MR. AMOEBA
THE SUN'S HARSH MISTRESS
KNEES TOGETHER

"Let's try this one." Greer settled in the darkest corner of the clean, stylish bar and tapped on a low bronze table. The walls of the tavern were faceted ramstone that reflected the firelight in a thousand different patterns, the floor was covered with amber and red lightning bolts that flashed at the pressure of a footstep. "What'll you have, Katie?"

"Red jack."

Greer punched the order into the mech waiter.

Two men who had been sitting at the long bar stood and approached them.

"Ladies," they said. "We're Free Traders in search of honest company."

"Yeah?" Greer said. "How honest?"

"We honestly hate Pelleas Karlson and swear to end his reign."

"Good enough. Have a seat. Have two."

The two corpulent, mustachioed traders, whose names were Onzerib and Douzerib, looked much too well dressed to consort with a spacer, much less plot political upheaval. But they certainly seemed interested in Greer, and listened intently as she pitched the *Falstaff*'s cargo.

Look at them, Kayla thought. *You'd think Greer was hawking herself instead of some tired old N-ware.*

At first glance the men seemed identical. Clones? They had the same faces and mustaches, identical mannerisms, matching smiles. The one on the left—Douzerib?—waved his hand in the air to punctuate a comment, and Kayla saw the flash of something dark and starshaped against his ruddy skin. A tattoo? So these glossy twins really were Free Traders?

She took a quick scan of their minds. *Hmmph. They're interested in Greer all right. But not in her body. They want her help. And the N-ware.*

The image of the N-ware cargo glowed in their minds, incandescent. They really wanted those armaments, and not merely to trade. No, they had other, darker uses in mind.

Behind their elegant facades, Onzerib and his brother boiled with anger, with hatred of the Trade Alliance and Pelleas Karlson. They were obsessed with bringing down Karlson's government and didn't seem to care what they had to do to achieve their goals. It was fascinating. These two had to be part of the most radical edge of the Free Traders.

But they also hated women. And in their minds, a dark plot had hatched for not only destroying Karlson but betraying Greer as well. It seemed simple malice, scarcely personal. Free Traders, they thought, should be men. If innocent people, especially women, died in the midst of their plot, well, it was too bad.

"I think we have a deal," Greer said.

Kayla stared at her. Somehow she had to stop this, to warn Greer what these men were planning.

Where would they strike? Kayla scanned the twins' minds desperately but could find no trace of a precise target outside of women in general and Greer specifically.

"We'll collect the goods tonight," said the left-hand twin.

Greer nodded. "Fine. And I'll meet you both in Vardalia."

"Greer, could I talk to you for a minute? Alone."

Her roommate frowned. Her expression said, *not now.*

"Just for a minute."

"Excuse me," Greer said to her companions. "I'll be right back." She stood up and motioned irritably for Kayla to follow her into the bathroom.

"What the hell's so important, Katie?"

Kayla met her gaze without flinching. "You're not serious about selling the N-ware to these men."

"No?" Greer seemed surprised. "Why not?"

"They want to use it. On other people. And on you."

"Is that so? Where, precisely?"

"I don't know."

"Then how do you know they intend to use it?"

"Please, Greer, listen to me. They're not traders. They're terrorists. Murderers. If you sell them those nuclears, you'll be condemning innocent people to death. They hate you. They hate all women."

"Don't be ridiculous." Greer laughed sharply. "Katie, your imagination is running away with you."

"It's not imagination, Greer."

Her crewmate's expression turned rock hard. "Then don't tell me anything more. I won't listen. I'm not interested in your mind-spy tricks."

"They're not tricks—"

"Shut up!"

"Greer, you've got to listen to me!"

"No. You listen to me. You should be damned grateful I haven't blown your cover. Now show a little respect by keeping your mouth shut, Katie, and listening. These guys are Free Traders. They're on our side. We owe them our allegiance and our silence. What they want to do with the N-ware is nobody's business but theirs."

"But—"

"We've got to dump that cargo, right? The deal's already made. The *Falstaff* needs that money. If you weren't such an innocent, you'd know that these guys have got subtler uses in mind for that stuff than blowing people up."

"Uses that you intend to help them with!"

"Maybe, if it's the right place."

"Like Vardalia?"

"Look, this is a perfect opportunity to take Pelleas Karlson down a notch or two. The last thing he wants is a bunch of nuclears being waved around on St. Ilban during the Trade Congress. It might ruin his lunch. I hope."

"He'll land on you with everything he's got."

"He's got to find me first." Greer was grinning.

"You're crazy. Rab was right. You don't even care if you live or die."

"I misjudged you, Katie. You're not ready for this. Okay. Why don't you run along? Go play with Iger."

"You can close your eyes. I won't."

Greer spun on her and her face was white with rage.

"You'll do what I tell you when I tell you. And you'll keep your mouth shut, regardless of what I ask you to do."

Kayla felt a sudden foreboding. "I thought you didn't want any part of me, or my mind tricks."

"I don't like them, but they might come in handy."

"For helping to kill innocent people?"

"Nobody's going to get killed."

"You can't guarantee that."

"No? And I suppose you can? Listen, I could tell Salome who you really are, and you'd be off the *Falstaff* so fast you wouldn't know what hit you."

"Greer!"

"Don't look at me that way, Katie. I'm no saint. This is war and I'm determined to win. I'll damned well help the twins use the N-ware to scare Pelleas Karlson green. And I'll have your help in the doing, hear?"

The implicit threat silenced all of Kayla's arguments. Mutely, she nodded.

Greer was halfway out the door. "Coming?"

* * *

"So, Greer," Salome said. "Did you make any headway on the nuclears?"

"We'll have it off the *Falstaff* tonight, Cap. Just keep the mechs away from the cargo bay between midnight and three."

Even Rab smiled at the news. "Well," he said. "Nice going, Greer."

She gave him a thin smile.

When we get to Vardalia, I'll be on her like a flea on a bambera, Kayla thought. *Those twins won't get near her.*

"Katie, are you daydreaming? I asked if you were ready to plot the course to the Cavinas System." Salome's eyes flashed impatiently. "It's a three-jump. You haven't done that many multiple jumps before. You ought to check out the navboard on the *Corazon* before we leave."

"Three-jump?" Kayla stared at her in alarm.

"Didn't I just say that? You seem out of it, lady. Better get on the ball." Salome stood up. "We leave tomorrow, 0900 hours. I suggest everybody get a good night's sleep."

Now Kayla had more than Greer's murderous colleagues to think about. How could she get her crewmates to St. Ilban without endangering them all—or dying in the process? She remembered much too vividly the nightmare of the last jump. Once before, luck—and the dalkoi—had rescued her, but she couldn't count on that again.

Or could she?

She paused and thought it over. Perhaps it was time to talk to Iger.

                              *   *   *

Kayla had been bedding down with Iger in his narrow bunk whenever they weren't on cross-shifts. This had occasioned some disgruntled comments from Arsobades, Iger's roommate, who, in order to accommodate their lovemaking, usually slunk out to sleep in the mess.

Third Child always kept them company, chirping quietly to itself. Did it sleep? Who knew? The dalkoi had grown accustomed to Kayla's presence and seemed to like her. She hoped it did.

That night, after she and Iger made love, Kayla prodded him in the ribs. "Hey, don't go to sleep."

He stirred, pulled her closer. "Mmm?"

"Iger, listen to me, Have you ever wondered what would happen if a load of N-ware got into the wrong hands?"

He opened his eyes and stared at her. "You've certainly got a strange idea of pillow talk," he said.

"Come on, have you?"

"Yeah. Sure. That's the kind of thing they raise Liageans on. We all remember what happened on Admanan, and swear never again. Never."

"Well, you know the N-ware we were carrying?"

"You mean the stuff that Greer got rid of?"

Kayla shifted so that she was snuggled comfortably up against his side. "Yeah. I saw the guys she sold it to. I didn't like their looks. Or their thoughts."

"You read their minds?" Iger sounded uncomfortable.

"Yes." It was no time to mince words. "They're real bastards. Terrorists. They're going to use it on Vardalia to scare the prime minister. And they don't care who they hurt, Greer included."

"So?"

"What do you mean, so? People's lives are at stake."

"They're not going to use it."

"You don't know what I saw."

"Katie, isn't it kind of late to be worrying about other people and their morality? I mean, we're living and working with smugglers. We're smugglers. Outlaws."

"But we don't threaten lives. Nobody's been hurt by what we trade."

"Yet."

"Iger, do you think I should call the Trade Police?"

"Not unless you want us all to end up on some penal colony."

"Yeah." *He's right,* she thought. *I can't go running to the police. I've got to handle this myself.*

"Forget it," he said. "There's nothing you can do. Chances are, those guys just want to use the stuff in some kind of bargaining ploy."

"Maybe."

"Definitely." Iger squeezed her gently. "Now could we talk about something else? Please? You know I can't wait until we get to St. Ilban. I've always wanted to see Vardalia. Dreamed about it. Promise me that you'll come see it with me."

"Yeah, sure," Kayla said, and paused dramatically. "If we get there at all."

"What do you mean?"

"I don't think I can do the jumps," she said. "You'll have to pilot us to Cavinas."

"A three-jump. I've never even handled one. You're the trained pilot."

"Look, you saw what happened when the jump engines came on last time. I was paralyzed. I've got jump sickness. We could all be killed."

"So tell Salome."

"I don't want to let her down. And I don't want to get kicked off the ship."

"Well," Iger said. "I promised Salome that I would

ride the tail scanner on the *Corazon,* but maybe I can talk her out of it."

"No," Kayla said. "I don't want to make her suspicious. But maybe there's another way. What if you were to lend Third Child to me?"

Iger looked at her as though she were crazy. "Why?"

"I think the dalkoi helped me fight the jump sickness last time."

"Third Child?" Iger sat up in bed. "How could it do that?"

"I don't know. But I'm sure it did. Got in between me and whatever it is that knots up my nervous system."

"Some sort of empath thing?"

"Maybe."

"You know, I'm beginning to think you've gone completely space-batty."

"Is that a no?"

"I don't know."

"Iger, you had goddamned better give me Third Child unless you want us all to die."

Iger shrugged. "Okay, fine. Take Third Child up to ops. Maybe you want to borrow some talismans from the rest of the crew, too."

She jabbed him in the side. "Don't be such a smartass."

Iger grabbed her hands and rolled over, pinning her to the bed. "If you're sick, take a pill. Or tell Morgan and let her fix something up for you."

"No, she can't help me. If she told Salome, I'd be screwed. And I've got nowhere else to go."

"I wouldn't like that." Iger pulled her closer.

"Hey, ease up. I can't breathe!"

"That didn't seem to bother you a few minutes ago." He kissed her neck gently, and then less gently.

Kayla closed her eyes. "On second thought, don't stop." She willed herself to ignore everything except his touch upon her and the feel of their two bodies, moving together.

* * *

At 0900 sharp, the crew of the *Falstaff* filed aboard the *Corazon*, made the requisite palm prints which identified them as crew, and took up their stations.

The ship, owned by Mammoth Enterprises, was bigger than *Falstaff*, newer, and built for speed. Sleek and clean, it contained not a trace of its previous occupants. The ivory-gray interior reeked of industrial-strength disinfectant and the stale metallic air that comes from months spent in dry dock.

"Have you seen the armory on this baby?" Arsobades said. "We have state-of-the-art disruptors. Hull-dissolving projectiles. Stuff I've only read about. What in Hades are we guarding?"

"I don't know. They wouldn't tell me."

"Truly? Must be something big. Try the computer and do some snooping."

After noodling around, Salome pulled up the ship manifest. "Well, we're empty."

"What about the *Cabeza?*" Kayla said. "That's where the important stuff has to be."

Salome scrolled through the list and gasped. The *Cabeza* was jammed to the rafters. With mindstones.

Arsobades swore softly.

Kelso let out a sharp whistle between his teeth. "A cool fortune there," he said.

"Sorry, folks," Rab said. "This is where I get off. Open the air lock, Salome. No mindstones for me."

"Don't be ridiculous," Salome said. "Who cares what we're riding shotgun on?"

"Salome, you know how I feel about this."

"Stop getting emotional, Rab. This is business. Period."

"What are all these mindstones doing way out here?" Iger asked. "I thought they never got far from Styx, let alone the Cavinas System."

Arsobades shook his head ruefully. "Probably stolen, then impounded from some stupid trader who needed repairs pronto and couldn't pay the bill. And turned over just as quickly by that pirate, the stationmaster."

"Company policy," Kelso said approvingly. "Don't let marketable goods sit in storage."

The minstrel rounded on him angrily. "Oh, yeah, fine. Delivering drugs to more pathetic victims may be business as usual for you, sport. But not to me."

Kelso started to protest, and Salome joined him, but Arsobades waved them both down. "I'll ride shotgun, Salome, as per our agreement. But you can bet that I'm going to keep an eye out for the bastard who's importing this stuff."

"It's not illegal, Arsobades."

"It should be."

"Gods," Greer said. "I wish I could get you as excited about the Free Traders. That's what's *really* important. Besides, we're not legally responsible for the other ship's cargo."

Rab smiled sourly. "Now who sounds like a lawyer?"

"And there's no hard data on mindstones to prove that they're dangerous," Greer said. "It's too bad about your wife, Arsobades. I'm sorry. But that was breen, not mindstones. And making trouble for Salome over this job won't bring her back."

"Try to relax," Salome said. "Everybody. Soon we'll be on St. Ilban, hand the stuff over, and book it back to *Falstaff*."

"What?" Rab said. "No downtime? Don't we have to give Greer the chance to stage a few political meetings? A little civil disobedience?"

"Oh, that's okay," Greer said casually. "St. Ilban isn't exactly my favorite place. Too close to Pelleas Karlson. The less time I spend there, the better."

Kayla peered at her roommate. Unsurprisingly, Greer was a better liar than she had thought. There was no hint on her face of what she was planning. Most likely, she was hoping to keep a low profile in St. Ilban and didn't want anyone to get suspicious and blow her cover.

"Who's the captain of the *Cabeza?*" Kelso asked. "He must be pulling down a sweet deal. Maybe even a percentage." He sighed dreamily, as though counting piles of credits.

Salome scanned the screen once more. "Cesar Vera. Longtime Mammoth employee. Believes in nepotism. It looks like his entire crew is related. But this is just a standard run for him. I'll bet he won't even draw hardship pay."

"A family ship? I'll bet they have some fun arguments," Rab said. "Knife-throwing in the corridors, at the very least."

Kelso looked disappointed. "Too bad it's not Vera's private deal."

"Who's the buyer?" Rab asked.

"I wish I knew."

Kayla had an uneasy feeling. Who would buy so many mindstones at one time?

"Tugs have disengaged," Kelso reported. "We're alone. Clear as a spring night on Liage. Nobody within half a parsec besides the *Cabeza.*"

"Katie," Salome said. "We'll want to jump in ten minutes."

"Right." Kayla silently crossed her fingers, where was that dalkoi? Hadn't Iger arranged for it to be here with her? "Uh, I'm taking a pit stop, Salome. Cover for me, okay?"

"Hurry it," Salome said.

Kayla lit out for the temporary quarters she was sharing with Iger—and Third Child. There. The dalkoi was crouched upon a pile of something in the middle of the room. Kayla looked closely.

"Dammit, Third Child!"

The dalkoi's perch was a loomed red and gold tunic

she had purchased on Vorhays. Or, rather, the remains of it. What had been a neat sweater was now a mass of unraveled wool and translucent pink fiber that the dalkoi had knotted around its toes and legs.

"What are you doing?" Kayla said. "Gods, why won't you leave my stuff alone?"

Third Child chirped and held up the knotted mess as though it were offering a rare gift.

"No," she said. "Come on. I don't have time for that now. I need you with me on the navboard, pronto. I'm going to do a jump and you've got to help me. Understand?"

The dalkoi made what sounded like an interrogative chirp and again pushed the wool toward her.

"Not now, Third Child. Please."

The dalkoi blinked at her, obviously offended.

"Oh, all right. I'm sorry. Bring your knitting. Bring whatever you like, but come on!"

With Third Child in tow, Kayla steamed back to the control room.

"Katie, there you are," Salome said, and paused, taking in the dalkoi. "Why did you have to bring that thing along with you? I thought it was Iger's pet. And what in the name of Andromeda is it wearing around its neck? A muffler?"

"I guess so." Kayla jacked herself into the navboard before Salome could ask her any other questions.

Whump!

Something bulky was covering her head and shoulders. It made her face itch. She felt as if she had to sneeze.

Third Child had covered her with the whole sticky mess of wool. But she had no time to complain or even do more than claw it down around her shoulders. The jump engines were heating up and she had to pour every ounce of concentration into the ship's maneuvers. It was especially tricky since they were practically jumping in tandem with the *Cabeza*. They went first, and then waited for their sister ship. If there were any pirates lurking at the jump points, the *Corazon* would encounter them first. Jumping with live weapons. It made Kayla's head hurt to think about it.

She was submerged in the false landscape of cyberspace, staring at the whirling bifurcated sphere which indicated the boundaries of different star systems. There, far in the distance, halfway to the eternally-receding horizon, that silver-white mandala was the Cavinas System with its two suns like eyes peering at her, yellow and green, from the center of the rotating display.

A three-point jump. She had never deliberately tried anything like it before. Her heart pounded.

She took careful aim as though the system were a target. She didn't want to land too near the suns. Xenobe and its moon, St. Ilban, were midway within the Cavinas System. She wanted to avoid Styx. There. She had it within her sights, a nice neutral location for the *Corzaon*. No planets. No asteroids.

Part of her was excited and eager. And part of her wanted to stay right where she was. Would she make it through?

—Third Child, stick close.

Was that an affirmative mindtouch or just her imagination? No time to think about it. No time to think about anything. She told the navboard to start the jump.

The world turned upside down. Colors were all wrong. The air was strange, thick, almost opaque. She could hear light, see sound.

Time stopped . . .

She was freezing. Burning. Couldn't move or breathe. They would all die. Her brain couldn't work, her hands couldn't operate the navboard. But what was that warmth creeping over her? She began to feel her toes again, to flex her fingers. She was awake and operational and working the board.

. . . And started.

Dizzily, Kayla stared around ops in relief. The first of the jumps was behind her.

She punched in the second set of coordinates and held her breath as the engines built back up to a roar.

She was in two places at once, three places, four. Which Kayla was she? The bottom dropped out of her stomach. Huge red cylinders came rolling at her down the walls, trying to crush her. She dodged one, vaulted over another. She was falling in white space.

Something seemed to cushion her landing.

She came to herself in her chair as the jump engines died away.

Third time lucky, she thought, *please,* and keyed the board for the Cavinas System.

Realtime dissolved. For a moment she hung, suspended, over a chasm. At the bottom she could see the icy glint of a thousand shards of broken glass pointing up to her. If she fell she would die.

She began to slide. But something was pulling at her, yanking her back, up, up, up the glassy slope and back onto flat ground. Something that had gotten in between her and the paralyzing effects of jump.

Cyberspace vanished and the universe winked on around her, familiar stars in configurations that Kayla had studied years ago on her vid cubes. The nighttime sky of the Cavinas System, the constellations of her childhood aeons ago.

Kayla felt a swell of warm wet emotion at the sight. The *Corazon* had emerged from jump into realspace not far from Xenobe, but not so close as to disrupt the gravitational fields of the gas giant. And there, coming around the far edge of Xenobe's pale green mottled belly, a crystalline star-mite. A tiny planet shining in the light of the twin suns. St. Ilban.

They had made it. Kayla was still jacked into the navboard when the realspace around them distorted and the *Cabeza* materialized nearby.

The protective aura shielding her began to fade and dissipate. Nearby, Third Child drooped in exhaustion.

—*Thanks.* Kayla hoped it understood.

"Smoothest jump yet," Rab said. "Way to go, Katie."

Salome beamed at her. "Beautiful."

Iger came pounding into the control room. "Katie," he cried. "I forgot about Third Child! Are you all right?" He paused and his face reddened as everyone turned to look at him.

"Hail, Romeo," Rab said.

Kayla held her hand out to Iger. "I'm fine. Really."

Abashed, he leaned closer, lowering his voice so that only she could hear him. "I came as soon as I could." He might have been about to say something else, but his words seemed to fail him as he stared at the woolen mess around her shoulders.

"What's the matter?" Kayla said. "What are you looking at?"

"Where did you get that?"

"This scarf?" Kayla tried to mash the itchy thing into some sort of cohesive shape. "From Third Child. It insisted that I wear it."

"Third Child made you an *oyo?*" Iger's voice cracked. "I don't believe it."

"Why not?" Kayla said. "What's so special about a nasty mess of sticky fiber that used to be a nice sweater?"

Iger smiled as though she were crazy. "Gods, don't you know? These are extremely rare. Priceless, really. I've only seen them in museums. On Liage they make them from Erfani grass. They're supposed to have strange magical powers. The dalkoi extrudes a fiber from its body and intermingles it with the rest of the weaving."

"Yuck," said Salome.

"Grass?" Kayla glared at Iger. "It used my best tunic!"

Iger nodded. "Sure. That makes sense. Third Child couldn't find any Erfani grass around here, so it used a substitute. Something that belonged to you. You don't realize it, Katie, but you've just been paid an incredible compliment. I know people on Liage who would sell their grandparents for a dalkoi oyo."

Rab sidled over. "Special scarf, huh? So, Katie, how about those magical powers? Did you feel anything magical? Sprout wings? Hear voices? Call creatures from the vasty deep?"

Kayla started to say something sarcastic, but she stopped as the truth of it hit her. Hadn't she felt protected, even insulated from the awful effects of the jump? And how could she explain it? She smiled mysteriously. "I'm not telling, Rab." She clutched the ugly woolen muffler tightly. "But I'm very grateful to Third Child for its gift and I'll wear it proudly, always." Especially during jump.

Third Child chirped in what might have been approval.

"I've heard of good manners, but this is ridiculous," Salome said. "Aren't you afraid you'll catch something from that nasty mess? Dalkoi germs?"

"Shh," said Rab. "You're just jealous, sweetie."

"Jealous, my foot!"

"Hey, kids," Kelso said. "I know this is fun, but we're being hailed by the St. Ilban port authority. Does anybody want to answer or should I just let them go ahead and open fire on us?"

* * *

No one on St. Ilban seemed to be expecting them or the mindstone shipment they were shepherding. At least, not officially.

They parked in orbit around St. Ilban, monitoring the increasingly complex communications between the *Cabeza* and the port authority of Vardalia.

"*Cabeza*, I told you, we don't have any landing orders here," the portmaster said. "Who's the buyer?"

Cesar Vera, the *Cabeza*'s captain, didn't answer him directly. "Could you check your records again?" Vera said. "You must have something there about us. We've come a long way."

"And you'll go back a long way, too, if you don't tell me who's going to sign for this shipment."

"All I have is a numbered account," Vera said. He sounded frustrated and even a bit desperate. "I've coded it into your screen. You should be getting that now."

A moment later the portmaster was back, sounding chastened and edgy. "Uh, roger on that account. Why didn't you say so? We give priority clearance to single-digit accounts. Go right ahead, I've cleared berth twenty-seven for you. You should be getting those co-ordinates directly. Do you require a tug?"

"Yes. And we'll have a sister ship coming down, too."

"Berth twenty-nine is free."

Salome looked up from her screen. "Must be somebody important buying those stones. Everybody sure fell to in a hurry. But I guess we'll never know who. Poor old Vera sounds like he's finished for the day. I guess we're done, too. Who wants to go down to Vardalia with me and do some shopping?"

"I'm going," Rab announced. "It's the only way I know you'll buy something I like."

"Me, too," said Arsobades. "Best music shops in the sector."

Even Kelso wanted to accompany the group.

But Kayla's attention was riveted on Greer. Her roommate was obviously intending to go on-world, and just as obviously planning to go alone. But Kayla had no intention of letting her get out of her sight.

"How about you, Katie? Katie? Hello?" Salome's voice was sharp with sudden impatience.

"Oh, yeah, thanks," Kayla said. "But I've got other plans."

Iger began to beam.

Greer gave Kayla a significant look and slipped out of the room.

Kayla began to follow her.

"Hey," Iger said. "Where are you going? I thought we had a date!"

Damn, Kayla thought. *Not now.* Aloud she said, "Did we? Oh, of course. Listen, can I meet you someplace in a little while? Good. By the docks? After lunch."

"Katie!"

But she was already out the door on Greer's trail.

Chapter Sixteen

Vardalia was a place of marvels. Kayla had seen the vid cubes and could recite facts from memory, but nothing had prepared her for the actual city.

The white-gold towers curved up into the clouds. The narrow boulevards thronged with sophisticated, well-dressed people. The lights of the orbital suburbs winked in the night sky. Long graceful necklaces of lights scalloped each street, casting an amber glow upon all nighttime activity. The music. The food. The thrum of life densely packed.

Banners hung from balconies and looped from building to building, high above street level, flashing messages welcoming delegates to the annual Trade Congress.

And the people! Out in the open air, right on top of one another. Kayla had never seen so many. It was terrifying and exhilarating.

How do they all breathe, jammed together? she wondered. *Why do they need so much light? Where do they get their food? And how do I find Greer among so many?*

A glittering palace carved from some sort of dark crystal rose up before her. Massive and graceful yet oddly brooding, it took up the center of a plaza and dwarfed every building nearby.

"The Crystal Palace," a holoplaque announced. "Home to the offices of His Honor Pelleas Karlson, and the grand Trade Congress."

Kayla stared at the glittering building and shivered. How many hundreds of people worked inside? How many noisy minds?

So many minds muttering and carping. She let her shields down very carefully, allowing only a narrow passage for a nearsense probe, searching for Greer's acerbic mind signature. And all around her a million minds chattered and clucked, sang and sobbed. And something nibbled at the corners of her shield, something subtle and dangerous. Was that another mind reaching out, trying to make contact?

—*Wait, little one. Not so fast.*

It was trying to enfold her, to capture her, to devour her. Kayla panicked, batting at the thing with her nearsense.

—*No, no. Get away. Stop it!*

She stumbled, nearly falling to the ground. No one around her paused or seemed to even notice.

The dangerous presence receded. Kayla shuddered, head swirling. That was too close, she thought. What in the galaxy had just tried to suck her up and finish her? Its mind signature had been huge, much too big for a single entity.

Groupmind.

The thought sent an icy shiver through her soul. It had never been tried, even on Styx. But there was no other explanation.

Was that what it had been? A groupmind, a linked group of empaths working in unison? She had heard such things discussed as theory. But was such a thing possible, was such a group here, scanning the city? How, and who were they?

A group of her fellows, scanning everyone in Vardalia. Perhaps they were right there in the central plaza, in that glittering evil palace.

Yes, and she had nearly been caught in the thing's net.

A nearby window. A multivid cube display re-

counting the history of the Trade Alliance and previous
Trade Congress triumphs. Kayla stood before it, eyes
blank, as her mind strained to detect any hint of the
mindnet, of the massed power of unknown empaths,
waiting to pounce.

Gone. Nothing. Not even a mindwhisper.

She was safe for the moment.

Bastards, she thought. *You won't get me.* Kayla spun
a seamless mindshield and locked herself behind it.
Any questing empath would slide right off its reflective surface and keep going.

God's Eyes, she thought. *This place is even stranger
than I thought.*

* * *

With all the crush on the street there seemed barely
enough room for people to get by one another. But a
determined group of street players had set up shop in
a scalloped doorway and were busily mimicking passersby, making elaborate transactions for invisible merchandise, pausing now and then to hold out an
upturned top hat for tips. Kayla thought she saw the
flash of a black starburst tattoo upon the wrist of the
smallest busker, a slender blonde girl wearing a blue-
and yellow-striped bodysuit. On her head was a floppy
red hat with multiple brims settling in petallike pink
layers. It fell over her eyes at regular intervals as
though set upon a spring and timer mechanism. There!
That tattoo again. Sure enough, it was the Free Trade
sigil.

Was the girl intentionally advertising her affiliation
or merely careless? As Kayla watched, a hawk-faced
old man darted out of the crowd toward the busker,
grabbed her hand, and exchanged several quick words
with her. The girl's face reddened. She nodded and
pulled her sleeves down, sealing them across her palms
to form open-fingered gloves.

Not much protection against a determined interroga-
tor, Kayla thought. *Watch out, sweetie.*

She was about to attempt another probe for Greer
when she saw a familiar face in the crowd, one that
turned the blood in her veins to frozen water as it triggered a dozen memories.

Handsome face, strong jaw, dark hair and eyes.

Yates Keller.

Here? It couldn't be. But it was. Oh, gods, it was.

He locked eyes with her and she knew, knew without
the slightest hesitation that he saw right through her
disguise, that he saw Kayla John Reed hiding behind
the short brown hair and ratty spacer garb.

She had to get away.

Keller gaped in disbelief. Then he seemed to gather
his senses, pointed at her, and his mouth formed her
name.

She dodged out of sight behind a fat woman and two
fat children, cut down an alley, jostling and bumping
people as she squeezed past. She had lost sight of
Yates, but that didn't mean he wasn't following her. He
might be only a few paces behind.

She turned a sharp corner and slid between two
vending carts, raced up a side street, and through a tiny
plaza, around a man laden with packages, and into the
shadows of another alley. Gasping for breath, she
leaned against a wall and waited, listening. No sound
of pursuing feet.

Kayla peered around the building and saw to her dismay that she had somehow circled right back to the
tourist-filled grand plaza by the looming crystal palace.
And in the center of the plaza, hard by the rotating
multilevel fountain with its leering crystalline cherubs and overwrought mermaids stood Onzerib and
Douzerib. There was no mistaking the twin mustaches,
the same smiles, the matching pairs of beady eyes.

Gods, Kayla thought. *Are they going to plant the
N-ware right here in the heart of Vardalia? Blow up
the Trade Congress and maybe destroy half the city? Is
that the "little disruption" that they've got planned?*

*And do they expect to lure Greer into the center of it?
I've got to stop them.*

Would a mindbolt do it?

Her mind opened a channel in readiness and she felt
the power coiling within her, ready to leap out and
blast the two men into unconsciousness. As Kayla
drew back to strike, something dark and terrible heard
her and crept near, something silent and relentless
came closer, closer, spread its dreadful invisible wings
to enfold her, and snapped shut. Everything went black
around her, and then it all went away.

* * *

The world came back one piece at a time. She was
alone in a room with pale walls, lying upon a cushioned pad. Her vision flashed on and off like a sputtering vid cube. The wall. The ceiling. A piece of her
foot.

The floor seemed to bulge upward and roll toward
her like a hard wave. Her head ached and her body
seemed paralyzed, rooted to the pallet, as though she
were in the midst of a major jump acceleration, forced
down and back by her own enormous weight.

Slowly, glacially, memory returned. She knew her
name: she was Katie, no Kayla, no, Kayla-who-was-
Kate Shadow-the-pilot. The smuggler. The outlaw. The
facts came forth, cold and glistening, from under the
ice. She had been hiding for a long time. But something had found her.

Her vision solidified. That was a relief. She scanned
the room. Where was the door, where were the windows? Was she in prison or in a hospital?

She reached out with her mind in a long narrow
probe and felt it bounce back at her. The walls of her
cell were shielded, impenetrable. Prison, then.

The outline of a door cut its way, glowing, through
the seamless wall as though someone on the other side
was drawing a picture with a laser, someone with a

steady hand. The door shot open and Kayla saw a face, a familiar face from long ago.

A name went with the ruddy face and brawny build: Johannes Goodall, the kindly Miners' Guild member who had tried to warn her about Beatrice Keller. A pear-shaped mindstone glittered in his right earlobe.

"Johannes, what are you doing here?"

He gave her a tight smile which his eyes did not share. "So it is you, Kayla. When I saw the brown hair I hoped—but no. Still, it's a pleasure to see your sweet face."

She sat up slowly and reached for his arm. "Tell me, tell me about Styx. How is Rusty? Dr. Ashley?"

"Fine," he said absently. "Real fine." He neither met her gaze nor completely looked away.

He's lying. "Is that so? Johannes, look at me, please!"

His face got redder. "I'll tell you the truth, Kayla. Things went bad in the mines. Real bad. A bunch of us were ruined by the mindsalt glut. Me, Miriam Crown, just about everybody you can name. Salt destroyed the stone market. Yates brought in mechs that could dig twice as fast as a man. We were useless. And after Beatrice Keller died—"

"She's dead?"

"Her heart gave out—surprised me that she even had one. Anyway, Yates took over, foreclosed on a bunch of stakes, and there we were without any means. Then he made us an offer: Pelleas Karlson wanted an empath squad. Yates would set it up so we could come to Vardalia and live like kings."

"But what about Styx? What about the Council?"

Johannes shrugged. "What good was any of it any more? Empty. Used up. There was a better life waiting here."

Kayla's spirits sank further. "And all you had to do was spy for the government?"

Goodall seemed genuinely stung. "It's not spying,"

he said. "It's security work. Very high up. We're an elite group. A patrol, sort of. A couple of us work the trade routes. The rest are here."

"And Yates Keller is the head of this elite patrol?"

"Don't look at me like that, girl. You're too young to know the tricks that life can play on you. Yates gave us another chance. I jumped at it."

"Did you."

"Yes ma'am." He smiled. "And it's been blue skies ever since. In fact, I thought you might like to join us."

Us.

Kayla shivered at the word. Could her old friend be serious? "Join you? As part of a groupmind? That's what it really is, Johannes, isn't it?"

"That's right." The ex-miner looked almost proud.

"So Yates asked you to come in here and recruit me?"

Goodall's smile faltered, but he nodded vigorously.

"Me, work for Yates Keller?"

The smile vanished altogether.

"You must be insane, Johannes. Yates Keller has driven you crazy."

"There's no need to be insulting." Goodall actually sounded hurt. "Yates told me to remind you that there are even worse alternatives."

"At the moment, I can't think of any."

"Now, Kayla-girl, don't say that. At least, not until you've tried it. The work's real interesting. You can make a good living, too. Better than in the mines."

"Yes, but you're living near Yates Keller, working for him."

He blinked, obviously confused, then looked away.

"No, Johannes, I'm sorry."

Goodall nodded, waved vaguely, and stood up. "Well, I tried. Luck to you, Kayla."

The door burned its way through the wall once again and allowed Goodall's burly form to pass through before it flared up, blazed briefly, and disappeared.

Almost immediately Kayla regretted letting him go. Perhaps she could have seized control of him, forced him to free her.

The door burned open, again. Yates Keller walked in.

All the old feelings came flooding back: attraction, anger, desire, and hatred.

"Come to gloat?" she said. "Or merely to stare?"

He sat down next to her and his face was a study in warring emotions. He looked more saddened than angry as he reached out, touched her face, and said, "Kayla. What have you done to your beautiful hair?"

The sound of his voice. She had to fight her reaction, keep herself from being drawn toward that warmth. *Chemicals,* she told herself. *It's only a chemical reaction.*

She pulled away and saw pain in his eyes.

"Why are you so damn stubborn?" he said. "It could be so lovely, really lovely, to have you here. All you have to do is say yes. Say yes, Kayla."

His voice. His smile. The touch of his lips. She remembered, and remembering, wanted him again. But what was he really offering? She was the one going crazy, to think about joining him. Crazy. Kayla glared. "You must think I'm a real fool, Yates."

He sighed as if to say, what am I going to do with you, and shook his head. "I could keep you in jail for the rest of your life, you know. Don't make me do it, Kayla."

"If I worked for you, it would amount to the same thing."

To her surprise, Keller smiled. "Touché." He sat down next to her on the bunk. "I don't blame you, you know. For that attack. I shouldn't have treated you so heartlessly back there. I'm sorry, Kayla."

She heard herself saying, "Well, so am I."

He patted her hand. "Good. Then tell me about your spacer's life. Why would you prefer it to the luxury here at the palace? You could live among others who are like you. Eat decent food. Don't you go crazy in those cramped quarters?"

His tone was disturbingly seductive. She pulled back all the way to the edge of the pallet. "Cramped? If I never went crazy in the mines, why should I mind close quarters now?"

"But you could have blue sky, the beauties of Vardalia, friends. Companionship. Why settle for recycled air and hydroponic glop, driving some space scow from station to station?"

"I already have friends," she said hotly. "I like space."

He rolled his eyes. "You would. Damned contrary, you Reeds. Always were."

"While the Kellers merely specialize in one thing—greed."

He pursed his lips but said nothing. Instead, he stood up and reached for a wall panel, and pressed the lower portion of it. A cup extruded itself and filled with a clear liquid. He pressed another panel and a scoop appeared. It was filled with purple crystalline powder which sparkled ruby-blue.

Fear. Kayla looked at the powder and was afraid.

"Is that mindsalt?" she said.

"Yes."

She waved it away. "If that's for me, I don't want it."

"We'll see." Yates poured the mindsalt into the cup. The liquid frothed up with an odd metallic sheen.

Suddenly Kayla couldn't move. Some tremendous force—the groupmind?—had blotted out her will. It was forcing her to open her mouth, to swallow the mindsalt-laced drink.

The stuff went down cold and sat on her stomach, a frozen stone in her gut.

Nothing happened.

Then her pulsebeat grew louder, louder, until the

walls began to move in and out, in and out. The floor of the room bubbled like some boiling pot. Yates was miles away, looming like some distorted monstrous being high above her.

The ceiling curved, the room narrowed, darkened, and she was back in the tunnels of Styx. Stalactites were falling, impaling everybody she had ever known, ever loved. Mother, Father, Salome, Rab, Iger, even Third Child. All killed by those gleaming, faceted spears glowing blue-red and deadly, cutting through their minds, their lives, their world. Mindstone spears.

The earth was shaking, walls tumbling, and the volcanoes of Styx belched fire and ice.

Far beneath the roiling surface, somewhere in the deepest of deep tunnels, Kayla and Yates lay naked, locked together in fierce embrace. Part of Kayla recoiled in disgust, but part of her wanted him, wanted it, wanted everything. *Hurry,* she thought. *Hurry, before I explode.*

In her frenzy she began tearing at him, ripping at his skin until it gave way, shredded, and came loose in her hands. Now he was a skeleton grinning at her mockingly. But she was a skeleton, too. They were frozen in a ferocious death-embrace from which she would never get free, never, never, never.

The stalactites bombarded them, dropping huge palm-sized gems, mindstones beyond price, beyond imagining. Each gem detonated in a flash of cold fire as it hit the hard tunnel floor. The mindstone bombs fell like some terrible hail, wreathing the writhing skeletons with tiny mushroom clouds and arctic blue flames.

The death's head that was Yates Keller laughed grimly at Kayla and said, "If you won't join us, perhaps you can be put to use. We need a powerful tripath like you. And if you won't help us willingly, there are other ways."

A gibbering, grimacing puppet-thing that looked like

Kayla capered before them, bowing, nodding, dancing like some marionette gone berserk.

"How would you like it if we made you into a mount?" The Yates skeleton snapped its bony fingers and the Kayla-puppet fell obediently to all fours, kneeling submissively. Yates jumped on her back and slapped her left haunch. Round and round they went in an arena filled with other skeletons, a room in which the only living breathing thing was the Kayla-puppet.

"No," Kayla cried. "Gods, no. No!"

* * *

The room came swimming back, the pallet, Yates, everything. The wild hallucination ended as swiftly as it had begun.

Yates watched her expectantly. "So," he said. "You understand me better, now."

"All I saw was blood," she said. "Death and murder."

"Death?" He looked genuinely confused. "No euphoria? The colors? The patterns? The incredible sense of power?"

"What are you talking about?"

"The greater awareness that comes from the salt? Didn't you feel that?"

"Nothing like it."

"Then what did you see?"

"A horror," she said. "I was in hell and you were there, Yates. Both of us."

"I don't understand."

She forced herself to lean toward him. "Listen to me, Yates. Let's have a truce between us, all right? There's a threat out there, a terrible thing. It could destroy Vardalia."

"Don't be ridiculous."

"Please. I'm serious. Two men from Mammoth Station are loose on this world with enough old style N-ware to wipe Vardalia off the face of St. Ilban."

He smiled condescendingly. "And I suppose they smuggled these lethal nuclears into the city?"

"Anything can be smuggled, anywhere. Even a major shipment of mindstones."

"How did you know about that?"

So Yates *had* been involved. It had just been a wild guess.

"Never mind," she said. "We've got to stop these crazy bastards before they kill us all."

"Even if anyone is berserk enough to attempt something as stupid as that, we'd catch them immediately," Yates said. "It's really none of your concern."

"You're a fool, Yates! We could all die."

"Nobody's going to die. But your life could be a great deal more pleasant if only you'd cooperate with us. Don't make me force you, Kayla."

"Force?" Kayla's temper stripped away her caution. "Oh, sure. Go on, then. Try to control me. You could never top me at home. Back there you were only a weak duopath. What'd you do, buy new powers with all your money?"

He said nothing, merely closed his eyes.

Something grabbed Kayla's mind and hung on with surprising tenacity. Where had Yates gotten such power? Kayla felt him pull her to her feet and compel her to walk across the room. Despite her best efforts, she couldn't break his control.

—What were you saying about strength, Kayla?

The door in the wall burned open and she was marched past its glowing edges. But her legs were numb and clumsy and she felt as though someone else were looking out through her eyes.

They moved swiftly along a corridor and down to the left, past closed rooms and walls with high windows that admitted light but nothing else.

They weren't underground as she had suspected. But Kayla had a difficult time ascertaining just exactly where they were. In the Crystal Palace itself?

Like the puppet out of her mindsalt-induced vision, she moved obediently across the cushioned floor. Pick up the right foot and put it down. Pick up the left. Now the right. Left, right. She lost all track of time. Where were they going? Kayla felt curiously passive, uninvolved.

Another door, burning in a wall. The chamber beyond was paneled in fine fuchsia silk embroidered with dozens of silvery flowers. The lighting was recessed and gentle, the cushioned chairs around the wide table dense and comfortable. And around it sat a group of empaths.

The groupmind. And somehow, Kayla knew the source of Yates' power, how he could control her.

So many familiar faces. Was there no one, no one at all left in the mines? None of them seemed particularly surprised to see her: they scarcely acknowledged her presence.

Each one of them wore a large mindstone cut in the pendeloque style, dangling from the right ear. The glow from the gems was nearly hypnotic. Kayla had to pull her attention away from them and back to the group.

Miriam Crown. Johannes.

And there, in the middle. Good old Rusty Turlay. But there was something odd, something terribly wrong about Rusty. He sat in their midst, eyes vacant, a thin line of drool snaking from the corner of his open mouth.

What's happened to him? Kayla thought. *And how can they just let him sit there like that?* But she couldn't ask. Yates still had her under control.

He forced her to join hands with those empaths to either side of her.

Kayla sank down slowly through the interstices of the empathic connections and felt raw power thrum through her body and mind. She rang like the strings of a fine harp as the groupmind opened, made room for her.

How marvelous. The complexity, the strength, the unity. Vardalia was a house with an open door to the groupmind. She coasted with it as it scanned the port, the docks, the main square. Sweeping, searching, endlessly vigilant. A miracle of coordination, a humming, awesome pleasure.

The streets were transformed: colors off-key, iridescent. Shadows were longer, angles sharper. Individual features blurred while minds turned luminous at a glance. Each person opened and turned like a flower with its face to the sun. The glow of the groupmind, its power, transfixed each subject mind for the instant it took to survey, analyze, and weigh its contents. Nothing was hidden. It seemed that no thing could be preserved and shielded from the blinding glare of the groupmind's truth.

A tiny thought whispered in the smallest remnant of the thing that was Kayla-alone: *But you hid. You shielded. You.*

Hush. Easy to ignore the mindwhisper. Cast it aside, silence it. The groupmind is all. Nestle into its embrace. Forget yourself. Forget everything but the all.

She floated as on a sweet cushion of air, drifted through the streets of Vardalia brushing one mind, then another. So might she have wafted forever, had the groupmind not arrowed down onto a small street urchin capering with her friends. The busker was wearing a striped bodysuit and floppy red top hat that drooped over first one gray eye and then the other. And on her wrist was a black sunburst, a negative star in supernova

Part of Kayla's mind came to full attention. Without thinking, she brought up shields so subtle that only a fully skilled tripath like herself would be able to see them, to contain the thought, the shock of recognition.

The Free Trade sigil.

Remember who you are. What you're doing here.

But images flowed over her, pieces of individual memory that formed the substratum of the mosaic that was the groupmind.

An iridescent shell. A gust of cinnamon-scented wind. A hand grasping a refining tool. A face, mouth stretched in fear. The wash of stars past a viewing port. A piece of unrefined ore. The same face, screaming. A perfect white rose. Screaming, screaming for help. Golden bubbling wine in a fine, fluted goblet.

Someone strapped to a table, a machine hovering over him as he shrieked horribly. The man was familiar. Rusty, right before he was changed.

And suddenly she understood. The awful price he had paid for Yates' favor. The groupmind needed a medium, someone to bind the other empaths into one seamless whole. An empath, yes, but one without free will or any other mental obstacles to full unity.

They had brainburned him. They had made Rusty little more than a vegetable, to be used as they liked. To ride and use him. A mount and medium for the groupmind, binding them together.

"How would you like to become a mount?" Yates had asked her in her mindsalt vision. Was that what he truly intended for her?

Kayla tried to pull out and away from the enchanted circle. But the groupmind beckoned. The sweet communal caress, blessed surrender of ego—lay down your burdens and be freed—was far more potent than she had imagined.

She saw her own face, mouth twisted in agony as she was strapped to the table, to the same table as Rusty before her. And above her, Yates grinned.

No. No. No. No.

Stay clear, she warned herself. *Don't give in. Think about something else. The twins, concentrate on finding them. Yes, ride the groupmind and keep watching through the groupmind's eyes and ears. Concentrate. You can find them again. This might be the only way.*

For what seemed like hours she overflew the city in concert with the minds of the other empaths. Two petty criminals were apprehended, a lost child was reunited with its mother, and a noisy disagreement between two rival traders was deflated. But still there was no trace of Onzerib and his brother.

—Rest period. The mindvoice broke through her concentration and Kayla felt herself being gently lowered back into her solitary head as the entrance to the groupmind was sealed shut behind her.

She was alone. Yates had released her, too.

She was sitting at the same table with the same group of people. Her forehead hurt and she felt drained of energy, incapable of lifting a finger, much less escaping. How much time had passed? Hours? Days? She had no idea. Beside her two empaths slumped in their seats, eyes closed. All around the table people sagged, sighed, and fell back in their chairs.

Round mech servers rolled into the room, beeping, lights blinking, bearing drinks on their upper trays. The empaths grabbed at them eagerly, gulping the bright liquid, holding their cups with shaking hands. As quickly as cups were emptied the mechs refilled them.

Kayla stared at the frothy liquid in the glass, wondering. It looked harmless, smelled sweet, sweet as a degli shake. Her mouth was parched, so dry. Everyone else in the room was drinking, savoring the liquid, and none of them seemed harmed. She took a cautious sip. It was sweet and minty, with a slight tang. Not bad. She took another sip. Rather good, in fact. She felt energy streaming back into her body, carried by the sweet metallic elixir.

Too late she realized that it was wine laced with mindsalt. Kayla's stomach turned over violently and she felt the urgent need to retch. *Fool,* she thought. *Ask first,* then *drink.*

The seconds ticked down as she waited for the dreadful effects of the drink to manifest. Her heart thudded and sweat dripped from her forehead. She got out of her chair and leaned against the wall, breathing hard.

Five minutes went by. Ten. Fifteen.

The sweat cooled on her upper lip and she wiped it off. Nothing, she felt nothing at all. There was no dizziness. No tingling or numbness or nausea. If anything, she felt stronger, sharper.

"C'mon, Kayla," Johannes Goodall said. He gestured impatiently to her empty seat. "Let's get going." All around the table the empaths were sitting down and joining hands.

They think I've joined them, Kayla thought. *Perhaps I should. It's so easy. So very easy.*

She held out her hands to the others beside her and, out of the corner of her eye, she saw Yates smiling in approval.

She sank down and down. It was like a warm wash of fluid moving across her body, the touch of a lover, or the whisper of a sun-warmed breeze. Submerged once again in the groupmind she surrendered herself to the power of the all. So thrilling, so much more alive than ever before. She would never come out, never leave them. Never.

Like a giant bird of prey the groupmind swooped through the city, trolling for minds. Some were quiet, others hysterical, but none were particularly interesting. Wait, what was that? An amusing anomaly: two minds almost exactly alike. Twins. And the part of Kayla that was still a single entity—a minute part—awoke and recognized the very target she had feared and searched for.

—Catch them! There they are!

To her horror and frustration, the mindnet moved on past the men and the quarter in which they were hidden.

Kayla knew then that Yates had been careless and overconfident. Security would not find the twins. The groupmind would not bother itself with phantom N-ware, not when there might be dangerous mindspies in the city. They would concentrate on sniffing out stray empaths while explosives capable of destroying the city were sitting right under their noses.

Now she struggled in earnest, striving to break free from the locked embrace of the groupmind. Strong, it was so strong, while she was so small. Helpless, she floated, suspended, forced to go where the groupmind willed.

The mindnet swept inexorably over the nighttime city and carried Kayla along with it.

* * *

Midnight. Whispers. Wind in the street and the sound of bootheels on stone, receding. Inside the Crystal Palace all was quiet, the silence of the tomb. All were asleep in the quarters of the groupmind: every empath nestled softly into his or her bed, dreaming, perhaps, of dark, safe places.

Only Kayla, locked in, was wakeful, eyes open but watching nothing. She reached with her mind, grasping one thing and then another, knowing that other portions of the city were still awake and alive with noise and smoke and song.

Farsense took her into the Musicians' Quarter, searching, prowling. From there she moved on to the bars and taverns, looking for her crewmates. She found them in a cavernous place, drunken, dancing, and carefree. At least, most of them. But there, on the periphery, sat Iger, nursing a beer, gloomy and sullen. Darting into his mind with a narrow probe, she saw that he missed her with an odd combination of resentment and concern. Was she really in trouble, he wondered, or had she merely slipped away for a rendezvous with someone else?

Poor Iger, she thought. *I wish I could comfort him.*

She sent him an affectionate impulse, saw his mood lighten slightly, and moved on. There was Greer, returned from her clandestine mission and sitting in the midst of a group of Free Traders, arguing economic strategy. Despite her crewmate's seeming concentration, there was a part of her mind filled with fear and fury, convinced that Kayla had betrayed her and gone to the Trade Police.

She's not far wrong, Kayla thought. *But it's not Greer I'm betraying, it's a million people—including her—that I'm trying to save.*

And there, sitting on a stool near the bar, head nodding drowsily, was Third Child, thinking its alien thoughts. At her mindtouch the dalkoi looked up, startled, and cast about the bar as though searching for her.

Silly thing, she thought. *Can you really tell that it's me probing you? Can you hear me?*

Third Child whimpered and flexed its toes several times. Kayla got a strong sense image of her face overlaid with anxiety. Even Third Child was worried about her.

But she grew tired of the bar and her mind ranged past her friends, out of the bar, and into the night.

In vain she tried to return to the twins. Where were they now? Had they already set their bombs?

Below her a thousand minds cycled in various sleep patterns, muttering and sighing. There was no fun to be had in spying on the subconscious discharge of a sleeping mind. Kayla's probe circled back to the great Crystal Palace. And found another soul awake at this late hour. Who?

The mind was well-ordered, disciplined, and powerful. A man, accustomed to power, great power. With a start, Kayla realized that she had penetrated the consciousness of Prime Minister Pelleas Karlson.

Triple refraction with double shadow edges. Distinct dichroism. Looks very promising. If we get the same results from these stones as we did from the rest of the hoard, we might just have our proof. Finally.

Karlson was working in what seemed to be a private lab within his quarters. He was clearly agitated, very excited. Kayla listened even more closely.

Yes, the indices are very close, almost identical between the step-cut gems. I thought the different ore sites would influence the results, but that doesn't seem to matter. Faceting rather than source seems to dictate readings—and, by inference, effects upon the wearer. Very good. The next step will be working with the un-cut gems.

Kayla wondered where the prime minister had gained his gemology background. He sounded as knowledgeable as any assayer she had ever met. Curious to think of the great man alone at night, peering at gemstones.

She looked closer still and saw that these were not merely gemstones but mindstones and of high quality. The very highest. In fact, something about them was unsettling and familiar. She knew those stones, knew them intimately.

My father's mindstones, she thought. Somehow, Pelleas Karlson has gotten hold of them! *I've got to get them back.*

She probed him for some sign of who had delivered the stolen stones but received only blurred images. He didn't know. Perhaps his assistant? The security chief? She would probe everybody in the palace if necessary.

First thing to do was find out where Karlson's apartments were. And when he was out of them, find a way in and take back what was rightfully hers.

Chapter Seventeen

Breakfast arrived on a mech server. Kayla devoured the fresh grain cakes and fruit. Almost as soon as she had licked the last bit of berry from her fingers, there was a knock at the door.

Yates Keller, accompanied by two armed guards, stood waiting in the corridor. He wore a crisp white and gray tunic shot through with sparkling green threads, and gray leggings that ended in soft boots.

"So you've decided to join us," he said. "Good."

"What are the guards for?" Kayla said.

Yates shrugged an apology. "I've got a meeting. They'll take you to the rest of your friends."

Before Kayla could pursue it further, she heard footsteps come up behind her. A female officer in a brown uniform saluted Yates smartly.

"We've gotten rumors of increased Free Trade activity. Provocateurs, loose in the city."

"Keep scanning," Yates said. "And double the patrols. I don't like having troublemakers roaming around Vardalia. It makes me itchy."

The third officer looked apprehensive. Evidently when Yates Keller felt itchy, everyone around him had the distinct urge to scratch. "Very good," she said quickly.

"Yessir. Oh, we've got a tail in deep cover on one of their leaders, a woman, Greer Ciaran."

Greer! Who was watching her?

"Shall we have him move, pick her up?"

"No, let's wait and see if she leads us to the rest of her comrades."

"Very good, sir."

"I've got a meeting with the prime minister," Yates said. "I'll check back with you afterward. Meanwhile, arrest anybody who even sneezes in a suspicious way. The Trade Congress convenes tomorrow and I want things to be peaceful as the grave."

"Yessir."

He hurried away.

Kayla worked six hours with the groupmind, sweeping the city, picking one brain and then another, then had six hours to rest before an evening shift. The empaths, she learned, worked in a staggered pattern to ensure continuous scanning.

During her down time she returned to her probe of the prime minister.

Karlson was a good amateur gemologist and she saw that he was indeed on the verge of determining and cataloging the specific effects of mindstones dictated by each faceting pattern. Through him she learned that half-step cut stones of alternating thirteen and fourteen rectangular facets on a flat base enhanced tranquillity and a sense of well-being, while the pendeloque or pear-shaped pattern of forty-eight facets, twenty-four on each face, yielded sharpened awareness and penetrating powers of analysis. And the mirabile cut with its exponentially increasing facets was by far the most powerful, yielding strange hallucinations and disorienting surges of telepathy and other mind powers.

She saw, too, that Karlson hoped to gain controlling rights in the Styx mines through Yates Keller, thereby owning the source of both mindsalt and mindstones. Karlson's opinion of Yates was that he was a contemptible weakling, somebody who could be bought—or sold—for the promise of power. Kayla agreed completely.

Why don't you go out? she wondered. *At least visit some vassal trader. Visit the mines in Styx.*

But the prime minister's mind was impervious to her half-serious suggestions. Patience, she knew, was all that availed her. And patience, eventually, rewarded her.

Pelleas Karlson did leave his apartments, she discovered, between the hours of four and five in the morning. He was a night rover, preferring the quiet of deserted streets and his own company to the hustle and bustle of the noonday square.

Kayla brightened at this revelation. Much better to make her way through a quiet palace filled with shadows than attempt to shield herself from the full retinue of guards, clerks, and importuning traders.

She cast a mindpeek at the security cadre: two guards dozed near Karlson's rooms. The night security chief was busy in another part of the palace. She paused as her questing mind brushed against a familiar image: a face she knew. But how? She probed more deeply and frowned at the ugly information. So. Her stones had come to the palace by way of the *Falstaff*'s communications officer, Kelso. Kels had stolen her hoard and hidden it, then decided to wait until they made landfall on St. Ilban before fencing the stones. Kelso's contact was a palace guard, a sublieutenant with ambitions.

Kelso, you?

Kayla felt a pang of sadness. But she hardened her will against her former crewmate. If she ever got back to the ship, she would settle matters with Kelso, but now she had other business.

With the skills learned from Barabbas, it was easy to pick the lock of her room. Once outside the door she cloaked herself in shadowsense. Anyone she encountered would notice only an odd movement of air, a strange diffusion of light.

Kayla crept through light and darkness past the quar-

ters of her fellow empaths and to the portcullis which
led to the main body of the palace. She paused at the
maze of passageways and tunnels. Which one to take?
It was so hard to see. Whether from neglect or econ-
omy, the subordinate routes were dimly lit, with alternating glow globes extinguished altogether. Trust in
mindsight, she decided. The way to the prime minister's apartments was through the left-most passage.
Her mind's eye led her surely through the gloom.

Soon she had left behind the gloom of the tunnels
for the thick red carpets and richly-embroidered draperies of the palace proper. The hallway was bathed in
soft golden light, and she began to pass guards at regular intervals, all of them staring straight ahead and
never blinking as she walked by not two feet away.
She felt a mischievous urge to tweak each nose but
quelled it and continued on her way. Farther along, a
crew of mechs were engaged in cleaning duties, and a
bald-headed clerk was sitting alone, head propped on
his hand, staring at a cube covered with orange numbers.

Quietly Kayla padded into the private wing of the
palace. The draperies became more sumptuous, the car-
peting even deeper and more luxurious. Racks of wall
globes gave way to single fixtures of exquisitely
carved crystal.

She passed under an arch covered by crystal filigree
and supported by pillars of black marble that gave off
opalescent glints, red-green-yellow. Down this way,
past the crystalline bust with laser-diode eyes. Into a
passage lined by green and silver tapestries.

There. The massive onyx door flanked by fluted am-
ethyst columns. Carefully she probed the apartments
behind the portal. Empty. She detected no other mind
in the vicinity. If he was true to habit, Karlson should
be gone for another hour. That gave her plenty of time.

She penetrated the prime minister's rooms easily and

stood for a moment in appreciative shock. He lived like royalty, did Pelleas Karlson.

The floor was bare, of a polished green stone striated by veins of gold. Jewel-bright fixtures jutted from the purple marble walls. The air was subtly perfumed and the sound of gentle chords, rising and falling from hidden mech instruments, gave a sense of tranquillity.

Broad wall seats lined a row of windows. Outside, Vardalia glittered like a jewel box whose contents had been upended and left to sparkle until dawn.

A huge holoportrait of Karlson dominated the far wall of the room and peered at her somberly from beneath jutting brows. Karlson's bald head glistened and his mouth was curved in a slight smile. But his dark eyes weren't smiling and they seemed to be following her as she walked across the room. Kayla wrinkled her nose at the picture. *I don't care if you are the prime minister,* she thought. *You have something that belongs to me and I want it!*

Several rooms led off from the main sitting area but none of them contained scientific equipment of any sort. Search though she might, Kayla couldn't find the prime minister's private gemology lab. Was it in a different part of the palace? Had she been mistaken?

No. She knew what she had seen. Her mindstones, they had to be here somewhere.

In a study filled with antique books a mosaic wall panel caught her interest. It was a depiction of the Cavinas System replete with twin suns in the center: a massive emerald and diamond in twin orbits. That tawny topaz cabochon over there had to be Liage, and the fire opal beyond it was giant Xenobe with her sapphire moon, St. Ilban. And here, this ruby-flecked geode—that was Styx. Kayla caressed the sparkling cabochon. *Home,* she thought.

Something clicked.

A slab of marble paneling swung back to reveal a room glittering with metal. The walls were lined by shelves loaded with vid cubes. In the middle of the polished black floor was a golden table gleaming with equipment and mindstones.

Mindstones spilled out of cartons and crates, casually scattered across the tabletop like so many gleaming marbles, blue-red, bronze, and green.

Kayla took one step forward, took another, and plunged her hands into the pile of gems. There were so many here. How would she ever find hers? Then her hands closed on a piece of soft cloth. She pulled it forth and saw that she held a sack, a sack of mindstones that bore her father's initials: RR. A dry sob welled up in her throat, but she fought it down. And as she tucked the sack into her pocket, an alarm went off.

The groupmind came rushing at her, rebounded off her shield, made another pass. She knew she couldn't hold out against it. Nor could she hope to defeat it.

But surely it had a weak spot, a vulnerable place. Wasn't there even one anomaly in a group of so many minds? There had to be. But in order to find it she had to risk everything.

She heard footsteps pounding in the corridor outside. No time to think. Kayla made her decision and as the mindnet swooped at her, she dropped her shields and gave herself up into its embrace.

Instead, she found herself in a space surrounded by glowing minds that she recognized easily. The groupmind was an intimidating entity, powerful, nearly invulnerable. But its member minds were not entirely shielded.

She plucked a stray fantasy from Miriam Crown's mind, blew ferocious life into it, and threw it at the group: A giant bird with mad eyes and spiked red teeth in a green beak, flying at their exposed faces, trying to pluck out their eyes.

As they cried out, Kayla hunted among them and

found one mind more pliant than the rest, less shielded. The flaw in the net. Rusty.

She bore down upon him with her nearsense. Pushed, then pushed harder.

Rusty gasped, flailed, tried to call for help.

I'm sorry, Rusty.

Kayla bore down on her old friend.

Suddenly she was in a dark and crowded space—Rusty's unconscious, the junk heap of his mind. She saw the scars, the damage that Yates Keller's machines had done. But she didn't have time to think about it. Kayla rummaged through the tangled piles of images and peculiar associations, unexpressed urges, and infantile fears. She lingered at this last segment, digging and then discarding one image as too obscure, another as too eccentric. but here, here was one, a primal fear, big enough to shatter a man, or a life. Surely it had shattered hers, once.

Kayla grabbed it up and pushed it, hard, hard as she could, at the minds of her fellows, injecting them with a bad dream of their own making, turning their worst fantasy into a potent, living, terrible weapon.

What was more awful to a group of miners than a cave-in?

Kayla gave them a quake such as had never been experienced before on any land, in any mine, or mind. The walls fell in on them, all of their carefully constructed defenses toppling, useless. No air, no light, no hope. Tons of rock came down to crush them, and fear, white-hot and sulfurous, smothered them, forcing breath from their lungs and obliterating every thought, every word in their minds.

Shrieking, the groupmind came apart. As it splintered, Kayla was caught by the awful wave, dragged under into the panic, the tumultuous fears, and felt her own mind begin to give under the onslaught. She was being pulled in every direction at once, was in every mind in the group. The strain was too great, she would crack. *Pull out, pull out, get away now!*

She broke free and with now-weakened flickering mindsight looked back at the carnage she had wrought, the scattered empaths reeling away from the table, clutching their throats. Only one figure was still, very still. Head thrown back, eyes empty. Rusty's face was oddly peaceful, and his mouth was curved in a smile of what could only be termed relief.

Rusty . . .

Kayla couldn't allow herself to think about him. She had done what she had to do. Fought off the groupmind and reduced it to broken components. She withdrew from its feeble presence and was once more looking at the rich furnishings of Pelleas Karlson's private apartments.

Weaving on her feet, her balance gone, senses untrustworthy, Kayla leaned against the wall as she propelled herself, hand over hand, toward the door. She pressed the keypad and stepped out into the corridor into a mass of guards.

There was little of her left, but she used up still more of herself as she showed them the icy flames, the bird with teeth, the nightmares born of their own minds, and she burned, screaming with them. But as they fell, she managed to pull herself past them and away.

Her legs felt as though they were going to give out any moment. Her head ached and her vision had odd shadows around the edges.

Got to stop, she thought. *Too much. Got to rest.*

Momentarily safe in a dim corridor, she leaned against the wall, panting. The sound of people rushing about, shouting, reached her and she knew she had to push on. Up the corridor and off to the side. But which way? Although the pain was great, she used a probe to find the closest exit.

There. Force the door. Outside. Keep moving.

The predawn gloom was giving way to rose and

gold, and a light wind brought fresh cool air to her lungs. Kayla hurried through the great plaza, oblivious to the merchants who were already dragging out their baskets of food and handicrafts, getting ready for another day's trade.

The mindstone sack bounced against her waist as she ran. Was it worth it to become a fugitive again? Yes, yes, for the last link with her parents and all that she had lost. She couldn't abandon it, wouldn't let Karlson use her father's best stones for his self-serving experiments.

Kayla was standing in a side street leading to the main plaza. People hurried by, taking no notice of her. She saw that all trace of her escape hatch had disappeared. Behind her was a wall of smooth stone.

She took a deep breath, inhaling the odd sweet and sour spices of city air. Part of her wanted to find a safe hiding place, to sink down and sleep until she had regained her strength. But she couldn't, not yet.

The twins, Onzerib and Douzerib. Greer.

Somehow she had to find them, stop that maniacal duo before they blew up the city or, failing that, warn Greer before it was too late.

She tried a nearsense probe. No good. Her head throbbed and a stabbing pain made her gasp. She had overtaxed herself. However she found the twins, it would be without the help of her empathic powers. Kayla rocked back on her heels, frustrated.

Wait, she thought. The *Corazon*. It had long- and short-range scanners. She might be able to use them to find the twins.

Kayla practically flew back to the port, hurrying along the slick pavements of Vardalia, dodging merchants and bureaucrats.

The ship was empty. Thankfully, Kayla made her way to ops and turned on the scanners. It took her a while to work her way through the symbols and sizes available for scan, longer still to detail the image to the point at which the machine would not merely pick out every mustachioed dark-haired gent in Vardalia. As Kayla was putting the finishing touches on the scan order, a familiar sound made her look up from the machine.

Chirping inquisitively, Third Child came padding into the room. As soon as it saw Kayla, it began to circle her, obviously hoping for a neck rub.

"Not now, Third Child. Sit down and be quiet."

Third Child didn't want to be quiet. Kayla finally used a firm mind command and the alien fell silent.

The scanner commenced its search, beeping occasionally and flashing green and yellow lights in mosaic patterns across its screen. Kayla settled back in her chair, watching and waiting, wondering all the while if she were too late.

A bell rang and the scanner displayed a magnified segment of city map in which a street had been outlined in red. Kayla knew that this was as fine a focus as the scan could manifest.

She copied down the address and prepared to set out. At the last moment, she pulled a disruptor from its wall mount and armed it. There was no sense in taking chances.

She was at the main port when the dalkoi caught up with her and started to follow her out the door.

"No," she said, and pushed it back inside the ship. "You can't come. I'm sorry. Wait for Iger, he should be back soon."

Third Child chirped indignantly.

She closed the port and hurried back to the main slidewalk into the city.

The neighborhood to which the scanner had sent her was a peaceful residential area set off in the southwestern portion of the city. The houses were lovely, well-maintained, and each one was as closed to her as a shielded mind.

Do I dare risk a mindscan? What else could she do?

Carefully, Kayla put out a narrow probe, sweeping the lower levels of the houses.

She felt a bit wobbly, but the scan spread out smoothly, touching a frenetic mind here, a somnolent one there, and two engaged in such furious lovemaking that it brought a blush to her cheeks.

But the scan was narrowing as though some shadow had fallen, sweeping up from both sides, blotting our her nearsense. Gone. Her powers were still untrustworthy.

The disruptor in her belt pressed uncomfortably against her ribs as her heart beat a frantic tattoo. The street yielded nothing. She would have to employ some other means of finding Douzerib and Onzerib.

Perhaps the bars of Vardalia? She had first set eyes upon the twins in a tavern. Instinct told her to look in rundown places in unfashionable districts.

Kayla wended her way back to the center of the city and began to follow signs toward the old town. Sure enough, the architecture soon changed from modern towers to squat buildings almost stooping with age. The street traffic was more colorful—and more ragged. She saw a pickpocket at work, and farther down the street a row of open brothels with sleepy whores yawning in their windows. And taverns, almost a dozen.

Kayla squared her shoulders and entered the nearest saloon. It was cool and dark inside. An old woman with a seamed face and white hair sat in a rickety chair, chin on her breast, dreaming by the fire. Behind the bar a young woman with eyes of different colors, one blue and the other light gray, watched Kayla with predatory alertness.

"I'm looking for someone," Kayla said. "Two people, actually."

"Do you want something to drink?"

Kayla gave her a sour glance and fished in her pocket for some credits. "Beer," she said. "A pale dry one."

The girl shorted her on the change, but Kayla decided not to complain. She took a sip of the tangy brew and said, "The ones I'm looking for are a couple of brothers. Twins. Mustaches. Fancy dressers. Have you seen anybody like that?"

"Nope." The bartender moved down to the far end of the bar and began polishing a tarnish-blackened spout with her filthy rag. The old woman by the fire snored quietly.

No help here. Kayla put her change in her pocket, finished her beer, and walked out without another word.

Where to next? Heart sinking, she looked up the street. At least six bars had their signs flashing in the fading daylight. With a jolt Kayla realized that she would never succeed in finding the twins this way.

Back on Mammoth Station, it had been easy to trace Greer, when a dozen bars were all she had to investigate. But Vardalia was a city, the nerve center of the Trade Alliance. It would take Kayla a lifetime to visit every bar here.

"Chirrup!"

Kayla spun around, not believing her ears.

The dalkoi stood in the middle of the street. People passing by turned to stare, obviously surprised by their first glimpse of the alien.

"Third Child! How did you get here? You followed me."

The dalkoi must have opened the *Cabeza*'s main portal. "This is no place for you," Kayla said. "Go back to the ship!"

A small crowd was growing around them. Before Kayla knew it, a police officer had appeared and was grabbing hold of the dalkoi.

"Where'd you come from?" the officer said. "How'd you get loose?"

"It's with me," Kayla said.

"Sure," replied the cop. "Looking to get a reward?

Well, now it's coming with me." He reached for the dalkoi. Kayla stepped between them.

"But that's my pet."

"Is it now? And I suppose you've got a permit for it, issued by the prime minister himself?"

"I left it on the ship."

The cop laughed nastily. "In that case, your pet will be waiting for you at district headquarters. Just bring your permit and we'll release him."

Kayla knew that if she left Third Child now, she would never see it again. "Why can't I take it with me and bring you the permit?"

"Rules. We don't allow these critters on the streets. They get jittery, cause accidents."

"You mean there are other dalkois on St. Ilban?" Kayla said. "How many? Where?"

The cop began to look edgy, then annoyed. "I ask the questions," he said. "Now get me that permit if you want to keep this thing."

Third Child apparently was following the conversation and in no way liked what it heard, because it began to shrill angrily, pulling away from the officer.

"Settle down or I'll have to stun you," the cop said.

Kayla wanted to scream. She couldn't allow the policeman to take Third Child away, and she didn't know if Iger even had a permit for the dalkoi. What's more, she didn't trust the officer alone with the dalkoi, not for a minute.

She could run, but the cop had a gun and would probably shoot her or Third Child.

Shadowsense. It was the only way. But she didn't know if she had the strength.

She tried to summon a shadowfield. Something sputtered briefly around the periphery of her vision and died. She tried again, with even less result.

Damn, she thought. Then, suddenly, as though something had intervened, a shadowfield of surprising proportion swooped down upon the unwary policeman. He stood, enveloped within the foggy mindfield, gaping blankly as Kayla stared in amazement. Where had it come from?

The dalkoi chirped.

No time to worry about that now. She grabbed Third Child by its vestigial shoulder and hurried down the nearest side street.

A series of zigzag cutbacks took them through alleys, past startled passersby and vendors, until she was convinced they were safe.

"Now," she said. "Go back to the ship and stay there!" She gave the dalkoi a shove with her mind. It squeaked briefly, but after a moment's hesitation, it began to waddle toward the port. Kayla watched it go with relief and sadness. "Take good care of Iger for me if I don't come back," she whispered.

When it was out of sight, she turned a corner and skidded down a narrow stone passage that was more stairs than street. Up a shallow incline. Around a bend.

Kayla's legs felt rubbery and strange. *Got to rest,* she thought. *Hide until my strength comes back.*

Farther from the city center. Away from the shadows of the Crystal Palace and the reach of its creatures.

Like a sleepwalker she stumbled up one street and down another, leaning against walls, propelling herself by her hands when necessary.

Just a few more steps, she told herself. *Just a few more.*

The street globes dimmed as the sun climbed in the sky. Kayla began to recognize the buildings around her.

I'm in the musicians' quarter. Arsobades ought to be around here somewhere. Her throat tightened. It was no use looking for her former crewmates. She would just get them in trouble.

There, behind the sign of a music shop, was a small overhang, and beneath it a dead space shielded by a planter. She crawled into it, curled up, and slept.

She awoke as a cold rain descended upon her.

Standing above her was a man with a gold and crystal tooth that caught the sun's light when he smiled. He held a watering can in his hand.

"This isn't a bed for street rats," he told her. "Off with you. Scat. I don't even let my musician friends sleep here. Bad for business."

Kayla stared at him boldly. "Musician friends? And what about friends of your musician friends? Friends of Arsobades?"

"Arsobades?" The man stared at her suspiciously. "And how do you know him?"

"Shipped out with him on the *Falstaff*."

"You? Hah! Where's your spacer suit? You don't much have the spacer look, girlie. And the *Falstaff*'s not in port."

"But I do know Arsobades."

"Everybody knows Arsobades. Be off with you." He shooed her away with his hand and she saw for the moment the edge of what looked like a Free Trader sigil peeking out of his shirt cuff.

"And are all Free Traders so quick to turn their backs on friends in need?" she demanded.

He stared at her as she pulled down the back of her tunic, exposing her shoulder blade and the tattoo that Greer had put there.

A muscle worked in his cheek.

"Come," he said.

He led her to a door at the back of the shop. "Down here." Together they descended into a basement, and from there to a subbasement. His expression was grave. He opened a small round portal and nodded for her to go through it. "Walk until you see daylight," he said. "You'll be at the far side of the quarter."

Kayla stared at him in amazement. "Tunnels?"

His mouth formed a grim line. "They were cisterns, once. Later, prisons and access routes. Abandoned for years, except by those who know how to use them. You should be safe in there."

He spread his hands and she saw again the black starburst tattoo of the Free Traders. "The Trade Police are no friends of mine. Go carefully, girl. Good luck." He shut the door behind her.

She was alone in the darkness once more.

Chapter Eighteen

Kayla walked quickly through the dank tunnel. Far away dripping provided a counterpoint to the beat of her footsteps. Occasionally she brushed against unseen cobwebs and recoiled as strands of feathery stuff caressed her cheek or pulled at her hair. All around her were strange rustlings and echoes, the squeaks and footfalls of small creatures. Her pace increased until she was nearly running.

Stay calm, she told herself. *It's like the tunnels of Styx, just wetter and dirtier.*

As she pushed her way through a narrow passage, she felt the unmistakable pressure of metal against her arms and the sound of chains sliding along stone. Was there someone there beside her in the darkness? No. The chains made a rusty song as they swung freely, to and fro. *Just some poor prisoner's manacles,* she thought, and shuddered.

Kayla walked for what seemed like hours. Was the tunnel sloping upward? She couldn't be sure. There, was the blackness softening, turning to gray? Yes, yes. And ahead was a glimmer of brightness, the promise of sunlight. A gust of fresh air hit her cheeks and she increased her pace.

Her long walk ended in a stand of bushes that sported fragrant yellow and purple flowers. Kayla peered out between the branches. She was in a corner of a deserted, tiny patch of greensward. At the boundaries, through the trees, glimpses of graceful buildings could be seen.

Kayla stepped out into the sunlight, took in a deep lungful of air, and cast away the shadows through which she had come. The smell of green and growing things reinvigorated her. She would find the twins. Yes, and turn their N-ware over to the authorities. And if she survived all of that, and her crewmates were still in Vardalia, she would, by the gods, try to go back to them. Maybe she and Greer would even be able to hash this thing out between them and make peace.

At the thought of her crewmates, a wave of longing swept over her. If only she were back with them, back in space, and had never heard of the twins or their N-ware! Never seen Yates Keller or the miners from Styx in their plush prison at the Crystal Palace. Never seen Rusty.

The mindstone sack pressed against her waist and she remembered that she would not have recovered that but for the trip to Vardalia. *Be grateful for what is,* she thought, *forget about what was, and keep moving.*

The tiny park emptied into a quiet residential street with well-kept buildings painted creamy yellow and orange. It was unfamiliar, this quarter, but she knew from her research on the *Corazon* that the twins were somewhere nearby.

House to house, she thought. *That's how I'll have do it.*

Kayla began with a needle-thin mindprobe. It formed up nicely and she was reassured by its strength.

She passed through one mind as it watched a vid cube and moved on to another fretting over accounts. Not here. Not there, either. One by one, mind by mind, she probed and passed on, up one street and down another.

Just as her control began to waver and the edges of the probe to blur, she brushed over two unmistakable nearly-identical mind signatures. In a small house on the corner. The twins. She had found them at last.

But her sense of triumph faded as she peered up at the smooth pink and green facade of the house. How would she get in? There were no windowsills, nothing to grab hold of, no access.

She crept along the alley beside the house but paused at the corner nearest the backyard. Several voices were raised in argument although their words were indistinct. Too many potential witnesses.

Side doors? There were none to be seen.

The roof, then.

She shinnied up a drainpipe in the corner, pulled herself hand over hand until she was standing on tiled shingles. The roof had obviously been neglected for some time: the tiles were cracked, some were missing, and at least a third were spattered with animal droppings bleached white by the twin suns. All around were other roofs and stovepipes. She walked carefully: the tiles were slippery underfoot and steeply canted: one misstep could send her tumbling down three stories to crack her head on the pavement.

In the center of the roof she found a trapdoor, but it was locked tightly, and, try as she might with every trick Rab had shown her, she could not trigger the combination to open it.

Kayla clambered toward the rear, wondering if she should climb down and try to pry open the back door. It was almost dusk. She might be able to slip in unnoticed. As she peered down, she saw triangular vents for what must be the attic. They meshed so neatly with the building's decorative tile pattern that she hadn't seen them at first.

The vents were narrow, scarcely as wide as her shoulders, but they were portals nonetheless.

On the street below the traffic was sparse. No one passing looked up to see a slender girl swing herself over the edge of the roof and disappear into the side of the building.

She was in a shallow shadowed room, a crawl space, really. There had to be a way down into the house proper from here, else why build this false attic at all? She scrabbled about on hands and knees, feeling her way.

Rough stucco tore at her hands and knees. Faint squeaks came from small beady-eyed creatures nesting in the far corners. The sweet-stale air was so warm that Kayla had no sensation of taking in anything with each inhalation. Her hand brushed through a pile of flaking debris in which things slithered and moved. Gasping, she recoiled, took a deep gulp of dead air, and forced herself to put her palm down again.

There, beneath her hand. A crusted metal latch. She pulled, it gave, and a heavy door slid back on squeaking rollers.

Kayla looked down into the house.

A tattered rug of faded blue-and-silver fibers sat upon the floor—miles below her. The hallway was empty.

Kayla lowered herself through the opening until she dangled by her fingertips. Then she let go.

Whump!

She landed in a crouch. Around her danced imaginary stars and too-real clots of dust. Overhead the attic door gaped wide. No help for that now. Kayla made her way down the hall and, beyond the threshold of a timbered doorway, spied a staircase. Probing, she found that there was no one nearby and down she went, quickly, quietly. The stairs were silent and her progress steady.

She crept from doorsill to doorsill, rounded a corner, and came upon both Onzerib and Douzerib, seated side by side before an enormous vid cube.

Onzerib leaped to his feet. "What in four hells?" he cried.

His twin jumped up a beat later. "Who are you? How did you get in here?"

Kayla smiled her broadest smile, as though she had finally found her oldest and dearest friends. "Don't you guys remember me?"

Douzerib squinted at her. "We've met before?"

"On Mammoth Station."

"Yes," Onzerib said, nodding slowly. "Yes, I remember. The crewmate of Greer Ciaran. Brother, you remember, don't you?"?

"Of course," Douzerib said. "Your name is Katie, yes?"

"That's right. And Greer sent me with a message for you."

"She did? What is it?"

Kayla cast a glance around the room. "Is this a secured space? We need privacy."

Douzerib gestured impatiently. "This way." He led her out of the room and into a small den lined by silvery interlocking plates. "Safe enough in here to whisper the combination to the prime minister's bank box."

"Are you sure? Can't be too careful." Kayla made a great show of checking the door for cracks, all the while trying to probe Douzerib's mind for a hint of where the N-ware was. Her nearsense sputtered and flared uselessly.

"I told you," he said. "This room is shielded."

"If you say so. Greer wanted me to tell you that the cargo which you purchased must be returned. It's not what you thought."

The twins exchanged quick looks. "What do you mean?"

"I can explain it more easily if I show you. Is the cargo here?"

"Not on the premises, no." Both sets of dark eyes were fixed upon her intently.

"Perhaps we ought to go where you have it, then."

Onzerib shook his head. "It's not safe right now. Too many patrols. They're searching for somebody."

Kayla paused, chagrined. She hadn't considered this added complication. But she had to find out where that N-ware was before she immobilized the twins. "Well," she said. "We can go there after dark, can't we?"

Again the brothers exchanged glances. "Yes, of course," Onzerib said. He gestured for her to follow him into another room. She nodded, gripped the doorway, and was halfway through it when she felt a strange leadenness creep down her arms. Her legs refused to obey her and her eyelids were too heavy to stay open. Swaying, she turned to the twin nearest her, and fell down, down, down, into silence and white space.

* * *

Kayla's mouth was parched dry as dust. She opened her eyes, wished she hadn't, lifted her head, and saw that she was someplace strange. A stone room, cold and damp. Her hands were secured behind her and her legs were similarly tied, forcing her into a painful ball. They must have used a contact sedative, she thought bleakly. Coated the lintels or walls.

"You wanted to see the merchandise?" said a smug voice. Onzerib. "Here it is. Some of it."

Kayla moved her head to one side and squinted up at him. Her heart thudded heavily as she took in her surroundings. Boxes and crates were stacked haphazardly, all with the universal sign for nuclear materials. She had found the N-ware, all right. Or, rather, it had found her.

A foot shod in gleaming black vat leather prodded her, not gently, in the side. "Liar! Fool, did you think we believed you for even a moment?"

Kayla tried to protect her exposed stomach and sides. "What are you talking about? Let me go! Greer will be furious when she learns about this."

The twins laughed. "Greer?" Onzerib said. "She'll

probably thank us. Your dear friend Greer has put the word out that you're a turncoat. Said that you deserted your crew and fled. You're not to be trusted."

"But that's not true."

"No? We don't care. You obviously took great pains to find us. Now you can wait for Greer—or the millennium."

"You're going to set off the N-ware." It wasn't a question.

They smiled derisively. "Not if our demands are met."

"What demands?"

"To force Karlson's government to remove tariffs on trade with the outer systems."

"And if he refuses?"

Onzerib shrugged. "Then there might be a small accident under the palace. A contained explosion. We wouldn't want too many people to be killed . . ."

"You are crazy," Kayla said. "What has Karlson ever done to you?"

"He destroyed our family."

"Family? But I thought you were clones."

"We are. But we were a six-clone before Pelleas Karlson hired our brothers. He was going to bring them to St. Ilban, to Vardalia. Train them in diplomacy. He promised much. What he gave was death. The ship he sent for them exploded—with them aboard."

She shook her head in disbelief. "Surely it wasn't intentional."

"What does that matter?" Onzerib said. "He put them at risk, didn't he? We've never been the same."

Douzerib nodded vehemently. "If he doesn't agree to our demands, then he'll suffer just like we did. It's only fair."

"What are you going to do to me?" Kayla said.

"We'll notify the Free Trade presidium. They'll decide what action to take. Probably turn you over to the Trade Police as a symbol of how we treat traitors."

She cast about for a way to stop them as they began walking out the door.

She attempted to seize them, to freeze their legs. But again her nearsense merely sputtered. Her own exhaustion and impairment, or, perhaps, something in the drug they had given her, was interfering with her already-weakened empathic powers.

The twins left her in the dark, alone. The sound of their footsteps faded.

In desperation, she thought of farsense. She hadn't tried that, yet.

She gathered herself and was gratified to find that farsense seemed to be working. She reached out, latching onto unknown sleeping minds somewhere in the city. —*Help!* she thought. *Please! Help me!*

No one stirred. Not one mind came awake under her empathic touch.

Straining, she reached farther. Beyond this quarter, this huddle of houses and out into the spaceport.

—*Salome. Barabbas. Somebody. Please.*

The familiar feel of her crewmates' minds nearly made her cry out in relief. But she had to contact their conscious minds or it was no good. One by one she tapped, knocked, pleaded. All slumbered on, not one responded. She was at the limits of her strength, her powers unraveling, when she remembered Third Child. If no human could hear her, perhaps the dalkoi could.

—*Third Child! Hear me. Wake up, Third Child.*

She didn't think she had the strength for it. The dalkoi would never hear her. Yet somehow her farsense stayed steady, as if some powerful force was feeding energy into and through her.

—*Third Child!*

She had a mind image of the dalkoi coming fully alert and casting about the room, mouth twitching. It heard, it knew.

—*Come to me, Third Child. You can find me, I know you can. Bring Iger and come right away.*

Before she could say more, she began to lose contact. In desperation she cast an impression of the quarter, the house, the street outside. Did it register? Did Third Child hear her and understand?

She closed her eyes and faded into a twilight realm between wakefulness and sleep. How long she languished there she had no idea. A sound roused her and she rose slowly to full awareness to find that something—someone—was making noise in the room behind her. The twins, come back to finish her? She'd fight them any way she could, even brainburn them, if she could manage. Kayla lay very still, marshaling her strength, when she heard a familiar sound.

Djeep! Djeeeep!

Someone was behind her, tugging at her restraints.

"Katie!" Iger's voice, at her ear. "What is this? What happened?"

His face swam into focus: skin permanently tanned, blue eyes, strong nose and slightly too prominent chin. A wonderful face.

"Gods," she said, her voice small and thick with relief. "You came."

"You were expecting me?"

"You. And Third Child." From the corner of her eye she saw the dalkoi sticking close, anxiously watching as Iger cut the ropes on her legs with a vibroblade. The blade's passage was nothing more than a humming shiver.

"I don't get it," Iger said.

"I called the dalkoi with my mind."

"You did? And it heard you?"

"We've got some kind of link. You said so yourself." She thought, but did not say, *And you do, too. You must have some sort of latent empathy. That's why Third Child stays close to you. And what makes you a good pilot, too.*

"So," Iger said. "You called Third Child and I got yanked out of a sound sleep and dragged into a strange part of Vardalia." He cut the ropes on her arms. "They tied you up good, like a bambera for market." He shut off the knife, and put it back his pocket. "How did you get messed up here?"

"It's a long story. But let's just say that I was stupid—in the extreme. The rest can wait. What we have to do now can't." She paused, surveying the room full of armaments. "We've got to get this stuff out of here before the owners come back."

Iger took in the room's contents and his eyes widened. "Hey," he said. "It looks like the old nuclears we traded away on Mammoth Station."

"Exactly. But it's not all of them."

"What's it doing here?"

"Greer sold it to two jokers who brought it here. Remember, I tried to tell you? They want to use the N-ware as a bargaining point with Pelleas Karlson—or so they say."

Iger shrugged. "What of it? That's their business, isn't it?"

"Iger, they're so crazy that they might just set the stuff off. I think they've already mined the city with some of the nuclears."

"Nobody's that crazy."

Kayla felt her patience evaporate. "Don't be naive. I goddam saw it, Iger. Saw their plans in their minds!"

"And who appointed you the savior of us all?"

"Me." She glared at him. "I didn't plan to get this involved. I only wanted to save Greer's life. But now I'm in too deep. Are you going to help? If not, thanks very much for rescuing me and you can go to hell."

For a moment they stood, gazes locked. Then Iger smiled slowly. "What do you want to do first? Get this stuff out of here?"

"We can't haul it all. And we don't want to get caught with it, either. Can't we dismantle it somehow?"

"N-ware as old as this? Are you an archeo-engineer? I'm not." Iger looked at the tightly packed cylinders and shook his head. "The last thing life on Liage teaches you is how to deal with a mess of nuclears."

Third Child had been sniffing the N-ware containers with obvious disdain. It paused, gave a strange, excited squeal, opened its mouth wide, convulsed, and vomited a thick, gluey purple mass onto the nearest cylinder. Almost immediately the mass hardened and darkened.

"Gods, what's happening?" Kayla said. "Is it sick?"

"I don't know." Iger peered closely. "No, I don't think so. The only other time I saw it do this was when a baby bambera died. Third Child covered it with that glop."

"Lovely."

"Maybe it's trying to help you, Katie."

"I don't see how."

"When this stuff dries, it's as hard as ferroceramic. Even a laser can't drill through it."

Kayla said, "Do you think it could cover everything in here with that stuff?"

"I don't know. There's a lot of N-ware and only one dalkoi."

For an hour they watched as Third Child covered crate after crate. Finally it sagged, exhausted.

"But that's only half of the nuclears," said Kayla. "There's still enough left to kill most of the city."

Iger gave her a sharp look. "Third Child has to rest. If you want it to do anything else, you'll have to feed it."

"With what?" Kayla held out her empty hands. "We'll have to go out into the city."

"And bring food back here?"

"I don't think we should risk leaving Third Child alone," she said. "Can you carry it? Throw your jacket over it so nobody sees it? There's got to be a place in this quarter where we can get food."

"If you say so." Iger shouldered the sleeping dalkoi and followed Kayla through the door.

* * *

They spent the better part of an hour searching in vain for a food stall, but the quarter was quiet and locked up tight. The dalkoi flopped like a lifeless doll in Iger's arms, eyes tightly closed.

"Nothing," Kayla said. "Damn it, we'll have to look somewhere else."

"But how do we find our way back here?"

"Let me worry about that. C'mon."

They took a twisting route up quiet streets and between two towering silver buildings that eventually led them to a small plaza crowded with shops and food stalls.

"Two plates of choba stew," Kayla told the counterman at a sidewalk stand. "Make it fast." She dug into her pocket and used the last of her credits to pay.

A bench in a quiet corner was shielded by red-leafed bushes and they settled there gratefully. At the rich scent of the food, the dalkoi roused, pushed its nose into the plate, and began devouring stew so quickly that Kayla was afraid it would regurgitate everything right there on the spot.

Somehow, the dalkoi kept every ounce of it down. When the plate was empty, Third Child sat back, looked at her with wide, bright eyes, and ventured an interrogatory quirch as if to say, "is that all?"

"Sorry," said Kayla. "No dessert."

Third Child blinked rapidly, leaned back, and bit a healthy mouthful out of the red-leafed hedge behind them.

"Hey," Kayla said. "Don't do that."

Iger grabbed at the dalkoi. "Are you nuts? Stop it."

It chirped and took another bite.

A woman peered out of an upstairs window, looked down, and cried, "My garden!"

Kayla jumped to her feet. "Let's get out of here."

"Stop them," the woman yelled. "Police! Get that wild animal and lock it up."

"Definitely time to go," Iger said. He grabbed Third

Child, heaved the dalkoi over his shoulder as it shrilled angrily, and ran down the street with Kayla right behind him.

They pounded across a small footbridge and into a quarter of broad boulevards. From there they passed into a park lined with yellow-flowered hedges. At the center of the greensward was a bandshell of elaborate bronze petals. A concert was taking place and a well-turned-out audience sat on carved benches and chairs in the warm breeze, enjoying the music. The men wore elaborately embroidered stretchsuits and matching visors while many of the women sported swirling coiffures in which mindstones glinted.

Third Child lifted its head, chirped happily, and jumped off Iger's shoulder. It landed in the lap of a large woman in a silvery tunic and pressed its head against a huge mindstone pendant at her throat. The woman cried out and tried vainly to dislodge the dalkoi as her companion, a thin woman with jet-black skin and pearl-white hair, made sweeping gestures with her program, attempting to shoo it away.

"Get it off me," the woman shrilled in a voice made brittle by fear. "Horrible beast." Tears ran down her cheeks.

"Third Child," Kayla shouted. "What in hell are you doing? Get over here!"

The dalkoi gave the matron one last affectionate rub and jumped down. The woman put one hand upon her pendant, grew pale, and put the other over her eyes.

Kayla reached out to grab the dalkoi's shoulder, but it ducked under her hand and dashed into a tightly-packed group of mindstone-bedecked music lovers.

As the dalkoi rubbed its head from one faceted stone to another, an odd effect took place. The stones' ruby-blue lights dimmed, faded, and vanished. They became ashen and pale, as though their inner fire had been snuffed out.

Third Child grew more animated by the moment. It

seemed to draw strength from each ruby-blue-green stone it rubbed against.

Is it possible? Kayla wondered. *Gods, can it really be? Is the dalkoi extinguishing the mindstones by absorbing their peculiar energy?*

Third Child made for an elderly gentleman wearing a white suit and a fine mindstone stickpin.

"Get away!" the old man cried, his hands flailing helplessly. "Stop it!"

Chirp.

The mindstone at the man's cravat was a mere ashen ghost of its former brilliance, all luster gone. And Third Child glowed with ever-increasing vigor, its skin giving off a faint lavender aura. The old man slumped in his seat, unconscious.

"Iger," Kayla said. "I don't believe it. Somehow the dalkoi's devouring the energy of the mindstones."

"He's not doing their owners much good, either. Let's grab him."

Cries of outrage drowned the orchestra's music. The conductor squinted over his uniformed shoulder, trying to make out the disruption of his concert.

"Thief!" cried a woman with flowing green hair.

"Criminal."

"Police, get the police!"

Iger grabbed Third Child around the neck and Kayla took its feet. Quickly they trundled their wriggling burden away from the bandshell and out of the park. They staggered down an alley, across a busy lane of traffic, and into another alley, emerging by a row of tattered shop awnings.

Kayla set the dalkoi on its feet. "I don't understand it," she said. "Why didn't Third Child extinguish my stones?"

Iger shook his head in bewilderment. "I've never seen it do that before, ever."

"Let's try to keep it away from mindstones."

"That shouldn't be hard in this neighborhood."

Kayla followed Iger's glance and saw young women and men, considerably less well-dressed than their elders in the park, sipping drinks at shabby tables set along the sidewalk and listening to a mechband. A festive, down-at-the-heels atmosphere prevailed.

Cafe logos shone from every window like crazy jewels and the street was washed by the coldlight glow of orange, pink, and green. This, then, was where the young and the poor and the disenfranchised came. The bohemians, the soldiers of fortune, the children of Vardalia's rich.

The street was strewn with garbage, bread rinds, scraps of clothing, cracked holo visors, and indecipherable urban debris. A medical cruiser idled at the curbside, orange lights flashing, doors hanging open. Vardalians were dancing in the strobing flashes cast by the cruiser's headlamps. As Kayla and Iger watched, the dancers formed a snaking line and wove dizzily in and out around tables, pedestrians, and slowly-moving vehicles, panhandling passersby as they went.

"Come join the dance!" cried a pale man in a green stretchsuit and purple cape. He waved at Kayla. "Yes, I'm talking to you." As he caught her attention he executed a dizzying array of complicated steps, paused, and bowed.

She grinned, waved back, and pulled Iger farther away from the flow of dancers. Third Child ambled along behind them as Iger looked back longingly at the dancers.

"The N-ware," Kayla reminded him. "We've got to do something about it."

"Relax," Iger said. "Listen to the music. Third Child took care of half that shipment anyway. With what's left they probably couldn't do much damage."

"I've already told you, they've planted some of it somewhere in the city. That could do enough."

"So report them to the police."

"The police won't believe me."

A pack of street urchins approached, saw Third Child, and slowed down, gaping.

"Weird," said a white-haired girl with a dirty face.

A tall, thin boy in strips of red cloth nodded rapidly and said, "Totally transcendent."

"What is it, Elzbeth?" asked a tiny boy with blue-stained skin. "A toy?"

The hulking young woman whose sleeve he tugged had frizzy gold-green hair and a heart-shaped mole on her cheek. She peered through a broken lorgnette at the dalkoi and shrugged. "I don't know you," she said. "Do you belong to the zoo?"

"Yael wants it," the little blue boy cried.

"Hey," Elzbeth said. "Can my brother have your thing?"

"It's a dalkoi," Iger said stiffly. "It's not a toy and it's not for sale."

"That's okay," the girl said graciously. "We don't have any credits anyway. But would you give it to us? We could sell it. It looks valuable. We'll split profits."

"No. I'm sorry."

The girl stared at him as though she couldn't understand why he was being so difficult.

Little blue Yael stuck out his lower lip. "Yael wants it!"

"Well," said Elzbeth. "How about a loan, then?"

Kayla began to feel uneasy. There was something oddly menacing about these children. "Let's go," she said to Iger.

"Let's go," the little boy Yael mimicked her. "Let's go, let's go, let's go." The child's voice rose until he was shrieking.

Someone tapped Kayla on the shoulder. She spun around. No one was there. She turned back in time to see Iger go down under Elzbeth's bulk while the three smaller kids yanked Third Child off his arm and away, around a corner. Elzbeth was on her feet in an instant and right behind them, laughing wildly.

"Third Child!" Iger yelled. "Hey! Come back here."

"Those bastards." Kayla tore down the alley with Iger right behind her, but the kids—and Third Child— had disappeared.

Kayla sent a probe arrowing after them. All she caught was a jumble of mind signatures, completely disorienting.

—Third Child! Third Child, can you hear me?

She received a faint thought-impression from the dalkoi, more of puzzlement than alarm. She couldn't tell which direction it came from.

—Third Child! Third Child, call again.

There was only silence and the mutter of a million minds.

"Great," Iger said. "Now what do we do? Put out a missing-dalkoi notice?" He sat down on the curb and rested his head on his knees.

"We'll find Third Child," Kayla said. "Those kids will get tired of it after a while. You'll see."

"What if Third Child decides that it likes them? I don't know how much common sense—how much sense, period—that dalkoi has," Iger said. "It might just decide that those kids are its new nestmates."

"We'll find it. We have to."

As they walked the street plunged into shadow, the glow globes broken into yellow hulls with jagged edges. Kayla and Iger walked past a row of burned-out buildings with plas-sealed holes where windows and doors had been. Somewhere a pipe was dripping and a tiny chittering sound which might have been insects or children giggling emanated from a dark corner. The stench of human waste assaulted them, making both Kayla and Iger gag, and they hurried past the ruin into a brighter, better-lit street.

The houses were larger, well-kept, and more impressive. Awnings sprouted here and there, neat yards enclosed doorways, and soon the area began to look familiar.

At one corner, Kayla turned left, stared at a house, and shook her head. "I could swear we were back in the Musicians' Quarter," she said. "But how can that be? I thought we were miles away."

Beside her Iger was silent and dejected.

She grabbed his arm. "Hey," she said. "We'll find Third Child. I promise."

"That dalkoi's been with me since I was a kid," Iger said. "If anything happens to it I'll never forgive myself."

Neither will I, Kayla thought. *Neither will I.*

Aloud, she said, "Come on. If we can't find it on foot, I'll bet the *Corazon*'s scanners can do it."

"Are you crazy? Even your supposed mind powers can't do that."

"Yeah, but the dalkoi is one creature. Unique."

"In a city filled with millions of people."

Kayla shook her head defiantly. "It can't be that difficult. I won't believe it."

"If you say so."

"All we have to do is find the ship. Which way is the port?"

They had barely taken a dozen steps when a familiar voice rang out. "So there you are."

Kayla whirled to see Greer standing in the doorway of a tavern. She smiled at her, but her smile of relief wavered when she saw the expression on her former roommate's face.

"You little bitch!" Greer's hand flashed out and caught Kayla on the side of the chin.

Her head rocked back but she took the blow, recovered, and instinctively prepared to return it.

"Hey!" Iger got in between them and grabbed Greer's arm. "What the hell is wrong with you?"

Greer's voice was bitter. "Nothing. That was mild compared to what the Free Traders do to traitors."

"She's no traitor."

"No? Why'd she run off? Ask her where she's been,

and who she's been talking to. Why have half the Free Traders in Vardalia been rounded up and deported? Your little girlfriend isn't what you think, Iger."

"I know all about it, Greer. And she isn't what you think she is, either." He pushed her back against the wall of the tavern. "Calm down. You've been drinking. Try to think straight."

Kayla still felt the impact of Greer's hand on her face and her temper smoldered but she fought to control it. "Greer, I didn't desert you."

"I thought you were going to help me. Where were you?"

"You wouldn't understand if I tried to explain it."

"No? Because you were telling the Trade Police all about my friends, weren't you? I should have known better than to trust you." The woman's eyes blazed.

"Greer, stop it. We've got a real problem here."

"Such as?"

"For starters, some kids took Third Child. We've got to get back to the ship and track them."

"Stole Iger's pet?" Greer's tone was mocking. "What a shame. Iger's getting a bit old for this kind of thing, isn't he?"

"Oh, stuff it," Kayla said, turning away. "Come on, Iger, she's too drunk to know what she's saying."

"Is that so?" Greer put her hand into her jacket and pulled out a pocket disruptor. "Then I guess I don't know what I'm holding on you right now, do I? And when I shoot you, I suppose I won't know it, either."

"Put that away," Iger said. "Are you crazy?"

"Yes. Remember, Rab said it. Said I was crazy." Tears glittered in her eyes and just as quickly were gone.

"Greer, put down the gun," Kayla said. "You know you don't want to hurt me." She sent a weak but functional nearsense whisper into Greer's consciousness. *Calm, calm, calm.*

Greet thrust out her chin, raised her gun, and squeezed

off a shot as—just in time—Kayla flung herself out of range.

Crash!

The shock wave brought down half of the tavern sign. A moment later the proprietor and half a dozen customers were on the pavement, pointing and yelling.

"Crazy spacer! You'll pay for that."

"Get the police. Get them, quick."

"Somebody take that gun away."

Greer got off another shot and the crowd scattered, diving behind mech vendors and under parked vehicles.

"She's gone wild," Kayla said. "I can't control her."

"Let's get out of here," Iger whispered.

The two of them backed down the street the way they had come. But Greer came after them at a half-run.

"Faster," Kayla said, gasping for breath. "She really means it."

They pounded away.

ZZZZZAT! Greer fired again. Her shot sent part of a wall crashing to the pavement behind them.

Kayla vaulted over a hedge with Iger right behind her. They trampled unseen plants as they dashed madly through one yard and into another.

"Don't slow down," Iger gasped. "Cut between those two buildings and take a left. We should be able to lose her in the Beggars' Quarter."

"I hope so," Kayla said.

"Can't you use those mind powers of yours to do something?"

"Something's wrong. It's not working."

"Great." He grabbed her hand. "Come on."

A grove of orange-flowered shrubs with an odd shadow behind it drew a flicker of memory from Kayla. Was that the mouth of a tunnel they were hiding?

She looked closer. Yes. A tunnel. Escape.

Brushing aside the prickly orange growth, she led her companion into the darkness.

"What the hell is this?"

"Shhh." She pulled him deeper into the gloom.

Iger said, "I don't hear anybody coming after us."

Kayla tried a cautious probe. "I don't either, but that doesn't mean anything," she said. "Let's keep moving."

Down and down the path led them. Kayla cast her sputtering nearsense ahead, not really trusting in its guidance but not knowing what else to do. Occasionally she brushed against small rodent minds and other tiny life-forms. But she sensed no threat from them, nor any from above.

Soon they came to a fork in the tunnel. Kayla paused and cast about, but her nearsense readings were inconclusive. Time to gamble on instinct. "Let's take the left branch," she said.

They passed a flickering glow globe and, a bit later, one that was fully operational. By the green-yellow light, Kayla and Iger saw pieces of metal, rusted chains, manacles, and odd sticklike objects.

Bones.

Were they human bones? Kayla suspected so.

"What was this place?" Iger said.

She gave him a hard look. "What do you think? A dungeon."

He prodded half of a skull with his foot. "So they locked people up in here and threw away the key?"

"They've got neater methods now."

"What do you mean?" Iger said.

Kayla told him about the palace and the groupmind. About Rusty.

Iger gaped at her. "Brainburning? A bunch of empaths spying on everybody? Pelleas Karlson hoarding mindstones? Now you sound like Arsobades."

"I didn't believe it before," Kayla said. "But I know what I saw. Karlson's obsessed with mindstones and more concerned about maintaining his power than taking care of Vardalia—or the Trade Alliance."

"He'd better be careful or somebody will take care of it for him," Iger said, clenching his fists. "Gods, if anybody back home on Liage heard this, they'd start a real secession movement. They're itching to free themselves from Karlson's rule anyway."

Kayla felt a sudden dizzying flash, as though a bright light had come on in her head. She saw Iger standing tall and dignified before a group of Liageans, arguing for the end of Karlson's rule. It could happen. She felt it in her bones. But how? She wasn't prescient. What, then, was showing her this vision? Was it the same force that had helped her before? *If so, help me now,* she thought. *Get us out of here.* She didn't know whether she was praying or hallucinating.

"Your secessionists might just get a chance," she said quietly.

She felt him turn toward her in the dark and knew she had confused him. "Never mind," she said. "We'll find Third Child. Just put one foot in front of the other and watch for daylight."

Chapter Nineteen

They emerged from the gloom of the tunnel into the tattered Beggars' Quarter once more. Iger looked around glumly. "Door to door? What do you think?"

Kayla shook her head. "I don't have a clue. Let me search again."

"Okay." He kicked aside a pile of trash and settled onto the curb.

Kayla knew her nearsense wasn't working, but she didn't have the heart to tell Iger. How were they ever going to find that dalkoi? She fretted while Iger sat, idly jiggering some odd bit of metal.

She tried farsense, but all she got for her trouble was a headache. Nearsense still sputtered gibberish. She was just about to give Iger the bad news when he exclaimed happily and held out the object he had been fiddling with: a mediscanner.

"Where did you get that?"

"Found it on the ground near that med cruiser we passed," he said, and stared hard at the palm-sized oval screen. "It's got an animal program, so I calibrated it for dalkoi."

Kayla leaned over his shoulder to see. "Is that a reading on Third Child?"

"I think so." Iger pressed a stud on the keypad and a map appeared onscreen. "Looks like it's not too far from here. Come on, this way."

The route they took led them through an industrial section where machines hummed and whirred behind anonymous stonelike facades. Piles of green and brown rock dust sat like so many loose pyramids in front of the buildings.

"I don't think those kids had time to bring Third Child this far," Kayla said.

"But the dalkoi reading is getting stronger," Iger said. "It's just up ahead."

Elaborate gates, fantasies in arched and swirling metal, but nearly overgrown with vines, delineated the boundaries of what looked like a private park.

"This backs right up to the center of town," Iger said. "I wouldn't be surprised if it's part of the Palace complex."

"And the dalkoi is in there?" Kayla gazed through the gate at the rows of neat green trees. "Where?"

"About a kilometer in that direction." He pointed beyond a stand of purple-flowered trees.

Kayla rattled the bars experimentally. "We've got to get in," she said. "Maybe there's an opening in the gate."

"Pry one open?"

"Only if we have to."

Luck was with them and they found a gap between two iron rods wide enough for a spacer to wiggle through. Two quick steps and they were shielded from any observers by thick undergrowth.

High above them in the trees, something shrieked. Kayla spun on her heel. "What was that?"

"Not Third Child, that's for sure." Iger consulted the scanner. "This way."

They passed enclosures filled with exotic beasts: low-slung, many-legged creatures with rounded heads and feathery hides, howling spider things that thrashed from one level to another in their transparent cage, quivering, jellylike domes topped by red eyes that never blinked.

Kayla came to the next cage. Stopped. Stared. Iger came up behind her and gasped.

"Gods."

Tawny and golden, ticked here and there with subtle shades of brown and lavender. One had white feet. All of them had large, liquid lavender eyes. There were at least five of them, and all were a head larger than Third Child.

For a moment Kayla stood, transfixed, as the dalkois stared back. The one with white feet ventured a soft, deep interrogative chirrup.

Iger swore softly. "Goddamned animal peddlers! All of these dalkois are here illegally. Got to be. No one on Liage would ever allow this many off-planet, especially a family cluster."

"A family?" Kayla couldn't take her eyes off them. "How can you tell?"

"Just a guess, but they're probably all related. See how they stand together in a tight circle like that? Clan behavior."

"I don't see Third Child. Could it be hiding behind them?"

Iger shook his head. "No, it's not here."

But Kayla couldn't respond. She was frozen as something touched her mind, something powerful, as strong in its way as the groupmind had been, but different, alien. The dalkois. They seemed to have a communal telepathic connection. Although they didn't communicate in words, exactly, somehow Kayla understood them.

—Release us.

—I don't know if I can.

—We have brought you here for this purpose, aided you when necessary. Release us.

—I'll try. Believe me, I'll try. But we're looking for another of your kind, Third Child. It's been taken.

—We know this one. An immature female. Her captors hope to sell her to the owner of this place.

—Do you know where she is?

—We will show you.

Kayla received a thought impression of a building in the Beggars' Quarter of Vardalia. It burned itself into her memory and then faded.

"We'll come back for you," she told the dalkois. "I swear it."

* * *

Iger followed her though the streets of Vardalia as Kayla played back the map in her mind that the dalkois had provided. A left here by that curving orange lamppost. A right near that vid kiosk with the broken screen. Two short commercial streets leading to a broad avenue and . . .

The buildings on either side of the street seemed to move in and then out. Out and in. Windows began to sag, melt, and trickle down the walls. The air was hot, foul, impossible to breathe. The world seemed to be turning inside out. Their stomachs leaped, trying to jump out of their bodies.

As quickly as it had begun, it stopped.

Iger turned pale. "What was that?"

"You felt it, too?"

They stared at one another in dismay and growing fear.

Another wave hit and left them both pale and trembling.

"Maybe it's an earthquake."

"I don't think so," Kayla said. "It's nothing like any earthquake I've ever encountered." She gulped air, trying to calm her throbbing pulse. "But something's wrong."

"What do you mean?"

"I don't know. Just wrong."

Again the street heaved beneath their feet, heaved and stretched, lengthening until it seemed to go on for miles, a white ribbon undulating and looping, bouncing Kayla and Iger like two pebbles from wall to wall.

"They're displacement waves," she said. "Some sort of powerful hallucination."

"Hallucination? They feel plenty real to me."

What can be causing such wrenching illusions, Kayla wondered. *Has the groupmind found another hapless medium to unite it? Or is something else going terribly, terribly wrong?*

A loudspeaker wheezed to life from somewhere high above them: "ATTENTION ALL CITIZENS. REPEAT, ATTENTION ALL CITIZENS. BY ORDER OF THE PRIME MINISTER YOU ARE INSTRUCTED TO REMAIN OFF THE STREETS AND IN YOUR HOMES UNTIL THE PERIODS OF SPATIAL AND TEMPORAL DISRUPTION END. THERE IS NO CAUSE FOR ALARM. REPEAT, REMAIN CALM. YOU ARE INSTRUCTED TO REMAIN IN YOUR HOMES. A TWENTY-FOUR-HOUR CURFEW IS IN EFFECT IMMEDIATELY."

"Max-A," Iger said sardonically. "That really makes everything easy."

"We've still got some time," Kayla said. "I don't think they'll be able to patrol the entire city, not right away. Come on. Stay focused." She stared at a row of dilapidated old houses. "Down this street. See that row of abandoned houses? That green one in the middle, that's where Third Child is."

Iger kicked at the door and it gave way with a dull splintering crack. Although there were several people on the street, no one so much as turned or glanced over a shoulder at the noise. After a moment's hesitation, Kayla crawled inside.

It was not as dark as he had expected: dust-filled light streamed down through holes in the roof.

"There's nobody home," Iger said.

"Third Child has to be here. The other dalkois told me."

"Hey, look at this," Iger said. He was pointing at a circular partition in a wall which looked oddly clean, almost new. "What is it?" He tapped his fingers against it and an odd metallic echo came back at him.

"I don't know," Kayla said.

Iger pressed his hand against it and it gave, sinking back into the wall until it had been completely subsumed.

"What the hell?" Iger said. "It looks like a doorway."

"A new doorway in an abandoned building?" Kayla said. She stepped inside. "Look!"

It appeared to be a towering ivory cylinder without doors or windows. A translucent tube filled with golden, shifting light.

"The dalkoi's in there," Kayla said.

Iger stared up the smooth curved face of the tower. "How do we get in?"

Kayla pressed against the wall and, to her amazement, her hand sank wrist-deep into the ivory surface. She pushed harder and sent it in up to her elbow. "Just follow me."

As Iger watched, she walked right through the wall of the tower.

"Hey, wait for me!"

They found themselves standing in the main room of a modest house whose walls were strained and buckling. The tower had been a projection.

Third Child was sitting in the center of the floor on a mound of moldering pillows. It wore a bright tattered blue crown on its head, a scrap of shiny fabric at its throat, and anklets of some fuzzy, iridescent fabric, which it seemed to be admiring.

When it saw Kayla and Iger, the dalkoi gave a loud chirp and proudly held out a limb to show off its finery.

Kayla wanted to laugh and cry with relief. She said, "Lovely. Oh, very, very nice. Had a good time, did you, Third Child? I'm so glad."

"You look like a clown," Iger said. "Take off that crown. Right now. Third Child, don't look away. Hey! I'm talking to you."

The dalkoi peered at its toes as though it hadn't understood a word of what Iger had said.

A skittering sound behind them made Kayla and Iger turn quickly around.

Stocky, sulky Elzbeth appeared, nearly eclipsing her brother, Yael, who trailed behind her like a small blue puppet. Their eyes grew wide when they saw the two spacers.

"You!" Elzbeth cried. "You've ruined everything."

Iger pulled the knife from his belt. Its golden blade flashed in the light.

The two children pivoted and ran. The last trace of either of them was the flash of Yael's blue-stained skin as he dashed, wailing, out the door right behind his sibling.

"Little cretins," Iger muttered. He put the knife back in his belt and patted Third Child on the head.

The dalkoi chirruped happily, and came over to Kayla for a head rub.

She petted it, realizing that she had grown more than fond of the odd creature. There was a strange affinity between them, she had to admit it. Like two lost bamberas.

It's my friend.

The realization surprised and humbled her.

"Yes, I'm very glad to see you," she said, and patted it again. "Now let's get out of here.'

* * *

Outside, in the city, hysteria reigned. Monsters were loose, and rumors of worse. Space/time distortions, ruined mindstones, crazed spacers. *Run, hide.*

With the dalkoi in tow, Kayla and Iger swam through the dizzying flow of agitated city dwellers and heard their fearful whispers, the multiplying rumors. Somehow they were safe in the midst of that frightening tide.

The corner of a towering white- and yellow-striped building came loose. But instead of falling and crushing fleeing pedestrians, it peeled away, curled in upon

itself, and became a strange half-alive thing which
shunted from clawed foot to clawed foot, raking its
pincers across the screaming crowds, as, panicking,
they fought to get away.

"Ignore it," Kayla said. "It's not real. It can't be."
She was tempted to tell him that she had seen worse
things, far worse, in the minds of former friends.

Iger glanced back nervously over his shoulder. "Tell
that to the woman it just ate."

"Come on."

A herd of gray and lavender bambera came whistling
out of a tube stop and ran straight up a polished bronze
wall, disappearing over the green lip of the roof. Third
Child squeaked and made as if to follow them, but Iger
restrained the dalkoi, looking all the while at Kayla.
"That wasn't real either?"

She smiled bravely. "Of course not."

"Watch out!"

The pavement in front of them shimmered, faded,
and disappeared. In its place was a flat and arid waste-
land of red sand and boulders, stretching toward distant pink mountains whose summits were hidden by
orange clouds.

The dalkoi squealed and pressed against Iger. "What
in nine hells?" Iger yelped. "Where are we? Where did
the street go?"

"The street didn't *go* anywhere," Kayla said. "It's
right here under our feet."

"Yeah? Can you feel it?"

"Well, no."

"Then how can you expect me to believe you?"

She said nothing except, "Just keep walking."

They crossed the red desert. They plowed through
fetid swampland. Strange creatures opened yellow
mouths lined with jagged teeth while somewhere high
above something hidden in the steaming green treetops
screamed uncontrollably.

They were fighting their way through razor-edged

vines when they heard an odd thumping noise. They paused and stared in the direction of the sound. Emerging through the vines and trees came a patrol, hacking its way through the jungle.

"You, there! Halt!"

Kayla ducked beneath a huge leaf with serrated edges.

The lead patrolman fired his disruptor. The shot whizzed past her and vaporized a tree trunk—at least, it looked like one. But for a moment in the afterglow, Kayla saw the hazy outline of a mech vendor as it melted to slag.

Third Child started to get up and Iger grabbed its leg, dragging it back into cover.

"Stay down," Kayla whispered. "Keep moving."

"Dammit," Iger said. "You can't hide behind hallucinations. It's a good way to get killed."

"How do we know that those patrolmen are even real?"

"They look pretty real to me," Iger said.

"Just keep going."

A shot sizzled overhead and vaporized a tree trunk just behind them. For a moment a storefront could be seen with its windows cracked and smoking.

"Still think that was an illusion?" Iger said.

"Gods, I don't know." Kayla hesitated. Another shot zinged past them. "No. That was real."

Sudden phantasms erupted up out of the pavement to snap at them with triangular red teeth dripping gore. The officers cried out, as, one by one, they fell prey to those teeth. Satiated, the creatures withdrew.

The scene shifted crazily and they were walking across a pockmarked lunar field of gray rocks and craters. Sharp black cinders crunched noisily beneath their feet. Suddenly a fat volcano thrust its angry mouth up out of the moonscape and began belching purple and green flames, pink and ocher smoke.

"An illusion, right?" Iger said. "Gotta be."

Kayla peered at it and nodded.

"You'll tell me if it isn't one, right?"

"Don't be a moron."

"Just thought I'd ask."

The disruptions came in pulses now, making them easier to deal with. Even Iger strode along uncomplaining as fiery hailstones pelted them and freezing tidal waves crashed down from the rooftops.

Through the fiery storms and floods a serene group of dalkois padded steadily toward them, tawny and golden, ticked here and there with subtle shades of brown and lavender. One of them had white feet. The group from the zoo.

Third Child gave a high squeal and ran toward the larger dalkois. They all screeched in unison and formed a tight cluster around the smaller dalkoi. At the same moment, Kayla heard the mindvoice of the dalkoi cluster speak to her.

—*Peace upon you.*

She felt as though some huge sheltering umbrella had settled above her and Iger. Around them the city was a maelstrom, but they were safe here, curiously remote.

—*You escaped? How?*

—*In the growing confusion we were able to influence a keeper to release us. Just as this immature female has been influencing so many of these events.*

—*Third Child is causing all of this?*

—*Affirmative.*

As if to emphasize the statement, Third Child made a strange, flat sound and a rumbling wave of pure empathic energy slashed through Kayla's mind and out.

—*I don't understand.*

—*The energies she consumed have almost overwhelmed her.*

—*You mean the mindstones?*

—*Affirmative. She is leaking emanations because of*

this psychic overload and is too young to have the control to quell these outpourings. We will assist.

Third Child gave another peculiar hiccup and the air directly in front of her glistened and began to fragment into mosaic pieces. The space between each fragment became distinct, vibrating with black energy as though the whole of reality were a jigsaw puzzle about to come apart. Just as suddenly, the dalkoi drooped in exhaustion and its eyes closed.

The puzzle pieces disappeared.

—She will sleep now.

With relief and even tenderness Kayla gathered up the sleeping creature, and removed Third Child's ragged crown and neckpiece. On a whim she decided to leave the iridescent cuffs.

"C'mon," she said to Iger. "Let's get back to the N-ware."

"You're kidding."

"Iger!"

"Are you out of your mind, Katie?"

"What about the dalkois? Are we just going to bring them along with us? We should hustle our asses back to port, to the *Corazon,* and regroup there."

"Iger, I've got to finish what I started."

"In a city under curfew, crawling with police?"

He was right. She knew it, but she also knew that time was running out for Vardalia. Oh, if only her mind powers were working. If only. Desperately, she turned to the dalkois.

—Help us. Please. The entire city may be at risk.

—Why should we aid our captors? We have no desire to remain here.

—Do you want to be destroyed?

—We wish to return to our homeland.

—We have a star ship that will transport you. But first there is this matter of the nuclears . . .

—Let us return to your vehicle and discuss it.

* * *

The *Corazon* sat quietly at dock, its supply lines working, the gate to its air lock open.

Kayla and Iger made for it, Iger carrying the sleeping Third Child, and behind them came the rest of the dalkois in tawny parade.

At that moment, Greer stepped out onto the ramp. Her olive-colored eyes widened in obvious disbelief at the sight of them. In a move too swift to follow she pulled a disruptor from the wall holster of the air lock and trained it on Kayla.

"Hold it right there," she said softly. "Not one more step."

Chapter Twenty

"Don't be an idiot," Iger said.

"Shut up." Greer leaned over and grabbed Kayla's arm. She seemed oblivious to the group of dalkois behind them. "I ought to just shoot you and be done with it, traitor."

Kayla shook her head fiercely. "Greer, you don't know anything that's happened. I didn't try to turn you in. I was trying to save you. To stop those twins. They're the ones who want to betray you!"

"Why should I listen to you? You're trying to turn me against my comrades." Greer's gaze burned into her. "I was going to give you one last chance, but I don't think so." She targeted her disruptor on Kayla's head.

I'll never be able to talk sense with her, Kayla thought. *Never.*

She lashed out, kicking Greer in the knee, hard. The woman cried out and fell heavily to the pavement but managed to keep her grip on the gun.

Kayla spun and booted the weapon out of Greer's hand.

Somehow Greer clambered to her knees and launched herself at Kayla, landing a fierce blow to Kayla's chin. Her head hit hard pavement and her vision blurred, but she fought against it, rolling out of range of Greer's next blow.

"Hey! What in nine hells is going on?"

Barabbas and Salome were on the ramp staring down in obvious bewilderment.

"Greer's lost it," Iger cried. "Watch out. She's going for her disruptor!"

Greer had pulled free of Kayla's grip, lunged to the side, and grabbed up the fallen gun. Before Kayla could stop her, she triggered it. Rab threw himself in front of Kayla, took the full force of the shot, and fell to the ground.

"No!" Rage and grief boiled in Kayla, bringing with it enough strength, enough madness to make her lash out at her former roommate. And the mind power was there, unexpectedly, waiting. She coiled it within, feeding it with her fury.

—*Wait. There is risk* . . .

She ignored the dalkois' warning and unleashed the full power of her fury on Greer's unprotected mind. The woman gasped and crumpled, fell to her knees, to her side, and lay still.

Nearby, Salome knelt over Rab, Iger beside her. "Rab," she called brokenly. "Answer me." Her long golden hair covered her face and veiled the face of her lover.

Rab lay on his back, eyes closed, skin pale, breathing rapidly. One look at him and Kayla knew he was mortally wounded. And she was helpless.

She had no mind power left, had exhausted it all in one foolish frenzied assault on Greer. And even if she hadn't used herself up, healing had never been one of her powers. Oh, if only . . .

—*You were warned.*

Kayla turned to face the dalkois. —*Help him, please!*

—*You had great gifts and have misused them. Now they have been taken from you. We can do nothing.*

—*I'm not asking for me. I'm asking for my friend.*

—*It is too taxing. Your friend is too damaged.*

—*You mean you could heal him?*

*—There is too much damage. We do not have suffi-
cient numbers.*

—Please!

—We regret . . .

—What if I could augment your powers?

—With what?

—With these. Kayla held up the pouch containing
her father's mindstones. *—The finest mindstones on St.
Ilban.*

—It may be possible. Show us.

With shaking hands she spilled the glowing gems
into her palm: blue-red and green facets refracted the
light of the double suns.

The dalkois gathered around her and bent their heads
to the glittering hoard.

—These may be sufficient. We will need a medium.

—I'll do it!

*—Place one hand upon your companion's head and
one above his lungs.*

Kayla gently moved Salome aside and positioned
herself as instructed.

"Katie, what are you doing?"

She had no time to explain.

—Open your mind to us.

"Katie!" Iger's voice, very near.

"Shh!" There was no time for interruptions. Kayla
focused all of her mind power, her very being, upon
her wounded comrade. Closing her eyes, she allowed
the dalkois to possess her. She was swimming through
a brilliant space of flickering light and shadow, strange
echoing whispers—the dalkois' groupmind?—and then
she was in Rab's mind, slipping in as easily as diving
into a quiet pond of water.

All was silent. Rab lay terribly still, blood pooling in
his heart. Death was close.

Kayla stood on the threshold of Rab's consciousness.
She could not, would not let him go.

Live, damn you! You can't make me care about you,

save my life, and then die. You can't leave me, leave all of us like this. I won't have it.

She poured energy, life, love into Rab. The outer world was lost to her, veiled by a red haze that swirled and rippled like some peculiar tide.

Heal.

She was outside and inside of him at the same time, triggering neural circuits, amplifying endorphin production.

Breathe, she thought. *Breathe and live.*

The red haze thinned to pale dawn pink and dissipated. Someone had grabbed her shoulder and was shaking her.

Kayla ignored them. *Come on, Rab! Come on!*

There, a twitch. And another. The heart spasmed briefly, stopped. Started again. A beat. And there, another. Faster. One. Two. Three. Four.

Rab blinked rapidly, opened his eyes. And moved, sighing gently, to raise a large hand and reach for Salome.

Kayla's eyes filled with tears.

Other hands lifted her to her feet. She turned to stare into Arsobades' sweaty face. Iger was just behind him.

"What did you do?" His voice was a hoarse whisper. "I heard the noise, saw Greer shoot Rab on the monitor. But what did *you* do, Katie?"

"Healed him, with the dalkois' help."

"Gods, what are you? A witch?"

"No." She took a deep breath. "Arsobades, I'm an empath."

His ruddy face went pale. "One of them. A damned mind spy!"

"No!" She held her arms out to him. "No, Arsobades, I'm no spy. Believe me."

He moved back, holding his hands up as if to ward her off. "Stay away from me."

The expression on the minstrel's face was a mixture

of fear and anger. Kayla couldn't bear it and looked away.

"Greer's gone," Iger said flatly. "Must've recovered from whatever you did to her and took off. I've got a fix on her with the mediscanner."

"We've got to catch her before she does something stupid."

"What about Rab?"

—*We will stand watch.*

Good enough. "Arsobades," she said. "The dalkois will help you take care of him." She left the minstrel glancing uncertainly from the cluster of tawny animals to his injured crewmate.

Iger looked grim. "We'll never get all the way back to that stash of nuclears, if that's her destination."

"I don't think that's where she's headed. What does the scanner say?"

"She's turning. Now she's going toward the Crystal Palace."

"The Trade Congress," Kayla said. "That's got to be it."

Something chirruped behind them.

"Third Child! Stay here with your friends."

Another sound. Obviously, Third Child had other ideas, like sticking close to her and Iger.

"Oh, all right. I don't have time to argue. But don't slow us down. Let's go!"

* * *

The grand plaza outside of the Crystal Palace was jammed with tourists, trade delegates, and gawkers. The twin suns poured harsh light straight down, but there was not an empty inch of pavement on which to cast even one shadow.

Kayla groaned at the size of the crowd. "Don't they know there's a curfew? I'll never be able to find Greer in this crowd!"

But there—beside the grand entrance, those two

cloaked figures. Weren't those the twins? And farther back, near the fountain, ducking out of sight—Greer!

Got you, Kayla thought triumphantly.

"Return to your homes!" a loudspeaker blared. "Clear the plaza. Repeat, clear the plaza!"

The mob continued to mill about the fountain, even as rows of police officers marched into view.

"This is your last warning," the voice shouted. "The prime minister has instructed you to return to your homes until further notice. If you defy curfew you will be arrested. Please leave immediately."

Kayla couldn't move in the crush. Somehow she had been separated from Iger, but Third Child stayed close, whimpering gently. She thought she saw the flash of a Free Trade sunburst across the back of a woman's hand, gone before she could focus. And there, on a man's arm. What were all these Free Traders doing here? Had Greer sent out a call to arms?

The police moved in.

There were screams and grunts of surprise as the cops began to grab people and drag them away.

Kayla forced herself to concentrate on the twins and Greer. She wormed her way through the thrashing bodies to the place where she had seen Onzerib.

A hand clamped down on her wrist. "There you are."

She looked up into Yates Keller's face.

"I don't know what you did," he said. "Or how you got away. But I've got a job for you now. As replacement for Rusty."

"Oh, no you don't," she said. A quick shifting of her weight, a firm grip on his arm. She bent low, toppling him over her shoulder and down, hard, on his own. Free Trader self-defense.

But Greer was suddenly right in front of her.

Behind her, Yates was getting to his feet.

Her hand brushed against a lump in her pocket. The mindstone sack. Gods, what was that in the bottom?

One last stone, overlooked. One last mindstone. And Greer had wanted to cause a diversion, hadn't she? Well, maybe she would just get her wish. In spades.

Kayla reached into the sack and pulled out the last of the stones. It winked, blue-red-bronze-green. The best quality, the finest stone her father had ever mined.

Quickly, before she weakened, Kayla held it out to Third Child. The dalkoi chirped in obvious delight, homed in on the gem, and rubbed her face against it.

The miniature ruby-blue stars winked out, dead, and a lump grew in Kayla's throat. The last bit of her birth-right, gone. Silently, she slipped the extinguished stone back into its sack and waited.

Third Child blinked, blinked again, and her violet eyes seemed to water. For a moment Kayla had the illusion that the dalkoi's head had expanded slightly. She belched.

Nothing happened.

The dalkoi chirped and looked cross-eyed. She burped several more times in rapid sequence.

And all hell broke loose.

Buildings reared up out of the pavement and collided like great stone dinosaurs. The very ground shimmered and melted, re-formed as deadly triangular shards of ice. Screaming, people were pushed, fell, and were impaled upon the jagged stones.

The air was liquid, running across the plaza in shades of yellow and green. The light of the twin suns poured down like rain.

Kayla waded through the mounting illusions and grabbed Onzerib's hand, pulled it around his back, and set her foot against his kidneys.

"Where's the N-ware?" she said.

"Calm yourselves," the loudspeaker shouted. "There is no cause for alarm. Proceed quietly and calmly to your homes. Repeat, there is no cause for alarm."

Kayla tightened her grip on the struggling twin and frog-marched him across the plaza, bumping into hys-

terical tourists and police, pushing past them right up
to the fountain and shoved him in, headfirst. Counted
to ten as he thrashed underwater and finally, she allowed him up to breathe. Coughing and sputtering,
Onzerib surfaced, water streaming from his matted
dark hair and elaborate clothing.

"I said, where's the N-ware?"

He shook his head and she pushed him under again.
But even as Kayla brought him up for air, the fountain
seemed to change shape, spouting quicksand in strange
muddy rills. Slowly, it sank back into itself like a
dying flower. Onzerib floundered like a fly caught in
the maw of a carnivorous plant.

Greer crawled out of the shadows of the deformed
monument, squinting and breathing heavily. "Let him
go," she said.

"No."

A pistol was in her hand.

Third Child burped.

The plaza was gone.

They stood deep underwater upon a purple sand
floor cleft by chasms which sent steam clouds gey-
sering up into the formless green heights. Overhead giant rocklike eel-things shimmied between the geysers,
pausing to hiss and hang open multiple jaws filled with
rows of uneven teeth.

Kayla lost her grip on Onzerib.

He scrambled away through a school of small red
disks which cloaked his motions and, in a sudden turn,
completely obscured him from her sight.

Greer swam directly into her path but was deflected
by the flailing limbs of a police officer who was struggling upward toward what he seemed to think was the
surface of the water.

A hand closed around Kayla's ankle.

She spun slowly in the water and came about to confront Yates Keller.

A policeman's gun went off.

Third Child burped.

The water wavered and vanished. They were lying, thrashing, on the cracked turquoise soil of an arid dryland that stretched as far as the eye could see.

Keller's thin-lipped mouth formed an oval of surprise and blood began to seep from the front of his chest. He writhed, obviously in great pain, and collapsed.

"Yates!" Kayla turned, saw Third Child nearby. "Help me reach him. I can't just let him die!"

The dalkoi's mindforce came gently into her mind.

Huge gas clouds filled with odd sparkling colors floated above them. One descended upon Kayla and the fallen Keller. At first she felt nothing. Then her senses seemed to rebel. She was hearing with her eyes, seeing with her mouth, breathing the sweetly scented air through her ears.

Now she was falling, falling deeper and deeper into a dark, endless spiraling cave. Grasping at the sides of it, tearing her fingers against the jagged surface. She would smash herself at the bottom and break into a million pieces.

But her descent slowed and she began to make out details in the darkness. There, a ledge. She landed upon it, going to her hands and knees in the red darkness. A small aperture allowed her to crawl inside the obsidian wall. She found herself perched within a giant theater where several plays were taking place at once.

In one illuminated circle, Yates Keller stood next to a stout balding man—Pelleas Karlson—and nodded as the prime minister spoke quickly and urgently.

To the left was another vignette, one of Yates standing beside a coffin which contained the shrunken, still body of his mother. But the third vignette—

Yates was creeping along a shining rock ledge, stopping occasionally to press something small and wet-looking against the living stone.

Kayla drew in her breath. Those were depth charges, used by Styx miners.

As she watched, Yates observed his handiwork, smiled, and withdrew. For a moment the cave was empty. Then two people walked into view.

"No," Kayla whispered. "No, please. Go back."

Her parents kept walking, tapping stones, unaware of their danger. Their doom.

When the first explosive detonated, the scene went dark.

The plaza came back in pieces: faces, hands, guns. Kayla was staring at Yates, watching him bleed, and knowing she could stop it.

He had killed her parents.

Blood was seeping onto the ground.

Kayla leaned close over him and touched his face. Did his eyes flicker? She couldn't tell.

"Yates?" she said softly. "Can you hear me? I hope you can. I know what you did. And I could save you. Yes, I could save you, heal you. And I know you would be grateful, maybe even sorry for what you had done. But I won't do it. I'm not that good a person. Not any more."

She turned away.

Another vision enfolded her: a brightly lit space that was empty save for her and Greer. Her former roommate lay on her back in midair. Blood dripped slowly from the side of her mouth. Her eyes were closed.

Kayla reached for her. "Greer! Answer me."

There was mind power yet within her and Kayla sent a probe lancing down into the mind of her crewmate.

—Greer? Greer, hold on.

Greer blinked slowly and opened her eyes. *—Is that you, Katie? Do you see, now? Didn't you ever wonder why your parents died?*

—I thought it was an accident.

—That's what you were supposed to think. But this Keller had your parents done. Didn't you just see that?

Never trust a Keller, Katie. Never. He wanted your holdings for his family. He never cared about you. And now he works for Karlson. His men are the ones who shot me. Greer gave her a death's head grin. Her eyes were empty, a skeleton's gaping sockets. Bones and splinters which fell to powder as Kayla watched. She was gone.

Kayla blinked.

The fountain. The Crystal Palace. Twin suns above her, tiles below, and Greer, red-stained and unmoving at her feet.

Kayla bent and put her arms around her crewmate. "Don't leave me," she whispered. "Greer, don't go."

The wounded woman didn't stir.

In peripheral vision Kayla saw Onzerib trying to sneak away around the fountain and her fury exploded.

She would destroy the twins, make them suffer as she had, destroy everything they held dear, everything associated with them, with Yates Keller, with the prime minister. Take the N-ware and use it! The towers would shatter and crumble, the very planet split wide open, the twin suns would burst into supernovae ...

NO.

It was a command of such power and resonance that she couldn't believe one mind was capable of its expression.

And then she knew: the dalkoi. Third Child, addressing her directly.

—*How many would you kill to seek revenge? And if you become a murderer, what then?*

—*What about my losses? My pain?*

—*Regrettable. But you are still alive. Do you wish to stay that way?*

—*Yes. Yes, I do.*

—*Then live. Seek life, not death.*

The red haze cleared from her eyes and with it went her furious blood lust. She saw again the shining mind signature of Third Child and knew she was right. The dalkoi was telling her to remember who she was.

—*But my parents*—

Even as she thought it, she knew.

More deaths wouldn't make it right.

But I'll find a way to get even with all who have hurt me. Damn Yates Keller and Pelleas Karlson and all who served them. Damn them to nine hells. To the surface of Styx.

Greer lay nearby, eyes empty and unseeing. Her mind was silent. Life had bled out of her onto the pavement stones.

Kayla leaned over and shut Greer's eyes. She felt a peculiar combination of remorse and relief. "Sleep," she said softly. "No more battles, ever. I'll show these sons of bitches. I'll do it for you, Greer. I swear it."

She stood up, the mindforce still powerful within her, and reached out, probing, searching until she found the mind signature of Douzerib.

—*You. You will dismantle the N-ware, and arrange to have it stored for me until such a time as I may need it.*

Her coercion, strengthened by the mindlinkage with Third Child, was irresistible and she felt the twin's mind give way easily before it.

The dalkois had been right. This wasn't the time—or possibly even the place—to use the N-ware. There never would be a time or place. But Kayla knew that she was stronger with it as a threat than without it. Perhaps Greer had been right all along. Perhaps the Free Trade cause really was her cause, too.

—*ENOUGH!*

It was too loud to be Third Child alone. The dalkois' groupmind had found her, and their command resonated in her brain.

—*WE HAVE MADE YOU TOO POWERFUL. THIS IS WRONG AND WE SEE THAT NOW. YOU WILL BE*

ALLOWED TO RETAIN SOME OF YOUR FORMER EMPATHIC POWERS, BUT THAT IS ALL.

—But . . .

The contact was broken.

Kayla was alone, in her own head, in the plaza by the Crystal Palace. Third Child rubbed against her as sirens shrilled in the sunlit air, and Iger walked toward her, his arms open in a welcoming embrace.

* * *

The mood in the *Corazon*'s ops was subdued. No one spoke much as they prepared for liftoff.

The dalkois were safely berthed below in restraints. They would be off-loaded at Liage before the ship left the Cavinas System. The cluster had offered to take Third Child with them, but she wanted to stay with Iger.

Kayla checked the navboard and saw with grim satisfaction that everything was in order. It felt good to be back in her seat again, back in ops. She looked up to find Salome's eyes upon her. Their expression was icy.

"What's wrong?"

The captain brushed back her long golden hair and crossed her arms in front of her. Her dark face was a study in suspicion. "I'd like some answers, Katie. I'd like to know what happened to you out there. Why did you disappear for days? What were you doing? What happened in the plaza? And what was all that about the N-ware?"

Kayla met Salome's cold gaze and set her jaw defiantly. "What difference does it make?"

"Look, I know you saved Rab's life with your weird mind powers. Arsobades and Iger explained all that. I suppose I should be grateful. But frankly, I don't know if I can trust you, or if I still want you here on my ship."

The words were like a knife in her heart, but Kayla maintained her composure. "Whatever you decide," she said quietly. "You're the captain. I'll get off here, now, Salome. If you can't accept that I healed Rab as an act of friendship, and that I'm not a spy for Karlson or for anybody else, then I won't waste my time trying to convince you. Or try endlessly to win back your trust."

Salome frowned and began to say something, but Rab leaned over and cut her off.

"Stow it, babe. I believe her." He held out his hand to Kayla. "Listen, Katie—or whatever your name really is. I trust my instincts. Didn't I hire you? So let me decide when to fire you, okay? You saved my life. I owe you one."

Kayla placed her hand in his large palm and smiled. "Okay."

"Dammit," Rab shouted. "She's family. Every family has its weird cousins. So what if she's an empath? We all have our flaws." He put his arm around Kayla's shoulder and turned to face the rest of the crew. "Salome, Arsobades, we've got to be clear about this. She's a damned good pilot and I say she stays."

Slowly, Salome nodded.

Even Arsobades gave a reluctant grin. "I'm for it," he said. "I can't pretend that you didn't scare me out there, Katie. But I think your heart's in the right place. And besides, we need a strong alto."

But Kelso looked from Salome to Rab with obvious displeasure. "I don't believe this," he said. "You guys are suckers. How do we know she didn't try to aim the cops at us? I say, don't trust her a millionth of a micron."

Kayla glared at him. "You're the last one to point the finger," she snapped. "Especially after you stole my mindstones! This is your spy, Salome."

Kelso's face turned red.

"Say what?" Rab said.

"Mindstones?" Salome stared at her, eyes huge.

Arsobades moved in closer. "Yes, Katie. What's this about mindstones?"

"My father left them to me. The best that he ever mined. And Kelso stole them. Sold them. To Pelleas Karlson's agents, who hired him as a spy."

"Hell, I didn't take them up on it," Kelso said quickly. "Don't look at me that way, Salome."

"So," Arsobades said softly. "You've been stealing from us and spying on us all along?"

Rab grabbed Kelso by the throat and lifted him against the wall. "You're finished on the *Falstaff.*" He turned to Salome. "Open the air lock. I'm putting this bastard ashore."

Kelso made choking noises.

"Y'know, Kelso, I always had a feeling about you," Rab said softly. "Not a good one, either." He dragged him out of ops and returned, moments later, empty-handed.

"Katie," Salome said, "I'm transferring all of Kelso's credits into your account. It's the least he can do to make it up to you."

Kayla watched the orange numbers dance across the screen: Kelso had been a frugal man, and there was almost enough in his account to match the worth of her lost mindstones. "Fair enough," she said.

A loud noise from across the room distracted them all. Third Child gave an odd three-tone belch. A wave of dripping green-winged spiders came crawling down the walls and hurried toward them.

The dalkoi belched again. The spiders became tiny soldiers marching complicated maneuvers between the command module and navboard.

Salome sighed. "How long is this going to last?"

"Until Third Child gets hungry again," Iger said. "I think."

"Please," Salome said. "Whatever you do, don't feed it any mindstones." She looked around the room. "Are we ready to go?"

"Yeah," said Rab. "And, Katie, do me a favor. Try

not to steer us into some star or passing comet the next time that critter burps."

"You watch your ass, I'll watch mine," Kayla said, and began to punch coordinates into the navboard. As she set their course to Liage, and then back to Mammoth Station, an odd lyric danced through her head: "Karlson can go to hell and wait, our taxes will be a trifle late. Free Trade, forever. Free Traders, free."

She hummed the song softly to herself. Someday the entire galaxy would sing along. She swore it on the deaths of her parents and Greer.

"Jumpspace in five minutes," she said. "Counting down." She hooked herself into the navboard and the engines beneath her roared to life.

Kris Jensen

The Ardellans:

☐ **FREEMASTER: Book 1**   UE2404—$3.95

The Terran Union had sent Sarah Anders to Ardel to establish a trade agreement for materials vital to offworlders but of little value to the low-tech Ardellans. But other, more ruthless humans were about to stake their claim to Ardel with the aid of forbidden technology and threats of destruction. The Ardellan clans had defenses of their own, based on powers of the mind, that only a human such as Sarah could begin to understand. For she, too, had mind talents locked within her—and the FreeMasters of Ardel might just provide the key to releasing them.

☐ **MENTOR: Book 2**   UE2464—$4.50

Jeryl, Mentor of Clan Alu, sought to save the Ardellan Clans which, decimated by plague, were slowly fading away. But even as Jeryl set out on his quest, other Clans sought a different solution to their troubles, ready to call upon long-forbidden powers to drive the hated Terrans off Ardel.

☐ **HEALER: Book 3**   UE2570—$4.99

With plague sweeping the native population, Terran Dr. Sinykin Inda answers the Ardellans' plea for help, only to be thrust into a conflict between anti-Terran and pro-Terran factions. And even as he struggles to save the natives, the Terran Union's control of mining operations is challenged by an interstellar corporation ready to destroy Ardel for its own profit.

FOREIGNER
by C.J. Cherryh

It had been nearly five centuries since the starship *Phoenix*, came out of hyperdrive into a place with no recognizable reference coordinates, and no way home. Hopelessly lost, the crew did the only thing they could. They charted their way to the nearest G5 star, gambling on finding a habitable planet. And what they found was the world of the atevi—a world where law was kept by the use of registered assassination, where alliances were not defined by geographical borders, and where war became inevitable once humans and one faction of atevi established a working relationship. It was a war that humans had no chance of winning and now, nearly two centuries later, humanity lives in exile on the island of Mospheira, trading tidbits of advanced technology for continued peace and a secluded refuge that no atevi will ever visit. Only a single human, the paidhi, is allowed off the island and into the complex and dangerous society of the atevi, brought there to act as interpreter and technological liaison to the leader of the most powerful of the atevi factions. But when this sole human the treaty allows into atevi society is nearly killed by an unregistered assassin's bullet, the fragile peace is shattered, and Bren Cameron, the paidhi, realizes that he must seek a new way to build a truer understanding between these two dangerous, intelligent, and quite possibly incompatible species. For if he fails, he and all of his people will die. But can a lone human hope to overcome two centuries of hostility and mistrust?

☐ **Original Hardcover**   UE2590—$20.00

☐ **Paperback Edition**   UE2637—$5.99

C.S. Friedman

☐ **IN CONQUEST BORN**   UE2198—$5.99

Braxi and Azea—two super-races fighting an endless war. The Braxaná—created to become the ultimate warriors. The Azeans, raised to master the powers of the mind. Now the final phase of their war is approaching, spearheaded by two opposing generals, lifetime enemies—and whole worlds will be set ablaze by the force of their hatred.

☐ **THE MADNESS SEASON**   UE2444—$5.99

For 300 years, the alien Tyr had ruled Earth, imprisoning the true individualists, the geniuses, and forcing them to work on projects which the Tyr hoped would reveal humankind's secrets. But Daetrin's secret was one no one had ever uncovered. Taken into custody by the Tyr, he would have to confront the truth about himself at last—and if he failed, all humans would pay the price. . . .

The Coldfire Trilogy

☐ **BLACK SUN RISING (Book 1)**   UE2527—$5.99
                                         Hardcover Edition: UE2485—$18.95

Centuries after being stranded on the planet Ema, humans have achieved an uneasy stalemate with the *Fae*, a terrifying natural force with the power to prey upon people's minds. Now, as the hordes of the dare *fae* multiply, four people—Priest, Adept, Apprentice, and Sorcerer—are drawn inexorably together to confront an evil beyond imagining.

☐ **WHEN TRUE NIGHT FALLS (Book 2)**   UE2615—$5.99
                                         Hardcover Edition: UE2569—$22.00

Determined to seek out and destroy the source of the *fae*'s ever-strengthening evil, Damien Vryce, the warrior priest, and Gerald Tarrant, the immortal sorcerer known as the Hunter, dare the treacherous crossing of the planet's greatest ocean to confront a power that threatens the very essence of the human spirit.

Kate Elliott

The Novels of the Jaran:

☐ **JARAN: Book 1**   UE2513—$5.99
Here is the poignant and powerful story of a young woman's
coming of age on an alien world, where she is both player and
pawn in an interstellar game of intrigue and politics.

☐ **AN EARTHLY CROWN: Book 2**   UE2546—$5.99
The jaran people, led by Ilya Bakhtiian and his Earth-born wife
Tess, are sweeping across the planet Rhui on a campaign of
conquest. But even more important is the battle between Ilya
and Duke Charles, Tess' brother, who is ruler of this sector of
space.

☐ **HIS CONQUERING SWORD: Book 3**   UE2551—$5.99
Even as Jaran warlord Ilya continues the conquest of his world,
he faces a far more dangerous power struggle with his wife's
brother, leader of an underground human rebellion against the
alien empire.

☐ **THE LAW OF BECOMING: Book 4**   UE2580—$5.99
On Rhui, Ilya's son inadvertently becomes the catalyst for what
could prove a major shift of power. And in the heart of the
empire, the most surprising move of all was about to occur as
the Emperor added an unexpected new player to the Game of
Princes . . .